THE SECRET LIFE OF
ELIZABETH I

PAUL DOHERTY

GREENWICH EXCHANGE

Greenwich Exchange, London

First published in Great Britain in 2006
All rights reserved

The Secret Life of Elizabeth I © Paul Doherty 2006

Printed and bound by Q3 Digital/Litho, Loughborough
Tel: 01509 213456
Typesetting and layout by Albion Associates, London
Tel: 020 8852 4646
Cover design by December Publications, Belfast
Tel: 028 90286559

Cover images © Alamy Images and Mary Evans Picture Library

Greenwich Exchange Website: www.greenex.co.uk

Cataloguing in Publication Data is available from the British Library

ISBN-13: 978-1-871551-85-3
ISBN-10: 1-871551-85-4

For Vanessa Cole an EAST END girl who became
Mayor of Redbridge and who loved every minute of it!
Her chosen charity, The Teenage Cancer Trust project,
is left to serve the young people of Redbridge.

Contents

Introduction   vii

List of Principal Historical Characters
    Mentioned in the Text   ix

Chronology of the Reign of Elizabeth I   xiii

Part I   1
Commentary on Part I   24

Part II   27
Commentary on Part II   44

Part III   47
Commentary on Part III   65

Part IV   58
Commentary on Part IV   95

Part V   100
Commentary on Part V   185

Introduction

The reign of Elizabeth I (1558-1603) fascinates anyone interested in history. The revelations made in the fictional setting which follows are based on hard evidence, primary sources, documents and memoranda which have been overlooked in the standard histories. These primary sources offer an alternative view on Elizabeth's reign. However, they do not detract from the reputation of that outstanding queen and most charismatic woman, but only enhance it. The author has provided a list of the principal historical characters mentioned in the text, an outlined chronology of Elizabeth's reign and a commentary after each section of the memoir.

List of Principal Historical Characters Mentioned in the Text

THE COURT OF HENRY VIII

HENRY VIII (1509-1547) – son of Henry VII, younger brother of Arthur.

MARY – Henry VIII's sister, married for a short time to Louis XII of France, later Charles Brandon, Duke of Suffolk.

THOMAS CRANMER (1489-1556) – Archbishop of Canterbury, presided over Henry VIII's divorce, executed by Mary Tudor.

THOMAS WOLSEY (1473-1530) – Cardinal Archbishop of York, Chief Minister of Henry VIII until 1529 when he fell from power over Henry's divorce from Catherine of Aragon.

THOMAS CROMWELL (1485-1540) – Chief Minister after Wolsey, fell from power after Henry VIII's inglorious marriage to Anne of Cleves.

CATHERINE OF ARAGON – Spanish Princess, Henry VIII's first wife, died 1536.

ANNE BOLEYN – second wife of Henry VIII, executed in 1536.

THOMAS AND ELIZABETH BOLEYN – Anne's parents.

MARY BOLEYN – Anne's sister, mother of an illegitimate child by Henry VIII.

GEORGE BOLEYN, HENRY NORRIS, MARK SMEATON – alleged lovers of Anne Boleyn.

KATHERINE HOWARD – Henry's fifth wife, executed for alleged adultery with Thomas Culpepper, 1542.

* * *

THE COURT OF EDWARD VI AND MARY TUDOR (1547-1558)

EDWARD VI – son of Henry VIII and Lady Jane Seymour.

THOMAS SEYMOUR – brother to Jane Seymour, uncle of the King. He married Henry VIII's widow Catherine Parr (who died in 1548). Entertained aspirations of marrying the Princess Elizabeth, executed for treason, 1549.

EDWARD SEYMOUR – Duke of Somerset, brother of Jane Seymour, uncle of the King, Protector of the Realm after the death of Henry VIII, fell from power 1552 and was executed.

JOHN DUDLEY – Earl of Warwick, Duke of Northumberland. He succeeded Somerset as Virtual Protector until the death of Edward VI in 1553. After the young King's death, Dudley married his son, Guildford, to Lady Jane Grey in an attempt to bypass the rights of Mary Tudor. The plot failed and Dudley was sent to the block.

MARY TUDOR – daughter of Henry VIII and Catherine of Aragon. Attempted to restore Catholicism, married Philip of Spain: her reign was characterised by plots, rebellion and persecution. She died in 1558.

* * *

THE COURT OF ELIZABETH 1

ROBERT DUDLEY – son of the above-mentioned John Dudley. Lover of Queen Elizabeth, later created Earl of Leicester, a dominant force in Elizabeth's court and council until his death in 1588.

WILLIAM CECIL – Elizabeth's chief minister, later created Lord Burghley. He virtually dominated Elizabeth's politics until his death in 1598 when he was succeeded by his diminutive and cunning son, Robert, a powerful force in the last years of Elizabeth's reign. Robert Cecil survived the Queen's death to become first minister of James I of England.

CHARLES HOWARD – of Effingham, Earl of Nottingham (1536-1624), held in great respect by Elizabeth and her successor James I.

JOHN WHITGIFT (Died 1604) – Archbishop of Canterbury at the time of Elizabeth's death.

SIR FRANCIS WALSINGHAM (Died 1590) – Secretary of State under Elizabeth, responsible for security both at home and abroad.

THE SCOTTISH COURT

MARY, QUEEN OF SCOTS (1542-1587) – daughter of James V, she married Francis II of France and, on his death, moved back to Scotland. She married the feckless Henry Darnley, whose murder led to civil war. Mary fled to England in 1568 where she became Elizabeth's prisoner and the focus of many plots until her execution in 1587.

JAMES VI OF SCOTLAND (Later James I of England) – Mary's only child who succeeded to the throne of England after Elizabeth, due to the work of men such as Robert Cecil and Henry Howard. James was married to Anne of Denmark.

SIR THOMAS BODLEY (1545-1613) – scholar, diplomat, bibliophile, responsible for refounding the library of Oxford University.

Chronology of the Reign of Elizabeth I (1558-1603)

1533   July: Robert Dudley born.
7th September: Elizabeth born to Henry VIII and his second queen, Anne Boleyn, proclaimed heir to the throne. State christening. Elizabeth was put under the charge of Margaret, Lady Bryan. Since Henry's first queen, the Catholic Catherine of Aragon, was still alive, Catherine's daughter, Mary, regarded Henry's marriage to Anne Boleyn as bigamous and Elizabeth as illegitimate.

1536   Death of Catherine of Aragon. Anne Boleyn found guilty on multiple charges of adultery and incest and executed. Henry VIII marries Jane Seymour, by whom he fathers a son, Edward. Elizabeth declared illegitimate, no longer heir to the throne.

1544   Mary and Elizabeth restored to the succession, after Edward.

1547   28th January: Death of Henry VIII, accession of Edward VI.

1547   Thomas Seymour marries the Queen Dowager, Catherine Parr, and soon begins a flirtation with her stepdaughter, the adolescent Elizabeth.

1548   Catherine Parr sends the Princess away from her household.
7th September: Catherine Parr dies following childbirth.

1549   17th January: Thomas Seymour arrested on charges of treason, which included plotting to marry the Princess Elizabeth without the consent of the Council. Elizabeth and her household are subjected to interrogations and "shameful slanders".
20th March: Seymour executed. Elizabeth resident at Hatfield.
Dudley, Duke of Northumberland, seizes power.

1550   Robert Dudley marries Lady Amy Robsart.

1553   6th July: Edward VI dies.
10th July: Jane Grey is proclaimed Queen.
11th July: Mary proclaims herself Queen and is swept to power.
19th July: Dudley, Duke of Northumberland is executed.
8th September: under increasing pressure from her sister Queen Mary, Elizabeth attends Mass.

1554   25th January: Wyatt's rebellion breaks out in protest at the marriage negotiations between Mary and Philip of Spain. It is suppressed, resulting in the speedy execution of Jane Grey and her husband, Guildford

Dudley, and the subsequent imprisonment and interrogation of Elizabeth in the Tower.

17th March: Elizabeth spends the next few weeks there [almost certainly without contact with Robert Dudley] until mid May, when she begins her journey north to Woodstock. She remains under house arrest in the charge of Sir Henry Bedingfield until the following year.

25th July: Philip of Spain and Mary marry.

1558   17th November: Mary dies, childless. Elizabeth is proclaimed Queen in London on the same day; the news is delivered to her at Hatfield by Robert Dudley.

1559   14th January: Eve of Coronation procession through the City.

15th January: Coronation.

10th February: Elizabeth replies to the House of Commons' petition urging her to marry: "in the end, this shall be for me sufficient that a marble stone shall declare that a Queen, having reigned such a time, lived and died a virgin". Nevertheless, marriage negotiations are opened with a range of possible suitors: Philip of Spain, Archduke Charles of Austria, and Prince Eric of Sweden. Elizabeth's relationship with Robert Dudley deepens.

23rd April: Dudley dubbed Knight of the Garter. Gossip about his relationship with the Queen circulates.

1559/1560 Diplomatic circles are rife with news of Dudley's ascendancy, about his wife's 'malady of the breast' and that Dudley intends to divorce or even murder her by poison. Lady Amy moves to different residences: Denchworth then to Cumnor Place, only thirty miles from Windsor where the Queen, Dudley and Court gather for Elizabeth's 27th Birthday.

8th September 1560: Lady Amy rises early and demands that she be left alone. She wants the ladies resident with her to go to Abingdon Fair. They object. Dudley and Elizabeth apparently spend the weekend hunting and feasting.

8th September: Sudden death of Lady Amy. Dudley banished from court to Kew during the inquest. Although the coroner returns a verdict of accidental death, many suspect Dudley of having her murdered (possibly with Elizabeth's connivance) in order to be free to marry the Queen.

8th to 18th September: A time of frenetic activity: Dudley dispatches Blount, his henchman, to Cumnor to discover what really happened. The Mayor/Coroner of Abingdon sits with the jury: Dudley and Blount are in correspondence with them.

October: Throckmorton, Elizabeth's ambassador in Paris, is busy warning Cecil of the real scandal being caused.

November: Interview between Elizabeth and Throckmorton's envoy, Mr Jones.

1561   Arundel and others harass Dudley. They scrutinise the verdict of the Cumnor jury.

June: The Spanish ambassador, de Quadra, records how Elizabeth and Dudley, sharing a boat with him on the Thames, joked that he himself might conduct a marriage ceremony between them on the spot.

1562   Queen dangerously ill with smallpox. (The Tamworth episode). From now on she is under renewed pressure to marry both from her Council and the Commons.

1564   The Scots ambassador, James Melville, visits the English court. His account of his conversations with the English Queen concerning the rival accomplishments and the appearance of Mary, Queen of Scots, lays the foundation for some of the later stories of the rivalry between the two. He witnesses Dudley's investiture as Earl of Leicester, during which the Queen fondles Leicester's neck.

1566/1567 John Appleyard, Lady Amy's half-brother, supported by Norfolk (who has quarrelled violently with Dudley) begins to hint that he is not happy with the Cumnor jury verdict. Appleyard is imprisoned and interrogated by members of the Privy Council. He makes a full submission.

1569   Northern Rebellion quashed. Discovery of the Ridolfi Plot leads to the imprisonment of Appleyard.

1573   Sir Francis Walsingham is made Principal Secretary of State. He begins to develop an elaborate intelligence network.

1575   Leicester entertains Elizabeth lavishly at Kenilworth, perhaps in a final bid to marry her.

1578   Leicester marries Lettice Knollys secretly.

1585 'Leicester's Commonwealth' published, an attack on Leicester by an anonymous Catholic propagandist, which claims that, in September 1560, Leicester had his wife murdered by Richard Verney and Anthony Forster.

1587 1st February: Elizabeth signs the death warrant of Mary, Queen of Scots.
8th February: Mary, Queen of Scots, is executed at Fotheringay. Elizabeth claims her secretary, Davison, sent the warrant without her consent.

1587/1588 Sir Francis Englefield writes to Philip of Spain regarding Arthur Dudley. The English agent in Spain, known as B.C., writes about the same to Cecil in England.

1588 12th July: The Spanish Armada sets sail.
September: Death of Robert Dudley.

1598 Death of William Cecil, Lord Burghley.

1601 8th February: Essex sent to the Tower for treason.
25th February: Essex executed.

1603 February: Elizabeth falls ill, soon after the funeral of her old friend, the Countess of Nottingham. Some time in March the Coronation ring is filed from the Queen's hand.
24th March: Death of the Queen at Richmond Palace.
28th April: Funeral of the Queen, Westminster Abbey.

Part I

My Mistress is dead. The Queen, Elizabeth of England, is no more. Glorious Gloriana has gone to her eternal glory, so swiftly, like the darting of a martin bird from beneath the eaves of my house. Yet, God be my witness, her going was shrouded in mystery. Her Majesty, being in her 69th year, was Queen – and a great one – reigning for 45 years, longer than anyone, even more so than her mother, God assoil her, who never survived four. In her last years Her Majesty grew conscious of her age and appearance. Everyone at Court, myself included, knew how it pleased the Queen very much for it to be seen, for it to be thought, and for it to be told, that she looked very young. At our final Christmas, when the Court was in its last blaze of glory, Mr Secretary Cecil presented her with a jewel set with rubies and topaz to match, as he told me, "the life of Her Majesty's eyes and the colour of her lips". False flattery aside, the Queen was still very majestic in her final years. Her face was oblong, fair but wrinkled, her eyes were small, jet-black and pleasant, her nose a little hooked, her lips narrow, and her teeth black; her hair was of auburn colour, but false. Upon her head she often wore a small crown. Her bosom was all uncovered, as we English ladies have it, until we marry. My Mistress' hands were slender, her fingers rather long and her stature neither tall nor low. Her air was stately and her manner of speech mild. She would speak very graciously, first to one then

1

to another, and her command of tongues was remarkable. She could converse in French and Italian, being also skilled in Latin and Greek. She was mistress of Spanish and Dutch. Foreign envoys could converse most easily with her. Whoever spoke to her must kneel. Now and then she'd raise some with her hands. Wherever she turned her face, everyone fell to their knees. I was no different. In her private chamber, she would crouch by me and whisper, one hand on my shoulder or knee. In public, however, she was the Great Queen, the Heart of the Blaze, the Source of the Glory, whilst I was a mere taper flickering before the Imperial presence. I must assure you of this, even to the end, despite passing moods, my Mistress' wits remained razor sharp. She could politic with the best but, as she once told me, she had no time for her brother princes whom she dismissed as "Antichrists of Ingratitude". To all her Court she was Beauty Incarnate, endowed with eternal youth. Woe betide any man, be he priest or lay, who broke that rule. Master Rudd, Bishop of St David's, found this to his cost when he preached the Lenten Sermon to the Queen in her Royal Chapel at Richmond during her 63rd year, the spring of our Lord, 1596. The good Bishop took as his text that verse from the 90th psalm, "So teach us to number our days...", and proceeded to preach about sacred, mystical numbers; how three was the number of the Trinity, seven of the Sabbath, and seven times nine, 63, the Great Climacteric Year. The Queen, as usual, listened to this sermon in her private closet behind a screen. She seethed like a panther in its cage. After the service was finished, it was customary for her to open the closet window and thank the preacher. But, Lord be praised, on this occasion, Her Majesty winked at me, opened the window and sharply declared that Master Bishop should keep his arithmetic to himself whilst all he'd proved was that the greatest clerks were not the wisest men. "God's teeth," she swore to me later, "Bishops should preach and leave such numbers to God." Her Majesty certainly entertained dreams of reigning long and her Court favoured her in this. On one occasion, Sir John Stanhope the Vice-Chamberlain, one of Master Secretary's creatures, a fawning greyhound of a man, presented Her Majesty with a piece of gold, big as an angel, dimly marked with some small, mysterious characters. Sir John informed me, so I could tell the Queen, how an old woman in Wales had bequeathed it to Her Majesty. He alleged the same old woman, by virtue of this piece of gold, had lived to over one hundred years. Now the old woman wished Her Majesty to hold the gold and live as long. My Mistress truly believed Sir John had bought it from some Cheapside chapman but told me to keep it in her special coffer, just in case. Be that as it may, in the January of the year of our Lord 1603, the Queen and I journeyed from Whitehall to Richmond. The Queen did not like Whitehall. I reminded her how she had been warned by the necromancer, John Dee, to be wary of that palace, while she and I always regarded Richmond as a warm winter box for her old age. My Mistress was in low spirits. At Whitehall she had premonitions, so she claimed, of an impending tragedy and shared them with her closest friends. Now, I saw none of these portents. I cannot say that, during these dreadful nights, the front of the heavens was lit by fiery shapes or blazing cressets. However, the Queen told Lady Southwell, with whom she was very private and confident, how one night, just before she left Whitehall, she had a vision of her own body, lean and fearful, in the glow of a mysterious fire. I cannot comment on the truth of this. Sometimes I was with Her Majesty, seated before a roaring fire in some wainscoted chamber with the wind rattling at the casement and the candlelight flickering like will-o-the-wisps in the dark. Other times, I was not. My Mistress did not wish to overtax me and would order me to withdraw. Certes, whilst she was alive, what she said to one of her ladies, would not be repeated to another. Whilst, as regards gossip between ourselves – well, we were like cloistered nuns with a tight rein on our tongues and a lock about our lips. On occasion, in those last days, she would whisper to herself about her mother and Norris, about sweet

3

Robin of Dudley and make the blessed sign against the shades of Mary of Scotland, Devereux of Essex and those other ghosts clustering about her. Her Majesty grew deeply melancholic and decided to see a true looking-glass: in twenty years she had not looked in a mirror but had a special one made to deceive her sight, it was kept by me in her private coffer. When I brought a true looking-glass, Her Majesty was shocked and fell to complaining about those who had formerly praised her. She did not blame me, for to me she was always lovely of face and fair of form yet, she was so offended by the sight, that former flatterers dare not come into her presence.

Her Majesty did not fall suddenly ill at Richmond these February days but, day by day, she decreased both her resting and feeding and, within a short time, fell very sick indeed. I do not wish to provide the symptoms, the different signs, because I am not too sure about the true cause of their malevolence. My Mistress had withdrawn down the lozenge-shaped, black and white tiled gallery to her own private chambers. Dark rooms, their walls covered in linen panelling, the cream plaster above rather dulled but still made glorious by vivid paintings or richly burnished tapestries. A place which clung like a shadow about us, lit and warmed by candles, chafing dishes and red-hot fires. This was the stage for her final masque, warm and close, whilst, beyond the walls, winter raged and the kingdom slumbered. A dramatic ending for Her Majesty as the night's candles burnt themselves out. Her extreme melancholy increased and, for two days and three nights she stood, or sat upon a stool, finger to her mouth around which, or so she told me, she could view a ring of golden fire. Mr Secretary Cecil came bustling in and said, "Your Majesty, to content the people you must retire to bed." To which she replied, "Little man, little man, the word 'must' is not to be used to kings and princes. If your father (Lord Burghley) had lived, you durst not have said it but, ye know, I am to die and this makes thee so presumptuous." She stayed on that stool fully dressed and none of her Council could persuade her to retire to bed or to eat or drink. I just sat and prayed. I had no authority; I could only wait like someone watching the moon pass through its different phases. Her Majesty complained of a heat in her breast, a dryness in her throat which kept her from sleep. Only the Lord Admiral (Charles Howard, Earl of Nottingham) at one time persuaded her to drink some broth and Her Majesty reminded me of how she had visited Lord Burghley, when he was dying, and fed him the same with her own hand.

The Queen still refused to answer any of the Council's questions even though there was a great deal of bustling to and fro. When the Lord Admiral earnestly persuaded the Queen to retire to her bed, Her Majesty quietly replied, "My Lord, if you had seen in my bed what I have seen, you would not persuade me to do that! I also have a premonition that once I lie down I shall never rise." She then dismissed the rest of her Council from her chamber but told Howard, the Lord Admiral, to stay. Once they were alone, she grasped his hand, shook her head and with pitiful voice said, "My Lord, I am tied with a chain of iron about my feet."

"Your Majesty," he replied, "what are these dire visions of the night? What do you mean? Be of good courage." He was aware how deep of night had crept upon their talk and wished the Queen to be at rest. However, Her Majesty shook her head and replied in a mournful voice, "I am tied, I am tied and the case is altered with me."

The Queen continued to sicken during the third week of March. Eventually she collapsed. We carried her to her own bed. She recovered a little when certain pustules in her throat erupted; so much blood and pus burst out, we thought she might choke. The source of these pustules was a mystery but she was full of phlegm and catarrh. We changed her gowns and placed her back in bed.

The Queen declared she felt a little better so I placed rosewater and currants on her bedside table. Nonetheless, the sickness returned. Her Majesty's illness and subsequent death at three in the morning of 24th March, were presaged by strange happenings and sinister occurrences. According to Lady Southwell, two ladies of her chamber moving the Queen's chair happened to look underneath and discovered a playing card, the Queen of Hearts, attached to the bottom of the chair with an iron nail knocked through the forehead of the image. The ladies dare not pull it out, remembering such devices were used by those who meddled in witchcraft and sorcery. Lady Southwell, she of the auburn hair and ready smile, allied to many of the Howard faction, told me this one dark-clouded morning when I'd returned to wait on Her Majesty. I saw the card and glimpsed the iron nail. Cruelty! Ingratitude! I gazed around at all those in the waiting chamber: little Cecil, all pert-faced and ready, Howard of Effingham, the Lord Admiral, heavy-jowled and bearded, garbed in his mantle of fur and ermine-edged gown with others of his tribe, including the Lady Mary Howard, fair-haired, fair-faced and black of heart. Someone like Master Holbein should have been present to paint them all, to catch the ambition glittering in their eyes like greyhounds hasty for the chase.

During those sombre days, the Court held its breath though many of the Lords of the Council were already in secret business with James of Scotland, the son of that Mary whom Her Majesty had sentenced to death. Indeed, certain of the Council had already taken aside Robert Carey, Lord Hunsdon's son. This fair-haired, rubicund-faced young man, a friend of James of Scotland (to whom he had been sent on embassy), was, by mere chance or so he told me, visiting the Queen at Court. However, as I learned later, in his journey south, Carey had stationed good horses, his swiftest steeds, at Doncaster, Witherington, and other places. Master Carey had also written to his friend the Scottish King how Serjeant Death, always strict in his arrest, would seize the

Queen and that "necessary end" would come swiftly enough to suck the honey from the Queen's breath. No one dares open the Book of Fate, so the likes of Master Carey and those others of the Queen's privy chamber should not have been the ones to leaf through its pages. As Her Majesty once said to me, "the web of life is a mingled yarn, good and ill mixed together", so who should dare, during such dangerous days, to pluck and sift one from the other? This was the drawing-out time when men spoke to each other in whispers as they realized our enchanting Queen's life might break off. I watched them all gather in the waiting chamber like ravens along a branch. A cold fear chilled my veins and almost froze my heartbeat. I dare not speak about the signs and portents, especially at a time when fear filled so many souls, a mere bush became a bear. I could not look at the seeds of time and say which would sprout and which would not. Nevertheless, the signs were there, even to the Queen's spirit becoming detached from her ageing body, before the twine, which wound them together, fully snapped. I have the following on good report from the Lady Southwell. One night, when the wax candles in the Queen's palace had guttered low, Lady Guildford, one of Her Majesty's attendants, a serious-minded woman, left the Queen sleeping in her bed and went three or four chambers off to search for something. Lady Guildford grew busy but, on hearing a sound, looked up and saw the Queen standing in the doorway staring at her. Lady Guildford, frightened lest Her Majesty be angry for leaving her bedside, hastened to excuse herself, whereupon the Queen vanished. Lady Guildford, her heart fraught with fear, hastened back to the Royal Chamber only to find Her Majesty sleeping deeply in her bed. I was not aware of such happenings; they occurred when I was away. On reflection, I wonder if they were stories to prove that Her Majesty's passing was ordained by God not by man. Nevertheless, I sensed the atmosphere, like dusk on a November evening when light and dark mingle and all sorts of danger might shoot from the swirling mist. The Lords of the Council, aware of such spiritual happenings, sent priests to her: the Archbishop of Canterbury and other clerics. When the Queen saw these she was much offended, angrily berated them and sent them packing. Afterwards she exclaimed to the Lord Admiral, "My Lord, I have had the greatest indignity offered to me that a Prince could suffer – to have sentence of death pronounced in my hearing as if I had lived as an atheist."

"Would you have other priests come?" the Lord Admiral asked.

"I will have none of such hedge priests," Her Majesty retorted. The Queen became much confused. She had consulted with a Catholic hermit and been most comforted by his presence and words. I remember him well – an old man out of Ireland who conversed long and hard with the Queen. On one occasion, my Mistress rolled on her side and glanced hollow-eyed at me. "Do I need such comfort?" she asked. "Is my going also ordained?" I could only stare earnestly back. I did not know what was wrong with the Queen. Her sickness was so sudden, strange and, despite even my urgings, she would have no physic. Think of me as some sea-object, washed back and forth by the tide of affairs, I could offer little comfort except remind Her Majesty that spiritual solace might help. Eventually, she relented. Her Chaplain, Dr Parry, arrived along with His Grace, Archbishop Whitgift of Canterbury. They stayed most solicitously by her bedside holding her hand until she died. Some reported how, by signs and movements of her eyes, the Queen did place her trust in God. I assure you she did. Nonetheless, before this occurred, the Lords of Council were not so trusting about the question of the succession. On the Tuesday before her death, being the 23rd March, the Lord Admiral standing on the right side of her bed, the Lord Keeper on her left, and Mr Secretary Cecil by the bed's foot, the Lord Admiral put Her Majesty in mind concerning her successor, a matter of sour nature to her. The Council had demanded that I and other ladies of the chamber withdraw but I listened at the door. The Lord Admiral explained how the three of them, in the name of all her

Council, had come to know her pleasure regarding the succession. Whereupon Her Majesty replied, for she had a tiger's heart in a woman's skin, "I have told you, and I tell you again, my seat is the seat of kings. I will have no rascal to succeed me. Indeed, who should succeed me but a king."

The Council Lords, not understanding this dark speech, looked warily at each another. At length, Mr Secretary boldly asked her what she meant by the words 'no rascal should succeed her'?

She replied, according to Master Cecil, though I did not hear this, "A king must succeed and who else can this be but our cousin of Scotland?"

Now, of course that was the reply Mr Secretary wanted – he was always ready to advertise it as such. Nevertheless he was like a dog with a bone. I heard movement but the voices beyond the door had fallen to a murmur.

"Your Majesty," Mr Secretary allegedly whispered, "is that your absolute resolution?"

"I pray you to trouble me no more," she replied, "I will have none but him."

About four o'clock in the afternoon, the above-mentioned Lords repaired unto her once again. Master Secretary clicked his fingers and told us to leave before asking the Queen if she remained firm in her former resolution about who should succeed her?

Her Majesty was unable to reply, whereupon Mr Secretary demanded, or so his report would have it, "We do beseech Your Majesty. Do you remain firm in your former resolution? That the King of Scots succeeds you in your kingdom? If so, show some sign to us."

Whereupon, suddenly heaving herself upwards in her bed and pulling her arms out of the sheets, the Queen held both her hands jointly together over her head in the manner of a crown whereby they concluded Her Majesty had chosen the King of Scots. In truth, such a gesture could mean anything. At ten o'clock that same evening, with the rain clattering against her casement window, the Queen fell into unconsciousness whilst the priests continued to send their prayers before her soul. In the early hours, I would say about three o'clock, the Queen died, her soul going forth mildly as a lamb, easy as a ripe apple falling from a tree. Lady Scrope, another of her attendants, immediately went to the window and dropped a ring to Sir Robert Carey, the agreed sign that our Royal Mistress was dead. Master Carey hastened off. He was met between the gates of Richmond Palace and told to hurry north as Master Secretary Cecil believed others of the Council might detain him as not everyone looked forward to James the Scot. Carey slipped away, took horse and rode to Doncaster where he had fresh mounts waiting for the journey into Scotland. Master Carey believed he was doing right because every subject's duty is the Crown's but every subject's soul is his own. Yet, there again, the devil can quote scripture for his own purpose and be seen as a saint when, in truth, he plays the imp: many thought Master Carey's haste was both unseemly and unwarranted. In which case, he was not the only one guilty of such lèse majesté. I can only report what I saw. After Her Majesty died, she lay between the sheets, head slightly back, eyes closed, her mouth slightly open. The priests, exhausted, had left. I could hear comings and goings in the chamber beyond, men and women arriving and departing, doors and casements being opened and shut whilst their Royal Mistress lay forgotten on the bed. I held a mirror to her lips but caught no breath, the soul being quietly departed. Such majesty, such glory, such memories all centred on that lifeless corpse whilst the Court withdrew and all eyes turned to another beginning.

Once the Queen had departed this life and, in doing so, had paid all her debts, the Lords of the Council hurried to London to proclaim His Majesty the King of Scots their Sovereign Lord. In their haste the Queen's body was left alone a day or two after her death so mean persons had access to it. I cannot comment on this because I withdrew from the death chamber; I was ill, sick at heart and weak in all my humours. My belly ached, as did my heart, and I only recovered my good spirits after Her Majesty's funeral. Nonetheless, I became most solicitous about what had happened to Her Majesty's remains. Only on the third day was Her Majesty's coffin sealed up and brought by torchlit barge to Whitehall, where it was watched every night by six good ladies. The coffin was laid on purple-gold cloths stretched over trestles. According to Lady Southwell who was in attendance, Her Majesty's corpse, though all nailed up and wrapped in a fresh cloth of wax within a broad coffin with leaves of lead and covered in velvet, swelled up and broke the coffin. Such a crack! It splintered wood and lead, as well as its wax-cere cloth, to the terror and astonishment of all who saw it. The corpse had to be trimmed up again in its royal casings to keep it secure and wholesome. Now, I have, God be my witness, made diligent enquiries on this matter. When Her Majesty died, the Lords of the Council decreed that the Queen's corpse ought not to be opened up and embalmed because that was Her Majesty's wish, and one she had shared with me. However, once most of the Lords were gone, Master Secretary Cecil secretly left instructions for Her Majesty's body to be opened to allow out the vapour of death. The surgeons, having been given a secret warrant, opened her to emit the fumes from the corpse. Why this contradiction? I do not understand it unless it was to hide some secret malignant act. True, Her Majesty had been ill, and was of advanced years, but I began to wonder if she had not been fed some delicious poison? Such compounds, masked in sweetmeats, are the movers of a languishing death, and often leave their mark which needs to be removed. I racked my memory to reflect on those final days. Her Majesty journeying from Whitehall to Richmond, rejecting food, refusing physic, becoming all tight-lipped and wary. So, who did feed her in those final days? The Lord Admiral gave her broth but, by then, she was already languishing deeply whilst she hardly touched the currants and rosewater I placed on her bedside table.

Her Majesty was in excellent health at the beginning of the year and been on her progresses, falling ill of a cold on the 12th January 1603. She moved to Richmond where she was soon healed. The Queen was attended by a swirl of people who came and went. God knows what she ate and drank then. On Monday, 28th February she began to sicken again and so continued until Monday, 7th March. At this time, notice of her cold was given to the Lords of the Council, the Queen continued sick till Tuesday, 15th March. On the following Friday, 18th March, she began to be very ill, whereupon the Lords of the Council were called to Richmond and continued there in full session until 24th of that month, the day she died. Now murder, even if it has no tongue, always speaks out and cries that question which rings to heaven, 'Who profits?' Is it not strange, a matter of morbid curiosity that Her Majesty's ghost was glimpsed before she died? That the Queen of Hearts was found nailed to a chair in her own privy chamber? I asked myself, did someone wish for Her Majesty's death? Blood, including that of kings, has been shed since Adam's time, whilst the murder of princes has been perpetrated, sometimes in a manner too terrible for the ear to hear or the soul to digest. In all cases the question of guilt remains and so does that of profit. Who profited then? I have considered this and reached one conclusion: the Yellow Jackets, the Howards of Norfolk. Rivalries aside, even though they were close to the Queen, the Howards nursed resentments against her. It was a Howard, Charles, Earl of Nottingham who, on the morning of her removal from Whitehall, first asked the Queen about the succession. I know, I heard him. My Lord of Nottingham was married, or had been, till her death that same February, to Catherine, daughter of Lord Hunsdon: she was the sister of Robert Carey, the man who stood by doorways, beneath casement windows, caught falling rings and appeared between the gates of Richmond Palace to receive news how Her Majesty had died and he should ride like Jehu for Scotland. Carey was no real friend of the Queen whatever he might boast in his writings or speech. Her Majesty had told me all about him. She had been mightily offended by Carey marrying a widow without royal approval. He only regained Her Majesty's favour after a stormy and terrible encounter, one I witnessed standing in the chamber beyond. Oh, strange it is and most curious still, how Carey, Warden of the Middle March of Scotland and a Member of the Commons from the County of Northumberland, should, by mere chance, travel hundreds of miles in the late winter of that year to be present when Her Majesty fell into her final sickness. Stranger still, when that Queen died, the same Carey had all the preparations ready to hurry across the Scottish March to be the first to inform her successor. Carey later claimed he acted to protect his own concerns. I met him once at Hunsdon House where he said to me: "I did assure myself it was neither unjust nor dishonest for me to do something for myself if God did, in His own good time, call Her Majesty to His mercy." Ah yes, I reflected but, Master Carey, you did more than that! According to a young Scot I later became sweet with, a message from Carey arrived in Edinburgh on 19th March to assure King James that the Queen could only live a few days more. He, Carey, would tarry in London to bring him first news of her death whilst he assured the Scottish King that he had already placed horses along the way to give him speed in his post. True, Fortune does blow in boats which are neither steered or have no sails but, for Master Carey, Fickle Fortune dealt ever so well. Carey's messenger arrived in Edinburgh on 19th March. Carey himself took two days of hard riding to reach the Palace of Holyrood. Let us say Carey's Mercury, his winged herald, took six days journeying, this meant he left London on 13th yet, according to the Lords of the Council, it was not until 18th March that Her Majesty began "to be very ill". Curious indeed it is, for a member of the Commons from the North, Warden of the Middle March of Scotland, to be given such a prophetic spirit that eleven days before Her Majesty died, at least five before she began to be very ill, Carey was knowledgeable enough to send messages, arrange horses and leave when he wished, to take the sad news to Scotland. God be my witness, he had better sight than I who sat by Her Majesty and willed her better. This Carey was lavishly rewarded by James but not as much as Howard, Earl of Nottingham and others amongst the Yellow Jackets; they had all been in close correspondence with James who sent them rubies out of Scotland as tokens of his affection. Oh, I have watched events. These Howards rose high when James rode south, being given preferment both in the Privy Council and elsewhere, so it became Howard this and Howard that. Her Majesty, however, privately told me she never liked the Howards, except for the Lord Admiral, even though her mother, Boleyn, was of Howard stock. Indeed, as I shall relate, Her Majesty was much concerned by the meddling of the Howards with her 'Sweet Robin', her beloved Robert Dudley, Earl of Leicester. She always deemed the Howards treacherous. She whispered privately to me how she believed they had some hand in the mysterious death of Lord Dudley's wife, Lady Amy, even trying to place her death, from a fall betwixt stairs, at Dudley's door.

The power of Norfolk was severely checked during Her Majesty's reign and I shall prove this. Thomas, the Fourth Earl, lost his head on Tower Hill in the June of 1572 for treasonably plotting with the Italian Ridolfi to free the imprisoned Mary, Queen of Scots and marry her. This traitor's eldest son, Philip of Arundel, suffered a similar fate 23 years later. Being a rank Papist, Arundel was imprisoned in the Tower; but he did not die resting his head on the headman's block, he was suddenly taken ill during the month of August 1595 after a dinner in the Tower. Some claimed he died of the rigours inflicted on him, others chattered about poison. Accordingly, as my journal, the gospel of her reign, will relate, the Howards had good cause to resent Her Majesty, to wish her gone and welcome James riding south. In truth, I saw their faces, hypocrites all. They came before Her Majesty crying "All hail", like Judas when they really meant, 'All harm'. However, to return to the events of those Ides of March when the Queen fell very ill. Who might inflict such mortal injury on her? Who would be the Brutus to give the killing blow? Such a person must have been part of her close company for that playing card, that hideous curse to be placed on a chair and pierced with a nail in Her Majesty's own chamber. I have thought long and hard, kneeling on my prie-dieu in my private chapel or toasting my toes in a fire-hot chamber. I have sat and reflected whilst the moon wanes and the stars flower and fade. Faces come before me, Howard's, Cecil's, but they were men kept at arm's distance. So who else? Who are left but the ladies of Her Majesty's chamber, those honeysuckles who ripened so well under the glow of their royal sun? Oh, it's so very true, pretty flowers, when they fester, smell worse than rotten weeds. Amongst Her Majesty's ladies-in-waiting was one Mary Howard, a lady watched most carefully by her Royal Mistress, a kinswoman of that same tribe and one who nursed grievous resentments against Her Majesty. Mary Howard! 'The country girl', I called her, sweet of face and coy of manner. A subtle smile whose fragrant ways and delicate manner hid a scheming mind and an arrogant soul. A conspiring Cleopatra with her blonde hair and clear, blue eyes, who paid such attention to her appearance. Now our Queen always revelled in her glory and laid keen emphasis on her splendid gowns which advertised her imperious, majestic nature. Her Majesty paid keen attention to what she wore as well as the appearance of those around her. In the early spring of 1594, Aylmer the aged bishop of Durham, dared preach in the Queen's presence against the vanity of decking the body too finely. Afterwards the Queen angrily declared to me that if the good bishop dared to preach like that again, she would not only fit him for heaven, he would walk there without his crozier and leave his furred mantle behind! Her Majesty was very conscious that clothes maketh the woman and bolster the power of the prince. She always insisted that I and other ladies-in-waiting wear only black or white so that the splendour of her own apparel would shine more vividly. Lady Mary Howard ignored this. She took to wearing a red velvet gown, its collar proudly powdered with glowing gold and precious pearl, a garment much admired by the rest. Lady Mary knew the Queen was displeased but, in her arrogance, refused to concede even though my Mistress warned her. Eventually, the Queen took Lady Mary into her own privy chamber: I accompanied them. My Mistress did not remonstrate with her but asked if she could borrow the aforesaid gown. Lady Mary Howard, all a-fluster, was constrained to agree. She handed her costly garb to the Queen who promptly dressed in it and paraded herself in front of the Court. Her Majesty was in a silent fury like a galleon slipping across the sea, all quiet but cleared for battle. Everyone could see the precious gown was too short for the Queen who was much taller than her lady-in-waiting. Her Majesty taxed her courtiers on what they thought; they all commended it highly. I kept silent. After everyone else had praised it, the Queen turned to Mary Howard.

"Is it not," Her Majesty asked, "too short for my person?"

"Your Majesty is correct," Lady Mary hastened to agree.

"Why then," the Queen replied, "if it becomes not me as being too short, I am minded it shall never become thee, as being too fine. So it fitteth neither of us very well."

The Queen returned the gown to Lady Mary who immediately hid it deep in her wardrobe and never wore it again until after Her Majesty's death.

The Queen was angrily minded towards Lady Mary for other reasons than a pearl-trimmed gown. True, in Her Majesty's eyes, a woman's soul may be in her clothes but Lady Mary Howard was guilty of more than that, a matter she often referred to during that fateful February. When Robert Devereux, Earl of Essex, former favourite of the Queen, rose to prominence and his star dazzled the Court and frosted all with its glittering gloss, Lady Mary Howard was much smitten by him. In time, as I shall describe, the Earl of Essex, because of his arrogance and plots against Her Majesty, fell from power and lost his head under the third stroke of the headman's axe at Tower Hill. This occurred two years previous in the February of 1601. Nonetheless, Her Majesty had not forgotten. I am a widow still because I followed my Royal Mistress' example; the Queen did not take kindly to any dalliance by her maids. She accused Lady Mary of an illicit relationship with her favourite Earl and never ignored any opportunity to humiliate her. The incident of the gown was only one amongst many. Lady Mary was bidden to trail the Queen wherever she went and hold the hem of her dress. Her Majesty treated Lady Mary as a servant, bidding her to serve her at table and fill her cup with wine. I do wonder if our Lady Mary, who was with the Queen during her progress in the spring of 1603, was the Brutus-in-waiting. I have tried to recall each day but it is impossible to describe each hour, and what happened, where and when. Her Majesty was on progress, cups and platters were filled and served; sometimes I was there, sometimes not. God knows who gave her what to eat and drink. Some might dismiss this as fanciful, the work of a cogging, cozening tongue, the venomous malice of a swelling heart. They will point out that, in the February before she fell sick, the Queen's own cousin and dearest friend, the aforesaid Catherine, the Countess of Nottingham died, for whose death the Queen wept bitterly and showed an uncommon concern. According to gossip, the Queen fell into a deep depression, a mood not lightened by the sawing off of her coronation ring, the symbol of her marriage with the kingdom; this had become so deeply embedded in her swollen finger, it could not be tolerated. Shortly after this, Her Majesty told me how she had written to Henry of France that the fabric of her reign, little-by-little, was beginning to fade.

Yet, to cry murder is not too fanciful. Let us return to the events of February 1603, the year of Her Majesty's death. February was a mournful month for the Queen. Two years previously the Earl of Essex had paid the supreme price for daring to touch the sceptre

of princes, losing both honour and life on the scaffold. In that last
February, so common report has it, after Catherine, Countess of
Nottingham, wife of the Lord Admiral, died, the Queen remained
in a deep melancholy and complained of many infirmities, a
thickening in her head, aches in her bones and continual cold in
her legs. Frailty of soul and mind also weighed her down and,
according to malicious reports, even her wits wandered. True she
could not abide discussion of government and state but delighted
to hear the *Canterbury Tales*. I read these to her often and they
pleased her greatly. At other times, I concede, she was importunate
and testy so that none of her Council, except Master Secretary
Cecil, dare come into her presence. These are not the actions of a
witless woman. Nevertheless, this was how Her Majesty was
depicted. The Venetian ambassador, Signor Carlo Scaramelli
reported how the Queen had become "quite silly and idiotic".
Seigneur Beaumont, the French ambassador wrote: "The Queen
has declared, 'I wish not to live but desire to die …' and is said to
be no longer in her right senses." I have sat many a night poring
over a cup of posset, staring into the fire flames whilst I invoked
these memories of yesteryear. Her Majesty learnt of these reports
about her wits wandering and asked me to investigate. I did so,
and the clerks of these ambassadors merrily sold their masters'
secrets for a bright smile and honeyed words. Accordingly, as I
shall relate, I was much surprised at their source. Master Secretary
Cecil even had the impudence to ask the Queen about her mind –
and if Her Majesty had seen any spirits? My Royal Mistress did
not even countenance a reply. In truth Her Majesty was weak but
strongly in her right wits. She did not wish to rush into the secret
House of Death or do that deed which ends all other deeds.
Certainly Her Majesty was most anxious. Even the Venetians
reported how she was worried about the succession and 'other
matters'? What were these 'other matters'? I shall tell you clearly.
Her Majesty was not so much grief stricken over the Countess of
Northampton's death as more angry about what that good

Countess had confessed whilst dying. The Queen had much loved Robert Devereux, Earl of Essex. In their honey days, she had given my Lord of Essex a ring and told him that, should he be in any dire necessity, if he sent that ring to her she would always respond favourably. The Earl fell from power and was dispatched to the Tower. After Essex was judged a traitor and condemned to the block, he had the precious ring conveyed secretly to the Countess of Nottingham to deliver to Her Majesty. The Countess, however, knowing how much her husband, the Lord Admiral, and Master Secretary Cecil hated the fallen Earl and desired his death, detained the ring, so my Lord of Essex was executed by due process of law. The Countess, on her deathbed, revealed this truth to Her Majesty and craved her pardon. The Queen, in mingled grief and fury, struck the dying woman and swore, "God forgive you woman, but I never can." No, I was not there, the Queen being closeted by herself with her dying friend. Yet I was with Her Majesty afterwards; I saw her face and listened to her ranting before she slipped into sickness – or was eased into it. I know what's gone is past all help and should be past grief. I cannot prove what I am going to say. The noiseless foot of time has moved on, but it may unmask falsehood and bring truth to light. I do not want to be bound in a dark room or suffer some mishap on a lonely road. Nonetheless, if I have to die, I will embrace the darkness like a lover and hug it close. Certain sins are so rank they reek to heaven yet leave no proof except a gossiping tongue. I have been, and shall be, more artful. I have kept away from reports of the Lords of the Council, and dined those clerks from the foreign embassies. They'll witness to what I say. Let them tell you my tale in their tongue. According to the Venetian envoy, Signor Scaramelli, after the Countess of Nottingham died, and before the Queen fell grievously ill, Her Majesty turned to considering how the Earl of Essex used to be her dear and intimate friend and might have been quite innocent after all: she burst into tears and dolorous lamentations as if for some serious sin she had committed.

I call a similar witness to a more sinister matter. After the Queen fell ill, she did not take any physic whilst the absence of physicians around her during those dangerous days is remarkable. Archbishop Whitgift, whom she called her 'little black husband', and Master Secretary Cecil, begged on their knees for her to seek a remedy in physic to which the Queen replied, "I know my own strength and constitution better than you my lords. I am not in such danger as you imagine." I, too, begged, for amity's sake, to call the physicians but she turned away whispering about Essex. In England I'll find no one to prove this – the proof lies elsewhere. Signor Cavalli, the Venetian ambassador in Paris, reported the Queen was most adamant in refusing physic; a statement repeated by Seigneur Beaumont who declared "the Queen takes no medicine whatsoever", whilst that loose-tongued gossip, Anthony Rivers, in a letter to an acquaintance in Italy, described how the Queen "fiercely resisted physic". Yet, 30 years previous, when the Queen was young and hale, the French ambassador, Fenelon, reported to his masters in Paris on 31st March 1572, "The Queen of England, with the permission of her physicians, has been able to come out of her private chamber." If Her Majesty called physicians then and entrusted herself to them, why not for this sickness during the last year of her life?

I shall tell you why. There is a strong tie between the execution of the Earl of Essex and the Queen's last melancholy. The Earl of Essex rose high, and whilst in the Queen's favour, the Earl showed, at least to his own satisfaction, how one of her physicians, the Portuguese Doctor Lopez, had been hired to kill her. The physician was investigated, tried, found guilty and executed. I am certain Her Majesty feared the same in those final days, but she dare not say it lest she be regarded as madder still. According to Anthony Rivers, the Queen resisted physic because she was "very suspicious about some of those about her being ill-affected". The Venetian, Scaramelli, is more bold and forthright. He declared:

"as the Queen's illness came from nothing but rage, and as her habit of life was sober and clean, some, forgetting her age, claim she may have been assisted to death. They even name the person and say that actions of this magnitude begin in danger but end in reward." I shall name such persons. The Howards wished her dead because Her Majesty knew the truth about the Earl of Essex and that ring. The same is true of that other person close to her deathbed, Master Secretary Cecil, who ignored the decision of the Council and secretly instructed my Mistress' poor corpse to be opened. Surely this was to let out the poisonous vapours! A man of great deceit, Master Cecil, a courtier from his cradle, his head constantly full of matters, his hands always full of papers. He was his father's son, great of mind but of stunted appearance. The Queen quietly mocked Cecil, often in my hearing. She called him her "pygmy", "elf", or "little man": he very much resented that. Master Secretary was a man of considerable subtlety, in secret correspondence with James, King of Scots; he had even drafted a proclamation in preparation for Her Majesty's death. Master Cecil must have been concerned that the Queen would tarry too long, that the French might land troops in England or some other claimant leap for the crown. Her Majesty had left no will and, although she named James her heir, she had warned the Prince of Scots "not to collect the fruit until it was ripe". Ten months before she died, she'd even threatened in Council that, after her death, her kingdom should become some kind of Republic. Cecil may have also been concerned about Her Majesty's efforts to reach an accord with the Papists. More especially, Cecil, too, was haunted by Essex's death. He must have grown concerned at how distraught the Queen had become after the Countess of Nottingham's confession and feared Her Majesty might remember his hand in that great Earl's destruction. Even worse, she might recover and find his correspondence with Scotland had crossed that line which divides loyalty to the crown from treason against it. After he became King of England, James the Scot boasted to Sully, the

French ambassador, who recounted the same to me, how he, James, governed England for several years before the death of the great Queen. How he had gained all her ministers who were guided by his direction in all things. Some will say Cecil is no traitor but, there again, once treason prospers it is no longer treason. Cecil was much frightened by his correspondence with the Scots. On one occasion, in the apple orchard of Hampton Palace, Her Majesty's 'elf' received a package from Scotland, a dangerous missive, handed to him in the presence of the Queen. Her Majesty was quite desirous to see what the packet contained. Cecil, cunning as a cat, took the packet and slowly drew his dagger to cut its strings. Abruptly, Master Secretary stopped.

"This packet," he declared, "has a strange and evil odour. Surely it has not been in contact with infected persons or goods?"

The Queen, fearful of contagion, ordered Master Secretary to place it at a distance and not to bring it into her presence until it was fumigated.

Accordingly, if Her Majesty was suspicious of her physicians, she must have been equally suspicious about those who controlled them, and who better than the Howards and Master Secretary Cecil? This answers the question posed by Juvenal, 'Quis custodiet ipsos custodes?' – 'Who shall guard the guards?' The answer, of course, is no one. Others will dispute this, pointing out how the Queen's mind was disturbed as she would not agree to physic. Her Majesty, however, was of good mind, her wits sharp enough to bid me discover the very source for such rumours, namely Master Secretary Cecil himself. She did many times say to him in my presence, "Cecil, I know I am not mad, you must not think to make a Queen Jane of me", a reference to a Habsburg queen who had fallen insane and been imprisoned.

In truth, Master Secretary Cecil either helped the Howards to assist Her Majesty into death or, for reasons of good politic, just looked the other way. What is the real truth beneath these seeming truths? I think Her Majesty was aided to her death by those at

Court, either by act or by thoughtful omission. The Yellow Jackets were eager for her death; Lady Mary Howard was their weapon, Carey their messenger. It's easy to distil a potion and mix it with the wine. So comforting for Master Cecil to sit and watch Her Majesty drink it. If the physicians were called, they could assist her even more into eternal night. She had to be gone to protect themselves and advance their interests with their Scottish Prince. They all wished her to die and not to linger long on the threshold between life and death. Her Majesty recognized that and, like the lion she was, bravely crossed that darkening threshold. She died, as she had lived, her own mistress, but one of great mystery, the possessor of many secrets, as I shall now relate. Her Majesty's death, or rather the manner of it, has stirred a pool of dark secrets. Elizabeth of England was the keeper of many mysterious happenings – she held the key to a chest full of so many enigmas, these worry me, deeply disturb my soul and agitate my heart. Well, and I can scarce write the words, I must now reflect on my great secret after accepting those manuscripts from Spain. If they struck at the Great Elizabeth of England, against who else did they lift the sword?

I will not speak alone on this matter. I shall call on witnesses, two in particular: Sir Thomas Bodley, my friend, my Virgil, he will lead me through this Labyrinth of lies, this Maze of secrets, around the icy, hate-filled pools of faction and the morass of deceit. Sir Thomas Bodley! He with the clever eyes and subtle wits. Sir Thomas has seen manuscripts others will never see. He'll come here with his faithful shadow, Master Reginald Carr. No, not one of the cozening, courtly Carrs, but a lover of books and a diviner of dark secrets. They will light the lantern-horns to brighten the dark passage of the years and send the shadows flitting …

Commentary on Part I

The identity of the lady-in-waiting of this memoir is unknown. It can only be guessed at, but she must have been someone close to Elizabeth. Her account of the Great Queen's last days is corroborated by manuscripts in the Cottonian Collection in the British Library which are published in J. Nichols, *Progresses of Elizabeth I* (1823), Volume III, pp. 607-609 and 612-613. They are possibly based on accounts by the Catholic Lady Southwell, who later fled the English Court.

J.E. Neale did reject such accounts in his scholarly work *The Sayings of Queen Elizabeth*, ('History', 1925). This has been taken up by historians such as Paul Johnson, *Elizabeth I: A Study in Power and Intellect* (Weidenfeld & Nicolson, 1974), p.438. Johnson rejects the "ugly rumours" and appeals to the diplomatic sources of France, Venice and others for proof of this. However, as I shall demonstrate, these same diplomatic sources are the origins of very ugly rumours, including the fact that the Queen may have been murdered. Moreover, the Chronicler John Clapham, a former servant of Cecil, quite categorically states in his chronicle how "The Queen's body was left in a manner alone … so, after her death, mean people had access to it." John Clapham, *Elizabeth of England* (edited by E.P. Read and Conyers Read, 1951), p.110. The references to the Countess of Nottingham's death are in Nichols, *Progresses*, III, pp.544-550.

Other sources, for example the French envoys, talk of Elizabeth being alone, of crying in the dark. (Thomas Birch, *Memoirs of the Reign of Queen Elizabeth*, 1754, Volume II, p.506). Others mention her being forlorn, melancholic, a description given by no less a person than the knowledgeable Bishop Goodman in his book, *The Court of James I* (edited by J.S. Brewer, 1839), pp.16-17. The death of the Duchess of Nottingham was a major blow to Elizabeth (Birch, Volume II, p.506 et seq.) Elizabeth did have her coronation ring cut from her finger (J. Bruce, *The Diary of John Manningham* (Camden Society, 1868), under the date 3rd April 1603). The Queen's decline was swift. She laid great emphasis on her appearance even as late as the Christmas/New Year parties of 1602-1603: J. Nichols, *Progresses*, Vol. III, pp.424-426 and John Harington, *Antiquae Nugae*, Vol. I, p.186. *The Calendar of State Papers, Venetian 1592-1603*, p.565 and pp.591-603. True, Robert Carey did write his own account of the Queen's death: *Memoirs of Robert Carey written by himself*, ed. Walter Scott (Edinburgh, 1808). However, these are very biased and depict him as the old Queen's favourite. Indeed he was a man with a foot in either camp trying to please everyone whilst promoting his own interests. Carey's actions were both duplicitous and self-serving. James VI of Scotland and Robert Cecil were truly in each other's pockets. The examples cited here are simply a few amongst many. Cecil's devotion to James and his haste to ensure his succession led to his disgraceful neglect of Elizabeth's corpse. The role of the Howards and, above all, Cecil in James' smooth succession to the English throne, are apparent in *The Correspondence of James VI of Scotland with Robert Cecil and others*, ed. J. Bruce (Camden Society, 1856). James used other people's seals to deceive Elizabeth. Cecil, to achieve the same, used that of a French duke. Carey was also Cecil's creature. He and his master were quick to provide the official version of Elizabeth I's last days and hours. I regard their account as highly suspect. Elizabeth was a very intelligent woman, a shrewd ruler, brilliant even in her faults. She had the measure of both Cecil and James.

The correspondence between them proves it often enough. Her threat that, after her death, England might become a republic is noted in the *Calendar of State Papers, Venetian, 1592-1603* (No. 1077, p.502). She also knew what was being prepared. On one occasion she wrote to James, confronting him with her knowledge that "her funeral had long been planned", *Calendar of State Papers, Domestic, 1597-1598*, p.487 and *Historical Manuscripts Commission (Cecil)*, Vol. VIII, p.385 and Vol. X, p.288. The incidents involving Bishops Rudd and Aylmer can be found in the writings of that inveterate gossip, the Queen's nephew, John Harington, *Antiquae Nugae*, Vol. I, p.189 and Vol. II, p.215. On Mary Howard – see the same source, Vol. I, pp.75-77 and Vol. II, pp.139-140. Historians', such as Johnson's, dismissal of the above-mentioned stories regarding the last days of Elizabeth should not be readily accepted. On 3rd April 1603, Giovanni Carlo Scaramelli wrote to the Doge of Venice how Elizabeth "has become quite silly and idiotic": *Calendar of State Papers, Venetian*, Vol. 9, p.562, No. 1166. She did refuse medicine, according to Martin Cavalli, Venice's ambassador to France (*Calendar*, above, p.563, No. 1167). Scaramelli relates how Essex's death weighed on her. He also adds the ominous lines, "that she (Elizabeth) may have been assisted to death. They even name the person." (*Calendar of State Papers, Venetian*, Vol. 9, p.566, No. 1169.)

Part II

Sir Thomas Bodley and Master Reginald Carr arrived on St Hilary's Eve. They had stayed the previous night at the Golden Griffin near Windsor, and left that tavern early in the morning before the lamps were dressed and the wicks lit. They came on horseback, gentle dark palfreys with silver-gilt harnesses. My servants met them on the steps and brought them in whilst ostlers walked their mounts to cool their sweat. Sir Thomas and Master Reginald were pink-cheeked and watery-eyed from the cold which had hardened the ground and froze the air so their breath hung like incense in a nave. They'd also hired a pack pony to transport coffers and chests, some of which were steel bound, the more costly ones covered in velvet and hidden away in leather sacks. At first there was the usual conviviality as they doffed their cloaks and hats whilst warming their hands and backsides before the roaring fire in the hall. Sir Thomas is slightly stooped, sharp featured, with an easy manner and careful grace, his eyes tell you little, his lips even less. He dresses all soberly like a Puritan Divine, although not all in black but in well-cut sombre colours. His velvet cloak was furred with sables, his doublet laced with thin ribbons of dark silk, his breeches of worsted, leather boots like those of a huntsman. He adjourned to the chamber I'd set aside to change, and as he put it, dress more seemly in a loose-fitting gown, cambric shirt, dark woollen breeches, with soft buckskins for his freezing feet. Master Reginald Carr, cheery-faced and bright-eyed as usual, offered to accompany him. Sir Thomas shook his head and murmured he should stay and keep me company.

My servants had arranged three high-backed chairs before the fire and warming cups of posset were standing on the side shelf of the inglenook. I took cloths, wrapping one round a cup and handed it to Master Reginald who sat on my left easing off his boots. He thanked me, put the cup on the hearth and went across to a pannier he'd left lying near the door. He fetched out a pair of blue, silver-edged slippers, put them on, pulling up his socks of pure wool, loosening the cords of his leather jerkin and the clasp on the linen shirt beneath. He talked as he did so, as if to distract me. He referred to the weather, the journey and the doings of the court where young Villiers had caught the King's eye. Master Carr is not a London man but from estates in the Mid-counties. I asked if he knew much about Lord Robert Dudley?

"Only from the manuscripts." He smiled across the cup.

Sir Thomas rejoined us looking all fresh, his grey hair, moustache and beard combed, dressed and oiled. For a while we joked about the seer, Simon Forman, who had boasted how a potion of snakes boiled in wine, made him look younger, fresher and took away his grey hairs. Master Reginald, his good-natured face all grinning, talked about more novel remedies for men's hair now on sale in London. How elderberry juice turned it black or, if you wanted it yellow, marigold would serve. We discussed the masques at court and the new fashions brought in by James of Scotland. How the King insisted on wearing thickly-padded doublets and breeches against the assassin's poignard or rapier as well as the use of corsets to create a thinner waist, and those ridiculous feathered hats the court fops were now disporting. Sir Thomas relaxed in the glow of the fire, before rising to walk round my hall, admiring the age-darkened oak panelling, polished to gleam like burnished gold: the gilt-edged panes and paintings, as well as my tapestries in their brilliant hues telling the story of

Daniel and Susannah, a tale I've always loved. He crossed to admire my furniture, particularly a little chair for a child, in carnation-red cloth edged with silver and tinsel. He commented on this before Master Carr coughed noisily. Sir Thomas quickly remembered my sad loss so many years ago and hurried to retake his seat before the fire.

The morning drew on. The skies outside turned from a leaden grey to a lowering black iron. We wondered when the snow would come and turned to our common love, books in all their beauty, bound in leather, calf-skin, or jewel-embossed in velvet. Sir Thomas explained he'd seen a copy of Boccaccio's *Amorous Fiametta*, on sale beneath the sign of The Red Keg at Westminster whilst he'd recently studied a copy of Ariosto's *Orlando Furioso*, translated by Harington, the late Queen's nephew.

"Well written," Sir Thomas smiled. "But the pictures?" He shook his head. "I'm not too sure whether he should be included in our Library. I have also purchased a copy of Lord North's *Lives of Plutarch* – as well as Spenser's *Fairie Queene*."

"The Second Edition?" I queried, "1596?"

"No, no." Thomas shook his head. "The first, 1590, with Spenser's letter to Raleigh."

" 'Two bodies'," I quoted.

"Pardon Mistress?" Master Reginald queried.

" 'Two bodies'," I explained. "Spenser claimed our late, lamented Queen had two bodies, the first of a prince, the second of a woman." There, I'd touched upon it: the true reason why these two men had journeyed through the depths of a cruel winter to shelter in a glowing hall ringed by ice-packed fields.

"We have it." Master Reginald put his cup down and glanced expectantly at his master, though Sir Thomas considered Reginald more a friend than a servant. Sir Thomas nodded. Master Reginald rose and went across to the leather chests placed on the side drawing table beneath the great window overlooking the lawn. He opened a chest and brought back a tome, bound in polished leather with a silver clasp. He undid this and handed it to me. I leafed through the virginal white parchment pages to the leaf bearing the title and the author's name, Nicholas Sander. I read on. *On the Origin and Rise of the English Schism.* I looked at the date – 1587. I pulled a face as my Royal Mistress would when confronted with a problem, a gesture I'd long imitated, mirror-like, a drawing down of the lips with a raising of the eyebrows.

"Sander was a Papist," I continued, handing the book back. "A Jesuit, hot and furious against my Mistress. You say the legend begins here?"

"No legend," Master Reginald intervened. "Sander publishes and proclaims the story about the Queen's mother, Anne Boleyn. How, when Henry VIII, of blessed infamy, fell in love with her, Sir Thomas Boleyn, Anne's father, hurried back to court and begged on his knees that the King not marry Anne. 'Why?' the King asked. 'Because,' Lord Boleyn replied, 'she might be your daughter.'"

"No!" My voice rose to a shout.

"It's possible." Master Reginald was no longer smiling. "Bluff Harry, our King, had a liking for Howard women, not just Lady Katherine, whom he married, then dispatched to the block for loving Master Culpepper. The story is," Master Reginald sipped from his cup, "that Lord Boleyn's wife, Elizabeth, formerly a Howard, was often visited by the King when her husband was abroad on royal business. Lord Boleyn claimed he was absent when Anne was conceived so, possibly, she was the King's own daughter."

I stared at the great hearthpiece and the curved wine stems, the clusters of grape carved either side of a rugged, wildman's face with popping eyes and smirking mouth.

"Would you put that in your Memoir?" Sir Thomas asked.

"That Henry VIII married his own daughter?" I mused, "that the great Elizabeth may have been the issue of an incestuous marriage?"

I pulled a face even as I reflected on what I learnt from other sources. How Henry VIII, according to the Chronicler Cavendish in his *Life of Wolsey*, quietly confessed to his own physician Sir George Owen that, when it came to affairs of the bed with Anne Boleyn, he was not like other men – a reference to a temporary impotence with Anne. I have heard of such a condition before. Certain men like their wives quiescent and Henry VIII, God punish him, wanted his wives placid. Fiery-eyed Anne, with her passionate heart and subtle ways, was a different matter. God knows how she affected Henry's mind which teemed like a bubbling pot. Henry impotent! Bluff Hal was a dangerous bull to bait: he'd blame everyone except himself, all and sundry would suffer his baleful mood. There were other matters too. Didn't George Boleyn, Viscount Rochford, after his sister fell from power and he and others were put on trial for their lives as her accomplices, make a strange confession? During his trial in Westminster Hall, George Boleyn held his own, battling against the King's judges who'd been told to stage a fair trial but still find him guilty. George Boleyn became reckless. He was passed a paper and asked to study the enclosed questions but not reply in public. The questions were simple. Had he ever said that the King was impotent? That Henry had neither vigour, nor strength to lie with his wife? Apparently evidence put forward during the trial claimed Anne Boleyn had secretly relayed the same to her brother. George Boleyn, however, ignored his judges. He did not keep it close but read the charge out in court to the great consternation of the King's judges and to the damnation of any hope of acquittal or pardon …

"My Lady?"

I broke from my reverie.

Sir Thomas drained his posset cup, stretching it out to be refilled. I grasped the cloth, lifted the jug and did so.

"Your thoughts, My Lady …" Master Reginald clinked his cup against mine.

"Impotence," I whispered. "The King's impotence! Bluff Hal had children by other women. He was smitten by love for sweet, dark Anne many years before they married." I sipped from my own cup savouring the sharp taste of the nutmeg. "Yet it all ended in tears, heartbreak and pain. In January 1536 Anne gave birth to a stillborn foetus and, so the gossips claimed, Henry declared he had been seduced and constrained to marry Anne by witchcraft." I glanced at my two visitors. "Did Henry's dark mind, estranged from itself, harbour sinister thoughts about his second wife's true status? How she had miscarried, not provided a male heir? Was Henry," I asked, "the elm and Boleyn the ivy, curling round him in a shower of dark secrets to sap the life from him?"

"I do not understand," Master Reginald asked. "I am not too sure what path you follow?"

"What path?" I asked. "Here is a King, infatuated with a woman. He breaks with Rome, sends his friends More and Fisher to the scaffold so he can bed Anne Boleyn, lie with her between the sheets and yet," I shrugged, "within years he is tired of her, claims he is like a gelding. Why so? Did he suspect Anne could have been his own daughter?"

I rose to my feet and, lifting a candle, excused myself and walked across to the darkened corner where the chill hung like a mist. I stared at the picture of Anne Boleyn fixed above the wainscoting. Sweet Anne with her abundant black hair gleaming like a veil, those alluring dark eyes and olive skin, lips full of blood and passion. My Royal Mistress had given it to me as a present, a reminder of her past. Underneath the painting, on a golden scroll, was Boleyn's motto, or at least one of them, 'Semper Eadem' – 'Always the same'. The phrase great Elizabeth used whenever she wrote to her beloved Dudley.

"So full of beauty." Master Reginald joined me, squinting his eyes at the portrait. He stretched out and touched the image of the White Falcon, Anne's personal emblem, painted in the corner of the portrait.

"The great Elizabeth," I murmured, "very rarely talked about her mother."

"Did she ever say," Master Reginald asked, "anything about what truly happened?"

I shook my head.

"I asked her once, about moving her mother's body, the head severed from the trunk, from St Peter's ad Vincula, the Tower Chapel, to a more worthy place. Do you know what she replied?"

Master Reginald simply stared at me. "She said, let the dead sleep. Don't disturb the past." I returned to my chair before the fire.

"Anne had beautiful hands," I continued, "as did her daughter Elizabeth. Imitating her mother, she liked to wear her hair floating down her back, interlaced with jewels."

"But the rumours?" Sir Thomas intervened, "the gossip about Henry and the Boleyn women."

"Rumours abound," I replied. "They grow thick and fast as weeds. Yet, Sir Thomas, you are correct: Henry had a weakness for Howard women and their soft, perfumed flesh. Thomas Jackson, a Chantry Priest, claimed the noble Henry had slept with Anne's mother as well as her sister Mary. Such a charge was repeated by Mistress Amadas, wife of the King's goldsmith, whilst Sir George Throckmorton made the same allegation about Henry and the Boleyns."

Sir Thomas pointed to Sander's manuscript, resting on the quilted stool beside me.

"Read that," he declared. "It contains a story, I forget the page. Anyway, Henry, in a jocular mood, asked Sir Francis Bryan, one of his roaring boys at court, a drinking companion, what sort of sin it was to ruin the mother, then the child? Bryan replied. 'It is a sin like that of eating the hen first, and its chicken afterwards.' The King burst into laughter and said to Bryan, 'Well, you certainly are my Vicar of Hell!'"

"A true story?" Master Reginald asked. Sir Thomas shrugged.

"Perhaps. Thomas Cromwell in one of his letters called Bryan the Vicar of Hell."

"And Boleyn's sister?" I asked. Sir Thomas gestured at the coffers and caskets piled on the drawing table.

"You'll find the reports about a boy at Syon Abbey on the Thames in the 1530s. The monastic record claims he was 'Our Sovereign Lord the King's son, by our Sovereign Lady the Queen's sister, whom the Queen's grace would not permit to reside at court.'" Sir Thomas sipped from his goblet. "Apparently the lad was an idiot, which is why Anne Boleyn wouldn't allow such a nephew to appear at court."

"So you are saying that Henry slept with Anne Boleyn's mother and sister?" I asked.

"It's possible," Sir Thomas proceeded. "If you study the manuscripts, the evidence is provided."

"And Anne herself?" I asked. "Was she licentious?"

"Jokes were made about her. King Henry nearly killed his own jester when the latter called Anne a ribaud, a loose woman."

"Yet, this is unfair," I gestured. "The Lady Anne was brought up at a court reeking of corruption. I have read Seigneur de Brantôme's book, *Lives of Fair and Gallant Ladies*, which describes the court of Francis I of France."

"Why that?" Master Reginald intervened. "What relevance?"

"Very relevant, Master Reginald," I replied. "The Lady Anne, together with her sister Mary, were sent to France when Henry VIII's sister married Louis XII. The French King Louis died soon after the marriage. However, Lady Anne and her sister stayed at the French court, a place of great licentiousness, corruption and deceit. Seigneur de Brantôme described the court." I wetted my lips. "Go into my Library, Master Reginald, you will find a copy of his work, *Lives of Fair and Gallant Ladies*, a searing indictment of gross lewdness. No young woman should have been exposed to such vice. The court at Paris was dominated by Francis I, a very devil, a Lord of the lustful flesh in his jewel-encrusted doublets and laced-stretched shirts, a venereal man who, by his own admission, drank the waters of many fountains."

"I have heard of this," Sir Thomas murmured. "Francis was seduced by every fleshly desire."

"The Court of King Francis," I agreed, "was lewd in every way. Francis himself was always interested in the love-making of his companions and courtiers. He loved to hear of what he called their jousting! Any fine airs the ladies might assume at their frolics; what positions they adopted, the expressions on their faces, the words they used. The walls of Francis' palaces were decorated with paintings of several lovely ladies touching each other, fondling each other, handling each other, rubbing each other, feeling each other, intertwining with each other. On one occasion, a leading dame declared after studying such paintings, 'We have been here far too long!' she exclaimed to her lover. 'Let's hurry into our carriage and go home to my place, because I cannot bear this heat. I must go and quench it. I'm too scorching hot.'"

I picked up my posset cup and turned it in my hand. "Francis had a favourite goblet with copulating animals on the side. As they drank from it his lady guests would see these; when they reached the bottom they would reach the scene of a man and woman intertwined making love. Francis loved to watch the shocked expressions on his guests' faces. In the court of France everything was about love, about men being stallions, of ladies being mares, more like a breeding farm than a court." I stared into the fire where the logs were splintering under the heat. "What chance did she have?" I murmured. "The Lady Anne Boleyn? Then she returned to England."

"From the pot into the fire," Sir Thomas observed. "How did that preacher describe fat Henry?" Leaning back, he closed his eyes.

I hid my smile. Sir Thomas Bodley, although a stout Protestant, had little love for Henry VIII. He held that fat knave responsible for destroying the great archives and libraries of England when he suppressed the monasteries.

"Ah yes, that's it," Sir Thomas opened his eyes. "Thou shalt find his court fouler and more stinking than a sow wallowing herself in any filthy place." Sir Thomas lifted a hand. "He was fully given over to the foul pleasures of the flesh and lewdry. Henry of England was no better than Francis of France." He sighed. "And Boleyn was drawn into the quagmire."

"It was love at first," I replied. "Henry was infatuated with her, though Anne was of a different sort from the rest. Being acquainted with the stories about her mother and sister, Anne was determined not to act the same way. Anne had her many faults," I continued, "but she also had her pride; she was passionate, strong and resilient. She would not become the plaything of the King. There were others who fell in love with her." I tapped my fingers on the arm of the chair. "One of the Butlers of Ireland, then Sir Henry Percy, heir to the Northumberland Estates. But," I shrugged, "as you know, Henry called Anne his sorceress and would not give her up. For almost eleven years she held out …"

"Around the throne the thunder rumbles," Master Reginald intervened, quoting the poet Sir Thomas Wyatt's famous line.

"Wyatt!" I exclaimed.

"Mistress," Master Reginald persisted. "Thomas Wyatt was the court poet of Henry VIII. After Anne Boleyn fell from power in May 1536, when she and her so-called accomplices were arrested and dispatched to the tower, Sir Thomas Wyatt was also detained. He never faced execution, being later released and restored to favour. In his defence he maintained that he had always protested his innocence. Wyatt claimed that, even before Anne Boleyn was crowned, before she secretly married Henry in January 1533, he, Wyatt, had lain with Anne and confessed as much to the King, warning him not to marry such a woman."

"Wishful thinking!" I retorted. "Wyatt did woo Anne. He composed poems to her, praised her for her sorcery, her dark beauty, her graceful ways, yet there is no proof that she consented, gave in to him. Perhaps that was frustration, anger on his part, trying to destroy Anne even before she became Henry's Queen."

Master Reginald nodded and refilled his posset cup. I glanced towards the oriel window, its thick mullioned glass gleaming between the lead strips. Outside the snow was beginning to fall gently, just a few heraldic flakes, warning of the storm yet to come. I was about to continue when Master Reginald knelt down and took a log from the stack. He placed it on the fire pushing it in deep with the poker to send up a stream of furious sparks.

"I have been to the Tower." Sir Thomas leaned forward. "Mistress, I have been closeted in its record room and muniment chamber. I have searched the records." He snapped his fingers. "Only the general indictment remains. The record of Anne's trial, as well as that of her brother and her so-called accomplices Smeaton, Weston and Norris have long disappeared."

"Destroyed by Master Cromwell?" I asked.

Sir Thomas shrugged. "They would not have made pleasant reading. Your Mistress Elizabeth may have also destroyed them. After all, they did depict her mother as a whore and even insinuated that Elizabeth was not Henry's daughter."

"When she was arrested in May 1536," I paused, hastily drawing my feet back from the sparks splashing out of the fire, "Anne was accused of adultery with a number of Henry's close intimate friends, Gentlemen of the Chamber, together with the musician Mark Smeaton as well as incest with her brother George, Viscount Rochford."

"Is there any evidence for that?"

"Come, come," I teased as Sir Thomas moved restlessly in his chair. "We, in this hall cannot do real harm. My Mistress is dead. Henry long gone to Judgement, whilst Anne Boleyn's corpse lies decaying beneath the paving stones of St Peter's Chapel in the Tower."

"Why?" Sir Thomas asked sharply. "Mistress, we are close friends, true; but why this close interest in long dead amours, affairs of the heart? What difference does it make?" At that moment, just for a while, I felt like telling him the truth, of going down the dark, backward abyss of time, to the great secret I nourished about my Mistress, locked away in that steel-bound coffer within my own chamber above stairs – but, now was not the time.

"True," I conceded. "I twist and turn, like a lurcher chasing this hare and that. Yet, Sir Thomas, you must suspect what I seek? Now the musician Smeaton went to the block, accusing Anne to spite her. The poet Thomas Wyatt, would have loved to have lain with her, whilst her brother George stoutly denied he had ever acted with any impropriety towards his sister. The same can be said of Weston, or any one else accused of adultery with her, except for one name which springs out at me. You know whom I mean? Henry Norris, gentleman of the King's bedchamber, one of the few men allowed to be with Henry when the King was by himself. Norris was arrested in May 1536 at the Greenwich Tournament held to celebrate certain festivities, the same tournament from which Anne was dragged to be taken by barge to the Tower." I paused. "Well, what have you found, Sir Thomas? You, Master Reginald? You've been digging like good terriers in the records in the Tower, teasing out the memories? I did ask you to concentrate on Norris."

"I've done more than that," Sir Thomas confessed. "I discovered a poem and bought it. It was written by Lancelot De Carles, Chaplain to the Dauphin, later Bishop of Riez, and first published at Lyons in 1545. Apparently this Lancelot, through the French ambassador in England, learned a great deal about what happened when Anne Boleyn fell from power. According to him, when Norris was arrested at the Greenwich Tournament, he was taken back to London by the King himself. Henry asked Norris to confess and, if he did so, would suffer no tribulation. Norris did confess that he had slept with the Queen but, when he was later arraigned for treason, he protested that he'd been tricked into confessing by the King's agents. He pleaded not guilty at his trial, though he did not deny the charge that he had circulated reports about the King being impotent and, more importantly that Henry might not be Elizabeth's father. The record of the trials of Anne Boleyn and her fellow accomplices are much mangled or destroyed," Sir Thomas conceded, stretching out his legs to catch the warmth of the fire. "However, in the Tower, I came across a schedule of documents, letters from the Constable of the Tower at the time of Anne's arrest, an official courtier, Kingston. He was instructed by Henry and Cromwell to have four women attending on Anne, amongst whom was a Mistress Coffin, King's Spy. Coffin was instructed to draw Anne into conversation and report everything she said to Kingston who, in turn, relayed it to Henry and Secretary Cromwell. According to Coffin, Anne Boleyn made the following confession regarding Norris. She conceded that she had recently challenged Norris why he hadn't married his sweetheart? Norris replied he would tarry for a time. Anne challenged him again. 'You are waiting for dead man's shoes,' she claimed, 'and, if the King should die, you would look to have me.' Norris retorted, that that was treasonable and he could lose his head."

Sir Thomas fell quiet.

"And?" I asked.

"Anne then said something to Norris. She threatened him that, if she wanted to, she could undo him."

I sat straight up in my chair, aware of the logs crackling in the hearth, the distant sounds from the kitchen.

"Sir Thomas, please repeat that."

Sir Thomas replied slowly, "Anne threatened Norris that, if she wanted to, she could undo him."

I glanced towards that dark corner where Anne Boleyn's portrait hung. I repressed the shivers coursing across my shoulder as if cold fingertips had stroked my skin. Memories came and went. Henry Norris had lost his head but his son, also called Henry, later succeeded to his estate including the Manor of Rycote near Windsor. There had always been a great friendship between Elizabeth and Henry and between Elizabeth and Henry's wife, whom Elizabeth affectionately called her "little black crow". Had the Queen herself known something? Were the rumours that Norris was Elizabeth's father true? Is that why my late Mistress was always partial to Norris' family and stayed with them regularly throughout her reign?

"There's more," Sir Thomas spoke softly, "isn't there, Master Reginald?"

His manservant nodded, picking up his wine cup he tapped it against his knee, narrowing his eyes as he recalled something.

"You know, Mistress," Master Reginald chose his words carefully, "that we have friends in the retinues of the French, Spanish and Imperial ambassadors and how careful these clerks are when it comes to records. Well, when King Henry wanted to divorce Anne, he ordered his creature Cranmer, Archbishop of Canterbury, to carry matters through. The Imperial ambassador at the time, a great gossip called Chapuys, in one of his letters to the Emperor Charles V, reports a slip made by Cranmer in his public declarations, how Anne Boleyn and Henry Norris had lain together and that Norris was the father of Princess Elizabeth."

"What!" I exclaimed.

Master Reginald spread his hands. "I have a copy of that letter. Chapuys tells his Master that Cranmer has declared the Princess Elizabeth to be the daughter of Norris, not Henry of England."

"A mistake." I shook my head. "Norris went to his death protesting his innocence!"

"And what was his innocence?" Master Reginald acted the lawyer, a role he could play so well. "That he had not slept with the Queen?"

Master Reginald leaned down, opened the small leather satchel and took out a scroll which he passed across. I pulled a candle closer and slowly read the letter of Ernest Chapuys, Charles V's ambassador to England. The missive was dated 19th May 1536, the time of Boleyn's downfall. It openly gloated over the humiliations of the Queen whom Chapuys called "The English Messalina or Agrippina". I studied the marked passage: "'I have just heard that yesterday, the 18th, the Archbishop of Canterbury (Cranmer) declared and pronounced by way of sentence, the lady's daughter (Elizabeth) to be a bastard and begotten by Master Norris and not by the King.'" I glanced at Master Reginald.

"If this is true, Boleyn and Norris played a very dangerous game!"

"True, but remember Mistress, Anne Boleyn and Henry were married in January 1533 when Anne Boleyn was already pregnant with Princess Elizabeth. She was born the following September, much to Henry's disappointment. He had prepared a rocking cradle and a small throne for a male heir. Within a year Henry was declaring that he was impotent, how he could not relate to his second wife and had already had his eye on other beauties. Now Anne Boleyn was a passionate, tempestuous woman. However, by 1533 she had led the King a truly royal dance and was growing older. For the sake of Boleyn, Henry had overthrown his first wife, Catherine of Aragon, broken with Rome, faced revolt in his own country, not to mention opposition from abroad." He paused. "I'm not saying that Anne Boleyn had a heart bursting with venomous malice or that she was as promiscuous as some Cock Lane whore. She was a woman growing older, married to a fickle despot, who insisted she produce a male heir ..."

"What if?" I gestured, "What if? Let me finish your song for you, Master Reginald. Are you saying Anne Boleyn became frightened?"

"Possible." Master Reginald nodded. "Even worse, did Anne become so terrified of not producing an heir as well as being aware of Henry's growing difficulties in bed that, before she married Henry and was crowned Queen, she took a lover, Henry Norris, to make herself pregnant as well as to avenge herself for

Henry's infidelities towards her? Norris was a suitable choice: loyal, faithful, of good stock, a widower who had already sired seven sons. He was a natural choice. Is that why Norris, infatuated with Anne, was reluctant to marry his own betrothed, perhaps waiting for Henry to die so he could marry Boleyn as, later, Thomas Seymour married the King's last wife, Catherine Parr?"

"And that phrase," Sir Thomas intervened. "If Boleyn wanted to, she could undo Henry Norris. She was, surely, referring to some great secret between them?"

"You see," Master Reginald added quickly. "Imagine Anne, 10 years after her return from France: she is growing older, she wishes to keep the King's affections, she is desperate to produce a male heir, but Henry has problems in bed. If she and Norris had congress, if they became lovers, they could both stoutly deny the charge of treason. Anne could say that she had never committed adultery. Norris could avow the same because the act had been consummated before Anne became Henry's wife or England's Queen. Yet, in the end," Master Reginald clapped his hands softly, "this is supposition, not firm evidence." He pushed back his chair. I, too, became aware of how hot the chamber had become.

"Mistress, why do you want to know this?" Master Reginald whispered. "What good would it do?"

Both men were studying me curiously.

"There's some great secret, isn't there?" Master Reginald asked. "Something you haven't told us."

I was about to deny it but I nodded slowly. "The great secret," I conceded. "The first part is, I want to understand my Mistress. I want to know what ghosts haunted her soul, what spectres from her past determined her actions. Secondly, yes, there is something else." I was about to continue when, deep in the house, a bell sounded, my cook's signal that the meal would soon be ready.

"Not now," I smiled. "Perhaps later, as we go further along the passageway, down the corridors of the years. Until then, gentlemen, let us rest our minds and feed our bodies."

"What secret?" Sir Thomas asked sharply. "Does it affect the King now? If there was someone behind the arras or pressing his ear against the keyhole?"

I shook my head. "The secret is about the past, Sir Thomas. I just want to know: I want to discover the truth. Did my Mistress, Elizabeth, who claimed she loved everyone, love anyone?"

"Dudley," Sir Thomas Bodley spat the name out. "It's Dudley, isn't it?"

I couldn't lie. I held his gaze and nodded. "Sweet Robin," I replied. "That is what Elizabeth, Queen of England called the man whom she couldn't abide to be absent from, even for a day."

"And the secret?" Master Reginald's face now flushed with excitement. "Dudley told you a secret?"

"No, Dudley, like my Mistress, took the secret to his grave."

Commentary on Part II

The legend which flourished about the relationship between Henry VIII and Anne Boleyn can be found first in the Jesuit, Nicholas Sander's, *The Origin and Rise of the Anglican Schism*. The relationship between Elizabeth Boleyn, Anne's mother and Henry is cited in the same source. David Lewis, in his 1877 edition and translation of Sander's work, demonstrates that the chronicler Raynaldi mentions these stories as early as 1536 – the year of Anne Boleyn's death. Lewis even asserts that, according to William Rastall, Thomas More also knew of this story. For the story about Francis Bryan – see Sander (p.24) whilst Sander (pp.28-30) records how the poet Wyatt warned Henry VIII not to marry Anne Boleyn as she was "lewd". On the lechery at Francis I's Court – see Seigneur de Brantôme's *Lives of Fair and Gallant Ladies* translated by A.R. Allinson (New York, Liveright, 1933). This is a scurrilous work but undoubtedly captures the lechery of the Court at a time when Francis I proclaimed himself "the world's greatest lover".

On the popular stories about immoral relationships between Henry and the Boleyn family, the principal sources are *Letters and Papers, Foreign and Domestic, of the Reign of Henry VIII*, edited by J.S. Brewer and others (21 Vols., London, HMSO, 1862-1910). For the lewdness of Henry VIII's Court, see *Letters and Papers*, Vol. XIII, pp.214-215 and Vol. XIII, pp.230-231. These allege the English Court was turned into a brothel where the King kept his ladies – *Letters and Papers*, Vol. XII, part II, p.253. On the immoral relationship between Henry and the Boleyn family: William Hoo, Vicar of Eastbourne, claimed in 1536 that the King was a drunkard and a lecher – *Letters and Papers*, Vol. IX, p.300. The Prior of Whitby alleged the King was ruled by a "common stew's whore" – *Letters and Papers*, Vol. V, p.207. Ralph Wendon, a priest, called Anne Boleyn "a whore and a harlot" – *Letters and Papers*, Vol. VI, p.733. Regarding Thomas Jackson's comments – *Letters and Papers*, Vol. VIII, p.262. On George Throckmorton – *Letters and Papers*, Vol. XII, Part II, p.962. Amadas, wife of the King's Goldsmith – *Letters and Papers*, Vol. VI, p.923. On Mary Boleyn and her illegitimate child – *Letters and Papers*, Vol. XIII, p.567.

Anne Boleyn seemed to have had a poor reputation: even her uncle the Duke of Norfolk called her "Une grande putaine!" – *Letters and Papers*, Vol. XIII, No 1. The Imperial ambassador Ernest Chapuys, was very hostile to Anne Boleyn. In November 1535 he called her "that devil woman, the concubine" – *Letters and Papers*, Vol. IX, p.777. Many of the records associated with the downfall of Anne Boleyn, her brother George and her alleged lovers, have been destroyed. However, Wyatt's warning to the King about Anne Boleyn is also mentioned by N. Harpsfield, *The Pretended Divorce of Henry VIII and Catherine of Aragon*, Camden Society, Second Series, Vol. XXI, 1878, p.253. Street gossip is also relayed by commentators like Charles Wriothesley, *Chronicle of England*, edited by W.D. Hamilton, Camden Society, New Series, Vol. XI, 1875, pp.189-226. Kingston, Constable of the Tower, was a great source of information for Henry VIII and Cromwell. His letters, badly burnt, can be found in the British Library (Cottonian Manuscripts Otho.C.X. Folios 225 and following). These are all printed with gaps in W. Singer's 1827 edition of *George Cavendish's Life and Death of Cardinal Wolsey*, pp. 451-457 and 460-461. On Anne Boleyn, Norris and her fateful remarks – *Letters and Papers*, Vol. X, p.793 and *Letters and Papers*, Vol. X, pp.782, 864, 896.

Another source of evidence are the Chapuys Letters (one of which is printed in the text) *Calendar of State Papers, Spanish*, Vol. VI, Part II, No. 55, p.126, *Calendar of State Papers, Spanish*, Vol. V, Part II, No. 54, p.121 – *Letters and Papers*, Vol. X, p.908. The gossip about Elizabeth not being Henry VIII's daughter but that of Norris, as well as George Boleyn's role in spreading such stories about the King being impotent and that Elizabeth might not be his daughter, can be found in M.A.S. Hume, *The Chronicle of Henry VIII of England* (London, 1889), pp.56-58. Mary Tudor, and her principal lady-in-waiting, Jane Dormer (as we will read), actively encouraged such rumours, *Calendar of Venetian Mss*, Vol. VI. I, p.270 and Carolly Erickson, *Bloody Mary* (1995) p.481.

Part III

A servant came in to announce that the Painted Chamber was ready, the places set. I raised my hand and waited for the man to withdraw, closing the door firmly behind him.

"Dudley took the secret to his grave, as did the Queen," I repeated. "I learned it from a strange source. Robert Dudley, Earl of Leicester, died in the autumn of 1588, shortly after the Great Armada had been defeated and Philip of Spain's hopes of conquering England were brought to nothing. You know the story well. How Drake and the others harried the Spanish Galleons up the east coast of England. How God sent a storm and wrecked the Spanish on the rocks of Scotland and Ireland. One galleon, *The Alacantra,* was wrecked within sight of the great ruined Abbey at Whitby off the coast of Yorkshire. The crew were fortunate – well, those who managed to struggle ashore. Elsewhere, other Spaniards were massacred. The survivors of the *Alacantra,* however, were arrested by the sheriff's men and dispatched to the dungeons of York Castle, being later sent south to the Tower. Some singular persons were on that galleon. One of these was an Englishman, a trained clerk, a scribe who had fled the country because he was a Papist. He had worked for Sir Francis Englefield, another English exile, who had managed to worm himself into the affections of Philip of Spain. Now this scribe, I will not give you his name, was lodged in the Fleet Prison, and treated most harshly. He had a sister living in England so he appealed to her. She, in turn, appealed to me. To cut to the quick, I had the man released under an amnesty and arranged for him to be sent back to France, from where he could travel on to Spain. The Queen did not care. This scribe or clerk was considered a little man. She had no quarrel with him and the Great Elizabeth never wanted innocent blood on her hands. I stood as guarantee for this scribe. I helped him as much as I could and entertained him before he left for Dover. He wished to thank me. He claimed he had lost all his possessions in the shipwreck. However, once he returned to Spain, he promised he would send me a gift."

"And did he?" Sir Thomas asked.

"Oh yes!" I smiled, "within the year a casket with a hidden casement. I learned her secret then. However," I pushed back my chair, "we must not disappoint our cooks."

We dined in the Painted Chamber, a long panelled room, between the hall and the kitchen. The oaken wainscoting provided a feeling of warmth as did the braziers and warming dishes set on dressers along one side of the room. My second husband had renamed the chamber. He himself fashioned the wooden panelling and above it, he hung images of the Kings and Queens of England in gold gilt frames. The flagstones were so cold that thick Turkey rugs had been rolled across them. The table dominating the chamber had been laid out for a banquet, covered with damask cloths, napkins and all the silverware from my cupboards: candlesticks, jugs, ewers, bowls, goblets, even the platters were of pure metal, as were the forks and spoons, the great salt cellar and spice dish. I was grateful to these two men. I wanted them to feast well on the fruits of my kitchen. My chamberlain had broached a special cask of Burgundy. He brought in the brimming jug, bubbling and winking, splashing the wine into the goblets whilst another served watery beer in earthenware beakers, the best pot for such a drink. The air was sweetly thick with all the savoury odours from the kitchen as we dined on roast lamb, capon, pheasant and quail, followed by quince tarts and some fruits left over from the summer stored especially in my cold cellar.

The servants hastened to and fro so we did not discuss what we had conversed so secretly about in the Hall. Instead, Sir Thomas regaled us with stories of the Court about the Queen, Anne of Denmark and her darling boys. He said nothing which could be reported back or at which offence might be taken. Sir Thomas is a cunning fox! He recognises that, even in a hall amidst the wild wasteland of the countryside, there are always those ever ready to listen to tittle-tattle gossip and sell it on to someone else. I sat at the head of the table, Sir Thomas on my right, Master Reginald to my left. They chattered and laughed, filled their stomachs, and relished the wine. Now and again I would gaze up at the lead-paned window high in the wall at the far end. The snow was falling, thick and fast, it would be at least a foot deep by nightfall. I was not concerned. The house was well provisioned whilst the herdsmen and shepherds had brought the livestock in.

Only when the servants had withdrawn and Master Reginald had secured the door, did we return to the matter in hand.

"Why are you so interested in Boleyn?" Sir Thomas asked abruptly.

"Oh come, Sir!" I smiled, "it's obvious. My Mistress lived and died, according to public report and private gossip, a virgin, a maid. What caused her to do that? Was it the ghost of her murdering father who executed Anne Boleyn and, when Elizabeth was only eight, dispatched little Katherine Howard to the executioner's axe? Did she have a horror of all things male, of marriage and children, or was it a veil to hide something else?"

"There are rumours."

"What rumours?" I retorted.

"Rumours that Henry VIII neglected Elizabeth, banished her from his court and did not wish to meet her."

Sir Thomas took a tightly rolled scroll from the inside pocket of his doublet and pushed it across. "This is a letter written by the

Princess Elizabeth to Catherine Parr, Henry VIII's last wife. The Princess had apparently been banished from her father's presence for at least a year, so she asked her stepmother to intercede. The letter is dated July 1544 and shows Henry had little love for his second daughter."

I have that letter now: even as I transcribe it, tears well at the cruelty which prompted this tender appeal. It reads as follows:

PRINCESS ELIZABETH TO CATHERINE PARR

Inimical fortune, envious of all good and ever revolving human affairs, has deprived me for a whole year of your most illustrious presence, and, not thus content, has yet again robbed me of the same good; which thing would be intolerable to me, if I did not hope to enjoy it very soon. And in this my exile, I well know that the clemency of Your Highness has had as much care and solicitude for my health as the King's Majesty himself. By which thing I am not only bound to serve you, but also to revere you with filial love, since I understand that your most illustrious Highness has not forgotten me every time you have written to the King's Majesty, which, indeed, it was my duty to have requested from you. For, heretofore, I have not dared to write to him. Wherefore I now humbly pray Your Most Excellent Highness, that, when you write to His Majesty, you will condescend to recommend me to him, praying ever for his sweet benediction, and similarly entreating our Lord God to send him best success, and the obtaining of victory over his enemies, so that Your Highness and I may, as soon as possible, rejoice together with him on his happy return. No less pray I God, that He would preserve your most illustrious Highness; to whose grace, humbly kissing your hands, I offer and recommend myself. Your most obedient daughter, and most faithful servant,
ELIZABETH

"True!" I agreed, putting the scroll aside. "There's some substance in this neglect. However, whether it is because Henry believed in the story about Norris, or because Elizabeth reminded him of Anne, to whom he very rarely referred, I don't know. Oh, Elizabeth was declared a bastard and excluded from the throne. Yet, later on, when Henry drew up his will, Elizabeth was named as third in succession after her brother Edward, and Mary. She was also used in the diplomatic marriage game. A little chesspiece on the board, promised to this Prince or that until fat Henry died, sobbing in his bed, crying for a priest, shrieking all was lost."

"And afterwards?" Master Reginald asked. "Are there not rumours about her and Sir Thomas Seymour, High Admiral of England?"

"Tittle-tattle," I retorted. "After Henry died in 1547, when Elizabeth was only 14 years of age, Catherine Parr, Henry's sixth wife, married Thomas Seymour, High Admiral of England and uncle of the King. Lord Thomas and the Queen Dowager set up house in Chelsea and Lady Elizabeth was placed in their care. Seymour was a rogue, a pirate, a roaring boy, full of life and energy with an eye for a pretty face. Elizabeth did not escape his attention. He often engaged her in playful banter and boisterous touch, coming into her bedchamber before she was fully dressed so that he could bid good morrow, ask her how she did and sometimes patted her on the back or buttocks with great familiarity. If he found her still in bed, Seymour would pull back the curtains and act as if he wished to join her, forcing my Mistress, then a mere child, to hide helplessly under the bed clothes."

"That's not true," Master Reginald intervened. "Elizabeth was a young woman of 14 years."

"Albeit still a child," I retorted, "much taken by the likes of Sir Thomas and his courtly ways and flattery. Occasionally he tried to kiss her in bed but, to be fair to my Mistress, she began to rise earlier than he did so she could be dressed and ready when Seymour entered."

And so the game changed! I closed my eyes recalling Elizabeth, during the last months of her life, telling me about Seymour with an air of wistfulness, a smile upon her face. Seymour was like a

stallion on heat. He even began to pay his morning calls attired
only in a short nightgown until Mistress Ashley, Lady Elizabeth's
companion, told him outright it was unseemly to come bare-legged
into a lady's chamber. Seymour, of course, swore his famous oath,
by God's Precious Soul, how he meant no evil. But, perhaps he
did.

"And the Queen Dowager?" Sir Thomas asked. "She must have
known of this."

I opened my eyes. "According to evidence, she not only knew
but encouraged it," I replied. "She, Lord Thomas, and the Lady
Elizabeth moved to another of their residences at Hemsworth
where the Queen Dowager joined her husband in trying to tickle
Elizabeth in bed. On one occasion, in the garden, the Queen
Dowager held Elizabeth whilst Seymour interfered with her gown,
cutting her petticoats into a hundred pieces."

"Catherine Parr!" Master Reginald exclaimed. "With her
puritan ways?"

"She was desperate," I smiled. "Like many an ageing woman
married to a younger, boisterous man, she thought if she joined
in such games she would humour her husband. Of course, the
likes of Lord Thomas, whom my Mistress called 'a man of much
wit and little sense', took such encouragement as more fodder
for the flame. He eventually tried to embrace young Elizabeth.
Catherine Parr found them together, and that brought the matter
to an end. Lady Elizabeth was sent elsewhere but, of course, Lord
Thomas, who took to mischief like a cat took to cream, became
involved in treason and paid the price, losing his life. In doing so,
he dragged down his own brother, Protector Somerset, opening
the way for John Dudley, Duke of Northumberland and father of
the Queen's great love."

"Wait a moment, tarry a while." Sir Thomas held out his goblet,
admiring the silver rim, studying more carefully the jewel inserted
in its base. "Don't the rumours not only allege that Elizabeth was
not Henry's daughter but also that her relationship with Seymour

was much more intimate? I read a manuscript," he declared, "part of a consignment from Spain, a memoir written by Lady Jane Dormer, Mary Tudor's principal lady-in-waiting. She married the Count de Feria, the Spanish ambassador, and later moved to live with him in Spain."

"Oh yes," I interrupted, "I remember Lady Dormer, sharp-faced, and hawk-eyed, she would have nothing good to say about my Mistress."

"Nevertheless," Sir Thomas pressed on, "Queen Mary often confided to the Catholic ambassadors about how Elizabeth was not her true sister, certainly not her father's daughter. When she was in Spain, the Lady Dormer repeated this, time and again. She also resolutely maintained that the Lady Elizabeth became pregnant by Seymour and a stillborn child, a girl, was born and carried secretly from the house."

"Nonsense," I declared, "Jane Dormer is a partial witness, a Papist who had no love for my Mistress and went to live in Spain. True, the rumours of Elizabeth's liaison with Seymour continued for some time. Yet, as for a dead child being born of the Princess Elizabeth! Well, Lady Dormer's memory is faulty. She has mingled fact with legend. It was Lord Thomas Seymour's wife, the Queen Dowager, who gave birth to a daughter, both died shortly afterwards. My Mistress," I continued fiercely, I could feel the heat and colour in my cheeks, "well, look at the documents, Master Reginald. When the Seymour affair came to light, Elizabeth wrote to the Council insisting that her innocence be proclaimed throughout the counties." I picked up the beaker of watered ale and pressed its coolness against my hot cheek.

"We did not mean to upset you." Sir Thomas Bodley put his own cup down and spread his hands in apology.

"My Mistress was no strumpet! That is not my great secret," I declared. "She was a scholar, a student of Italian, Latin, French, Greek and Hebrew. She knew different tongues; look at her letters, sharp of wit and keen of mind. Of course, she'd seen the dangers of marriage, her own father, her mother, her aunt, her protector, Lady Parr, even her own sister, Mary." I closed my eyes. "Yes, she was a student of the classics. Elizabeth of England had studied Xenophon's *Cyropaedia*. Have you read it, Sir Thomas? You should do so. It was written five hundred years before Christ was born. The book summarises a discussion between the young Cyrus and his father Cambyses. The point of their discussion is about leadership. How the leader should create an image which becomes so sacred, it holds his followers spellbound. That is what my Mistress, Elizabeth of England did. She wouldn't even allow a painting of herself to be made or published without her express permission. When she became Queen she was very much aware of men and what they thought about female rulers. She was disgusted by the Scottish Calvinist, John Knox, with his blaring mouth and inflammatory pamphlet *Against the Monstrous Regiment of Women*, whilst she'd heard of the preacher, Thomas Becon, who declared: 'Queens, for the most part, are wicked and ungodly, superstitious and given to all forms of idolatry and filthy abomination.'" I sipped the cool ale.

"In that my Mistress and I were one." I held my hand up displaying the rings on my fingers. "Three times married, Sir Thomas! I, too, know the world of men. Elizabeth was fierce on that. She saw herself as the Virgin Queen, calling herself the most English woman of the realm. She told her first parliament, displaying her coronation ring, how she was married to the realm and that every one of them who was English, were her children and kinsfolk. She promised to be a good mother, better than any stepmother they would have. She called herself the Kingdom's Saviour, who saved her subjects when they hung heavy on the bough ready to fall into the mire. She informed Sir James Melville, the Scottish ambassador, that she would remain single and not be commanded by any man. She repeated the same to the French envoy, adding that the only reason she needed a husband was to produce an heir whilst he could always do some evil to her! Oh yes," I continued, "Elizabeth was more than aware of the mocking tale about spinsters being doomed to marry apes in hell. Nevertheless, she declared publicly, for all to hear, that to remain a spinster was best for her: 'If I were an old maid with a pail on my arm, I would not forsake that poor and simple state to marry the greatest Monarch' and that she preferred to be a beggar woman and be single. On one occasion, almost in tears, she exclaimed that, for her part, she hated the idea of marriage even more, for reasons which she would not divulge to a twin soul if she had one, much less to a living creature."

Master Reginald laughed softly, tapping the table with his hands. "But surely she wanted children, an heir to continue the Tudor line?"

"She was just as witty and sharp on that," I replied, "as she was on everything else. Elizabeth reminded her parliaments that children are not often like their parents and, just because she was a good ruler, it did not mean that any child she had would follow her path."

"So," Sir Thomas declared lifting his head, "one solution creates another mystery. Did Elizabeth of England resent the act of marriage because she could not bear children or could not tolerate the act itself?"

"Legend!" I scoffed. "Legend, heaped upon legend. The Spanish ambassador reported to his Master Philip how Elizabeth was not healthy and could not have children whilst another ambassador claimed she had many."

"But not just the Spanish," Sir Thomas intervened. "Didn't her own nephew, Sir John Harington, declare, 'In mind, Elizabeth ever had an aversion and, as many think, in body, some indisposition to the act of marriage'. Bess of Hardwicke, that sharp-tongued Countess of Shrewsbury, told her prisoner, Mary, Queen of Scots, that Elizabeth was not like other women which accounted for her failure to marry."

"Bess of Hardwicke," I countered, "was a liar and could not

say one good thing about any living soul. I was Elizabeth's lady-in-waiting. Oh yes, I've heard the tawdry tales, even the poet, Ben Jonson, claimed Elizabeth had such a thick membrane across her most privy and sacred part that it made her incapable of men, even though, for her delight, she tried many. That was just gossip. In 1566, eight years after my Mistress succeeded to the throne, a nephew of the French ambassador, De la Forêt, had a discussion with the Queen's doctors. During the course of this, the Frenchman remarked how he was pleased Elizabeth did not marry a prince of his own country because she'd given out that she was sterile. Now I was present when this discussion took place. One of the doctors, and I shall keep his name secret, claimed Elizabeth herself was the fount of such stories. Nevertheless, he would go on oath that Elizabeth of England was capable of bearing 10 children, adding there was not a man in the kingdom who knew her constitution better than he. Moreover," I tapped my nails against the goblet, "I have firm proof of this. You have great admiration for William Cecil, Lord Burghley, the Queen's Secretary?"

Bodley and Carr nodded in agreement. "In March 1579," I continued, "when her Majesty had reached her 45th year, Master Cecil was considering the possibility that Elizabeth might marry Alençon of France. He was anxious to discover if Elizabeth was capable of bearing children. He interviewed her doctors and made the most delicate enquiries amongst her ladies-in-waiting. He wrote down his conclusions in a memorandum which is still extant. I have it still. Master Cecil reached the conclusion that Her Majesty was very apt for the procreation of children."

"If that is the case," Master Reginald declared, "it strengthens the suspicions for her having had a child by some man, secretly, illegally. The rumours certainly swirled." He continued in a rush. "Time and again, particularly amongst the Romish ambassadors, those of France, Spain and Venice; gossips claimed Elizabeth had a daughter hidden away whom she was more than prepared to marry to some foreign prince."

"What daughter?" I retorted, "when and where?" I did not, at that moment in time, wish to go down that path.

"Never mind the smoke," Master Reginald was now all keen. "If there's smoke, there's fire surely. The stories of a child persist. Elizabeth liked the tune." He gave a half laugh. "It does not mean she liked the words. Her Majesty wanted to lead the dance in every sense: she actively encouraged rumours about herself. Would she marry? Wouldn't she marry? Whom would she marry? When would she marry? Could she bear children? Was she barren? It was all part of the game; she played the same in matters of diplomacy. Elizabeth was greedy for marriage proposals. The Spanish ambassador once declared, 'I don't think anything is more enjoyable to your Queen than treating of marriage although she assured me herself that nothing annoys her more. She is vain. She would like the world to be running after her but she will probably be remaining, as she is, a maid.' Elizabeth loved to flirt, she liked to divert the Great Powers and foreign princes with the prospect of marriage. She was also aware of the consequences of such conduct yet very proud of her reputation. Oh, the stories circulated in the Shires. I have read the indictment in 1572 against a knave called Berney. He claimed Elizabeth was a vile woman, who desired nothing better than to feed her own lewd fantasies and to cull any of her nobility who were perfumed and courtly enough to please her delicate eye. Nine years later another rogue, Henry Hawkins, was punished for saying the Queen had five illegitimate children, whilst Edward Francis of Dorset was found guilty of claiming the Queen had three bastards by different nobleman, two sons and a daughter. Others of higher station should have known better. Bess of Hardwicke claimed Elizabeth had slept with Sir Christopher Hatton, the Duke of Alençon and with Alençon's friend, Simier. Yet," Master Reginald shrugged, "Elizabeth always surrounded herself with her ladies of the bed chamber. The Queen herself declared how her life was open, she had so many witnesses and she could not understand how such bad judgements could be formed of her. She claimed she was watched by a thousand eyes yet such remarks are simple dust upon the water. Sir Christopher Hatton, whom she deeply admired, swore deeply and with vehement assertion that he never had any carnal knowledge of her."

"What are you implying, Reginald?" Sir Thomas asked. "That her late Majesty was a virgin? Lived a virgin? Died a virgin? Then what's the mystery? Why the intrigue?" He pulled a face. "So her Majesty may not have liked men, may not have even liked sexual congress. She may have been a maid from the first day of her reign to the last, where is the great mystery?"

"She was certainly puritan in her manners," Master Reginald replied evasively. "I have searched long and hard. She kept her own maids-of-honour under tight rein; God help any who fell in love or became enceinte by a gentleman at court. Many a lady lost royal favour; many a man fell from power because of the marriages they contracted against Elizabeth's wishes." I nodded in agreement. "Lady Mary Shelton," Master Reginald continued, "were not her fingers broken by Her Majesty who threw a candlestick at her when she married secretly? And weren't Bess Throckmorton and Walter Raleigh sent to the Tower when their secret marriage was discovered? And you, my Lady?"

I sat cradling my cup, pressing it against my cheek, staring down at a stain on the damask table cloth. The servants had gone. The turn-spit boy had brought his lute and now stood without the door plucking mournfully at the strings. The sounds took me down the years, kneeling before her Majesty begging her permission to marry and Elizabeth, ruffling my hair, softly agreeing that I should.

"You don't understand," I murmured.

"I don't understand what, my Lady?" Master Reginald's voice was sharp. I gazed full at him. Was he my friend? Had he come here to help or was he seeking information on behalf of his Royal Master, King James? I dismissed the thought as unworthy. Sir Thomas Bodley and Master Reginald Carr are my close friends, bound to me by the love of books, manuscripts and of secrets long past. I have known them many a year. They understood my fascination for my Royal Mistress and were so skilled in obtaining books, ledgers and manuscripts. Sir Thomas is closely favoured by James of Scotland in the establishment of his great library at Oxford. He has the key to many a door and coffer. What did it matter to James of Scotland, his Danish Queen and their strange court if the Great Elizabeth once did that or the other?

"What does it matter?" Sir Thomas echoed my thoughts. "What are you implying, my Lady? If Elizabeth lived a virgin and died a virgin, where is the mystery?"

"It's Dudley, isn't it?" Master Reginald insisted. "It's Dudley at the beginning and Dudley at the end. Tell us the truth, Mistress."

I drained my cup, and placed it carefully down. "I've eaten well," I replied, "I've drunk my fill. I need to retire. You have brought the manuscripts?" Master Reginald lifted his hand as if taking an oath.

"We have brought them, my Lady but, please, answer my question, Dudley this or Dudley that?"

I smiled and hunched my shoulders. "Dudley all the time," I whispered, "from the very beginning to the very end, always Dudley, the rest was just a sham!"

I stood up, excused myself and left the Painted Chamber. I went towards the great staircase leading up to my bedchamber. My maids came hurrying in, they'd been filling their stomachs in the buttery and now appeared all worried as if I needed their help. I shook my head, waved my hand and gestured them away. I ignored the rules of hospitality. Sir Thomas and Master Reginald would make themselves comfortable. I slowly climbed the staircase. Now and again I paused, resting against the woodwork. I stared through a window. The snowflakes were falling, fast and furious, covering everything in a white shroud. I reached my own chamber and went in. The servants had lit the lamps, the dark polished wood and coloured hangings glowed comfortably whilst beyond the mullioned window a storm raged.

I sat in my favourite chair and sank back in time. Dudley was watching me. Dudley, tall and slender with russet hair and sharp nose, full-lipped, long-legged, slim-waisted, the very devil incarnate! Eyes all laughing, though hard and piercing – no wonder my Mistress loved him! Dudley the dancer, smooth and expert, lithe and easy! Dudley the horseman riding a mount splendid in array, marvellous at the charge; Dudley plucking at a lute, Dudley reciting a poem, Dudley festive, Dudley all sombre, yet always the same to my Mistress. I extinguished the candles, lay on my bed and stared up into the darkness. The shades and shadows returned. Dudley the Queen's great love! The man to whom she pledged her heart. Such a contrast! Such a paradox! For thirty years he dominated our lives. In truth he should have been the Queen's enemy. He sprang from ill stock. His family had been hostile to her, yet Elizabeth loved him more than any other man. She disguised it, she hid behind a farrago of nonsense but, if she loved any one, it was Dudley. True, Elizabeth herself said he came from three generations of traitors. His grandfather had been executed by Henry VIII. His father had led a revolt against Mary, Elizabeth's half-sister, and paid for it with his life. His brother, Guildford, married Lady Jane Gray and joined her in the slaughter yard at the Tower. Robert Dudley, however, was unique. He had a lust for life, an eagerness for taking things as they were. I'll always remember his eyes. In her correspondence Elizabeth constantly referred to him as her "eyes". Dudley claimed they had both been born on the same day in the same year but that was not true. He was born two months earlier than the Queen. Nevertheless, from the start, their souls were enmeshed.

My eyes grew heavy, my limbs slack. A servant knocked on the door. I ignored the interruption as, in my mind, I hastened back to the court of the Great Elizabeth. Dudley, Earl of Leicester, Adonis Incarnate, clad in his white silk hose and cream doublet, a laced ruff around his neck, a pearl earring hanging from his ear.

Dudley claimed he and Elizabeth had known each other since the age of eight. Perhaps that was true, they were both in the Royal Nursery, each taught by Sir Roger Ascham. In childhood we create permanent friendships, those alliances which never die. That was true of Elizabeth. She shouldn't have even been friendly with her "eyes" yet, this is my great secret: a deep passion burned between Elizabeth and Dudley from the very start which may have brought great happiness. It certainly caused sharp sorrow.

The haunting tunes of the past, the songs of the court, the plucking of the strings by the royal musicians seemed to grow all about me. Elizabeth in all her majesty sweeping through palace chambers, Dudley beside her, his hand touching hers, the Queen glancing so coyly at him. Dudley's hands on Elizabeth's shoulder, Dudley sitting beside her in Council. Dudley in the dance or the masque. Always Dudley! I remember Elizabeth passing through London on a mist-filled morning. She paused, dismounting from her horse, to meet Dudley and, standing on tiptoe, kissed him passionately. What was his singular attraction? God only knows! Perhaps Elizabeth, my Mistress, was fascinated by Henry VIII's reddish hair, bold eyes, his impetuous, lustful disposition. Dudley was the same, a man full of life, boisterous and lecherous. A skilled dancer, learned and, like Elizabeth, passionate about horses and hunting. Oh true, a darker, sinister vein ran through him. Dudley could be devious, cunning and ruthless, a noble who could keep passion in his pocket. A killer, a silent assassin, if provoked. So what was the cause and root of their deep, mutual passion? Heaven only knows. They certainly shared the same past and, perhaps, because of that, believed they shared the same future. Dudley had vaunting ambitions. Perchance he saw himself as King and the father of Kings. Like a spectator at one of Master Marlowe's plays, he watched the imperial drama of Henry VIII's children play out. Edward died. Mary died. Elizabeth, the Protestant heir, was left supreme. Dudley must have dreamed his dreams. Master Cecil knew this. In a memorandum drawn up before Mary Tudor died, that subtle secretary listed those people who should be informed immediately Elizabeth succeeded to the throne. Amongst these was Robert Dudley, the soldier, the poet, the horseman, the cavalier who, when Mary Tudor died, rode a white courser to Hatfield to tell Elizabeth that she was no longer a prisoner but Queen of England. Dudley who nourished hopes that he would be the Queen's consort, married to a woman whose life had been entwined with his since a very early age. Only one real obstacle separated him from this golden dream. Dudley was married!

Eight years before Elizabeth succeeded to the crown, Dudley had been betrothed to Amy Robsart, the daughter of a Norfolk Knight, a lucrative marriage which brought some estates and money when Dudley was only a youth with no aspirations to kingship. In November 1558, when Elizabeth became Queen, Dudley's chain was Amy Robsart, a Norfolk Lady, gentle, retiring, yet still his wife and the greatest hindrance to her husband's ambition. I turned on the great four poster bed and glanced at the window covered by a flurry of snow. Some men were talking in the yard below. A dog howled, a servant cried. I returned to my dreaming. When her Majesty succeeded I was not with her. I was only a young wife with my second husband, steeped in country matters before I was summoned to court. Nevertheless, even then I'd heard of Lady Amy, or rather Dudley's great passion for the Queen and his desertion of his wife. It became the constant chatter at Court. How, if the Queen was to marry, she must avoid foreign princes and marry Dudley her Master of Horse.

I moved on the bed, lying back peering up at the tester. In later years I often asked the Queen what had truly happened during such stirring times. Her reaction was always the same. She'd shake her head, lift a hand and press her fingers firmly against my lips. "What happened then is best not told," she'd whisper. "What happened was, in the last resort, for the good of the Kingdom."

Now, an old woman, I recalled those words and thought of Cumnor Place in Oxfordshire, a grey-stone building with its outhouses, granges and parks. Lady Amy, Dudley's wife, rising early that Sunday morning, 8th September 1560. The subsequent events of that day would change the Kingdom, ruin lives and determine for ever what would happen to the Queen. I never met Lady Amy. I attended her funeral. I followed the gorgeous cortège to St Mary's Church, Oxford. I watched her coffin being lowered into the vault but I never met her. According to common report Lady Amy was a simple girl, full of life, desperate for her husband's affection. She must have watched in wonderment as Robert Dudley moved from one step to another, being raised high, Master of the Queen's Horse, Knight of the Garter, whilst she lived like a novice, relegated to a convent. The Queen never met her either. On that Elizabeth was obdurate. The wives of favourites never attended Court. By 1560 rumour had it that Robert Dudley would divorce his wife and marry the Queen Elizabeth who, at 27 years old, was ripe with passion for her Master of Horse. Then, abruptly, the dream became a nightmare. As I've said, Her Majesty had retired to Windsor to celebrate her birthday with masques, music and dancing. Little did she realise that, only a short distance away at Cumnor Place where Dudley's wife sheltered, events were to occur which would shatter her life forever.

Restless, I rose and walked to the window casement. The storm was still raging, the snowflakes falling thick and heavy. I could hear the sounds of the house, servants coming and going, Sir Thomas' shout, Master Reginald's laugh. They would stay here for a while. I felt tempted to go down and ask Master Reginald for the parchments he'd brought but I acknowledged I must wait. I stared through the lead-paned window and recalled that September, some fifty years ago, when the leaves were turning green-gold, the grass still sprouted long and lush and the hunting was good ...

The memories turned me restless. I walked out on to the gallery. It was dark and deserted. Only capped candles provided pools of light. I paused at a sound, but it was only Boabdil, our house cat, engaged in his bitter war against the mice and rats. The oriel window at the far end caught the glow of candles and the different coloured panes of glass shimmered, beckoning me on. I walked down past the different paintings, now and again trailing my fingers against the polished panelling. The gallery was cloaked in dark silence, only the creak of floor boards disturbed its stillness. I recalled local legends. How this gallery was reputedly haunted by a young woman who, many years earlier, had paced up and down waiting vainly for her lover to come. The poor girl allegedly hanged herself. I paused where the grisly deed was supposed to have occurred. I whispered a prayer and reflected how all our souls had their galleries and chambers haunted by fearsome spectres. Mine certainly were and the ghosts came thronging in.

Commentary on Part III

For Elizabeth's letter to her father in 1534 – see *Syllogae Epistolarum*, edited Thomas Hearne, Oxford, 1716, pp.164-165. For Elizabeth and the Seymour affair – see S. Haynes, *A Collection of State Papers from the year 1542-1571 left in the care of William Cecil, Lord Burghley* (1740), pp.97-102. The testimony of Jane Dormer who went to live in Spain as the Countess de Feria, is in Henry Clifford's *The Life of Jane Dormer – Duchess of Feria*, edited by Joseph Stevenson, London, Burns & Oates (1851), pp.80 and 86.

Elizabeth's determination to control paintings of her is well documented: J.E. Neal, *Elizabeth I and her Parliaments*, Vol. I, London, 1969, pp.44-45 and Public Record Office, *State Papers*, 12-31, No. 55. Walter Raleigh claimed that Elizabeth ordered any painting which did not have her authority to be burnt – see C.A. Partrides' edition of Sir Walter Raleigh's *History of the World* (London, 1971), p.59. Elizabeth did project herself as having two bodies: the Virgin Queen concept is best conveyed by the poet Spenser in his later edition of *The Fairie Queen*. Spenser drew directly on Elizabeth I's own words. In her first parliament she declared: "In the end this shall be sufficient, that a marble statue shall declare that this Queen having reigned such times lived and died a Virgin". J.E. Neal, *Elizabeth I and her Parliaments* (1953 edition), Vol. I, p.49. Elizabeth's view that she was married to the

Kingdom of England and that she considered all her subjects as her kinsmen is best caught in the remarks she made to different ambassadors such as Sir James Melville, the Scottish ambassador. Melville's accounts can be found in Thomas Thomson, *Sir James Melville, The Memoirs of his Own Life* (The Ballantyne Club, 1829). Some of Melville's remarks must be taken with more than a pinch of salt. Another source was the French ambassadors – their accounts can be found in Alexandre Teulet, *Relations Politiques de la France et de L'Espagne, avec L'Ecosse au xvième siècle*, (Paris 1862), Vol. 2, p.217 et seq. The Spanish ambassador's comments can be found in the *Calendar of State Papers, Spanish*, Vol. I, pp.63, 73 and 180. For the Imperial ambassador – see Victor Klarwill, *Queen Elizabeth I and Some Foreigners* (1928), pp.80 and 193. Another source for Elizabeth's anti-marriage remarks, as well as her determination to live as a virgin, can be found in the *Nugae Antique* by John Harington, edited by Henry Harington (1804), Vol. I, pp.233 and 259; the *Calendar of State Papers, Spanish*, Vol. I, pp.63 and 180. Ben Jonson's salacious remark about Elizabeth can be found in his *Conversations with William Drummond* (Shakespeare Society, 1842), pp.484-485. The incident involving the French ambassador in 1566 can be found in the Public Record Office, *State Papers*, 31/3/26, folio 156. The Spanish ambassador's report that Elizabeth simply wanted everyone to go running after her is in the *Calendar of State Papers, Spanish*, Vol. I, pp.463 and 468. Cecil's memorandum of 1579 on the Queen's childbearing potential can be found in Conyers Read, *Lord Burghley and Queen Elizabeth I* (London, 1960), pp.210-211. Mary, Queen of Scots' scurrilous letter relating scandal about Elizabeth is published by J.H. Pollen, *Queen Mary's letter to the Duke of Guise* (Publications of the Scottish History Society) Vol. I, XLII.

There are many examples of Elizabeth's harshness with her ladies over their love lives. When Ann Shelton married John Scudamore, Elizabeth yelled and shouted at the poor woman, threw things at her, and broke her fingers with a candlestick – *Historical Manuscripts Commission, Rutland*, Vol.I, p.107. On Elizabeth's hostility to Bess Throckmorton's marriage to Walter Raleigh, C.A.L. Rowse, *Raleigh and the Throckmortons* (Macmillan, 1969), Chpt. 9. On Anne Vavasour, B.M. Ward, *The Seventeenth Earl of Oxford* (John Murray, 1926), pp.102-126. On Elizabeth and Dudley in general, a most readable account is Elizabeth Jenkins' *Elizabeth I and Leicester* (Victor Gollancz, 1961). For Cecil's realisation, even before Elizabeth succeeded, of Robert Dudley's growing importance – *Calendar of State Papers, Domestic*, Vol. 1, p.3. For a swift, readable account of Dudley's life, the best is the article in the *Dictionary of National Biography*. Dudley's letters, which are printed in many sources, are constantly signed "The Eyes – OO". *The Calendar of State Papers Elizabeth, Foreign*, Vol. I, p.96 describes Dudley's skill as a horseman and jouster at a tournament in the autumn of 1559. On Dudley's pre-eminence between 1558 and 1560 – see *The Calendar of State Papers, Spanish*, 1558 to 1567, pp.57-58, 63 and 112; *The Calendar of State Papers, Venetian*, 1555 to 1580, pp.81 and 85. Dudley's letter to Sussex of that fateful weekend (7th September, 1560) describes how he and the Queen have been hunting all day – British Library, *Cottonian Manuscripts, Titus D*, XIII, folio 15.

Part IV

I returned to my own chamber where heating pans and braziers glowed, and leaping candles drove back the shadows. My chamber, where I had spent so much of my life since I left the court, with its four-post bedstead, gorgeous hangings, Turkey rugs and gilt-edge portraits along one wall, on the other, thick oaken shelves for my most precious manuscripts and books. At night, or when I am particularly lonely, I take one of these old friends down to leaf through its pages, admiring the illumination, studying the pictures or reading a chapter on this or that. But not that night as I slipped through the door of time into another place, the great Castle of Windsor, September 1560. The Castle was bright with glowing light whilst the Queen Elizabeth and her entourage shimmered like butterflies in their gems, pearls and precious stones, dancing to the tune of the rebec, tambour, flute and sackbut; whirling figures full of life in their robes and silks slashed and edged with lace.

I prepared for sleep, pulled back the curtains of the four-poster and lay down, head back against the bolsters staring up into the blackness. So many figures whirling there, faces come and gone, hearts full of important matters now the dust of history. I fell asleep. When I awoke the darkness seemed deeper. I rose and glanced at the hour candle in its heavy iron holder. The hours had passed. I remembered the phrase 'Judas non dormit' – 'Judas did not sleep'. Was I being a Judas, about to betray my Mistress? Prove that she was an assassin, who murdered another man's wife so as to take that man as her own husband and make him King? I was slightly cold, my limbs ached. I sat on the edge of the bed and coughed for a while. I washed my face at the lavarium, the water was icy cold. I dried myself, dressed afresh, put on my slippers and gathered my furred cloak from its peg. I went down to the solar where the servants had been busy, the candles were lit, the fire burning bravely. My steward, Catesby, using his fingers to communicate, explained how Sir Thomas and Master Reginald had risen from their late afternoon slumber about an hour beforehand. The snowstorm had subsided so they'd gone outside. I decided to follow, going through the main doors onto the top of the steps. Master Catesby brought a lantern horn. I stood looking up at the sky. The clouds were breaking up, the stars gleaming like icicles. Biting cold, the breeze carried the scent of the dog-fox and the mournful music of the owl which nested in Fairlop Copse and was now desperately hunting along the frozen hard banks of the stream. I heard voices. I raised the lantern a little higher, moved to the edge of the steps and peered through the murk. Sir Thomas and Master Reginald must have gone down to the herb garden. I decided to join them and was about to return for a pair of leather boots when their voices grew stronger and they emerged from the darkness.

"Mistress!" Master Reginald hurried towards me slipping and slithering.

"We did not wish to disturb you. We went out to take the air. Despite the snow we can still smell the perfumes of your herb garden. We were discussing the properties of sweet woodrough. Sir Thomas is thinking of buying a number of ancient leech books ..."

Chattering in this manner, they came up the steps and we returned inside. The servants took our cloaks. We went into the solar where an oval table had been moved nearer to the fire. Lights and candles had been placed on the table. The great Catherine wheel had been lowered and its lamps lit whilst miniature perfumed sacks, thrust between the burning logs, burst to bring back the memories of summer. They acted as a fresh memory prick for that golden autumn of 1560. I remember how sweet the castle smelt, clean and scrubbed for the Queen's Birthday visit. I had recently joined the Court, proud of my youth and my new fashion, now so ridiculous! The Spanish Farthingale, with its black and red colours, deep pointed bodice and long sham sleeves slashed to reveal the lace of the undergarment. I remember taking care not to stain the laced cuffs or chafe at the high ruff constantly pricking my chin. Yes, I was ever so proud! My auburn hair all piled high under a feather decoration whilst pearl drops shimmered from my ear lobes. I used to walk behind the rest of the ladies as we processed solemnly down this chamber or that so the Queen could watch a masque, or listen to some music and, of course, dance.

"My Lady?" Sir Thomas and Master Reginald had taken their seats opposite.

"My Lady?" Master Reginald repeated.

"My apologies, the wine of dreams!" I smiled, trying to hide my poor teeth which now make me so embarrassed. "The sweet wine of dreams," I repeated. "We all prefer that to the hard, harsh bread of reality. You have brought the documents?"

"Of course." Sir Thomas smiled. He seemed more merry than he had earlier in the day. He leaned against the table, ringed fingers playing a dull beat on the wood. "The Spanish clerks handed some over, whilst the Tower scribes never realised what I was looking for. It was so easy to extract document this or copy that."

"We have also been very busy at Hatfield," Master Reginald winked at me, "going through the Cecil papers and manuscripts. We were invited to assess the worth of the Hatfield Library." He sighed dramatically. "It is wonderful what you discover when you open this coffer or that."

"September 1560." Sir Thomas' voice was harsh. "My Lady, the day draws on, we have many matters before us."

"Sunday, 8th September." I declared.

"Tell us, Mistress, how it was." Sir Thomas shrugged. "If you recall I was a simple student who'd fled abroad to avoid Papist Mary's executioners."

"How it was?" I replied. "Elizabeth had been on the throne for two years, free from prying spies and wagging tongues. She was master of her own house and ready to lead everyone a dance they would never forget. Philip of Spain and his sister, Margaret, Duchess of Parma, Ruler of the Netherlands, watched Elizabeth as hungry cats would a mouse-hole; their ambassadors were always at court. First de Feria and, when he left, that cunning ferret, Alvarez de Quadra, Bishop of Avila." I licked my dry lips and gestured towards the tray, bearing a flagon and some goblets on a small table against the far wall. Master Reginald hastened to his feet and brought back the tray, pouring out for each of us a cup of sweetened apple water.

"Master William Cecil was Secretary to the Council," I continued. "His friends and allies served abroad: Chamberlain as ambassador to Spain, Sir Nicholas Throckmorton was our envoy in Paris. Civil war raged in Scotland. More dangerous, Mary of Scotland was also Queen of France, lording it in Paris, quartering her arms with those of England. By the early summer of that year," I shrugged, "Master Cecil had countered the danger, certainly from Scotland. The currency was being reformed whilst, in matters of religion, Elizabeth kept to her policy. She did not wish to make windows into men's souls."

"But the pressing matter?"

"The pressing matter," I replied. "Would Elizabeth marry? Whom would she marry? The Commons were insistent on this, time and again reminding her that the Kingdom needed an heir, but Elizabeth only flirted. Oh, yes, Sir Thomas, Elizabeth was the world's greatest flirt. Remember her motto 'Video et Taceo' –

'I watch and remain silent'. Nobody knew what the Queen would do. There was a Swedish Prince, Arran of Scotland, an Archduke …"

"And Dudley?"

"Yes," I replied. "Yes, Dudley, Sweet Robin."

"Why did he have such a hold on the Queen's heart?"

"Master Reginald, I've told you, he was part of her soul. In life you meet someone perhaps, just once, and they make you feel complete. Robert Dudley did that for Elizabeth. To begin with, he was her ideal man, almost six foot tall, dressed like a fop but with a casual grace, his feathered cap always tilted to a jaunty angle. He was well read, loved music and, above all, had a passion for horses, which Elizabeth shared. I met him within a day of arriving at court. I'll never forget that thin face, the moustache and beard carefully barbered, the sharp nose, above the cynical mouth. Yet it was his eyes, watchful, wary. He brimmed with life, full of tricks and conceits. He adored Elizabeth and, Elizabeth equally adored him."

"And the cloud across their sun?" Master Reginald asked.

"You know the cloud," I retorted. "Elizabeth was free to marry, Robert Dudley was not. In 1550, when he joined his father to suppress a rebellion in Norfolk, young Dudley had lodged at the house of Sir John Robsart, Knight of the Shire of Norfolk."

"I have something on that," Sir Thomas intervened. He opened the leather wallet and drew out a piece of parchment. "A memorandum of Cecil's, how Dudley and Lady Amy's marriage began in lust but ended in discontentment. The marriage took place at Sheen on 4th June 1550 amidst great splendour; even young King Edward VI was present. He recorded the event in his journal. 'Sir Robert Dudley, son of the Earl of Warwick, married Sir John Robsart's daughter after which wedding there were certain gentlemen who strove to be the first to take away a goose's head which had been hanged alive between two cross posts.'"

"It began badly enough," I murmured. "Stained with blood,

and it ended in blood."

"Many people thought the same," Master Reginald spoke up. "When Elizabeth became Queen, and Dudley her favourite, people wondered what Dudley would do with his wife." He turned to Sir Thomas who was sifting papers from the wallet.

"In April 1559," Sir Thomas picked out one piece of parchment. "The Spanish ambassador reported to his masters 'My Lord Robert stands high in the Queen's favour but it is publicly rumoured that his wife is sick and Elizabeth only awaits her death to marry Lord Robert.'"

"Was she ill?" I asked. "I'd heard rumours how, eighteen months before she died, she was suffering from some malady of the breast."

"I don't think so." Sir Thomas passed across more pieces of parchment. I picked them up and realised they were letters signed by Amy Dudley.

"Read them," Sir Thomas offered. "That is not a Lady suffering. She's going about the business of her estates and sending for expensive garments and items of dress. I bribed a servant of the Dudley Household; Lord Robert's accounts are still extant. We find the same there, food stocks and clothes being sent to his wife. You see," Sir Thomas warmed to his theme, "the Dudleys had no fixed home of their own. Lord Robert travelled with the Queen and, of course, the Queen never allowed a favourite's wife to attend court. Accordingly, Lady Amy moved from house to house, first to a place called Denchworth and eventually to Cumnor Place in Oxfordshire, a comfortable manor house, once the summer residence of the Abbots of Abingdon. The house was shared out, owned formally by Mistress Owen, Widow of the Royal Physician, Sir George Owen. She leased it to one of Dudley's men, Sir Anthony Forster and his wife. They lived in one part of the house whilst Lady Amy and her principal lady-in-waiting, a Norfolk woman, Mistress Pirto, occupied the north-wing. According to what I've learnt, it was a harmonious, peaceful existence though," Sir Thomas tapped the table, "if you study those letters, you soon conclude that Dudley hardly visited his wife and, when he did, left abruptly, to deal with weighty matters of state. So, to answer your question, Mistress, was the Lady Amy ill of some malady?" He shook his head. "I truly doubt it," he continued. "Dudley was married to Lady Amy Robsart but there seemed to be little passion between them whilst that between himself and the Queen burned fiercer every day. Rumours spread throughout the country. Scurrilous stories circulated both at home and abroad. No doubt that Elizabeth, now Master of her own House, Queen of her own realm, free from the suspicious prying of her sister, had fallen headlong, deeply in love with Dudley. Yes, Mistress, I would say the word was infatuated but," he pointed a finger, "you must have seen that for yourself."

"I was merely a child," I replied, "a mere chit who stayed in the outer-rooms. The Queen had a hard hand with gossips. I heard the rumours; but I would agree, Sir Thomas, gossips claimed Dudley's chamber was next to the Queen's, that she could not bear to let him out of her sight, how she visited him day and night. I certainly remember that when we moved to Windsor. We arrived at the Castle on Thursday, 5th September. The Queen was all excited about her birthday, promising Sir Robert that, as Master of the Horse, she would expect the fastest mounts and the most skilful hunters as she intended to hunt and enjoy herself in the forest surrounding the castle. Some of the court had moved there earlier, others later joined us. They came in, horses clattering or carriage wheels rattling. Master Cecil arrived ill-browed with anger, shoulders hunched. He'd recently returned from Scotland where he had negotiated a good treaty, a peace which would force the French to withdraw. However, since his return, he'd found his place in the Queen's affections, indeed that of the entire council, filled completely by Sir Robert Dudley."

"And de Quadra was there?"

"Of course! Like some haughty crow with his beetling brows

and olive face. He had a slight limp. We always knew he was coming, that cane forever tapping the floor! It so irritated the Queen."

"You seem to remember it well?" Master Reginald asked.

"Fifty years ago," I replied "yet, it seems like yesterday. The castle, the dancing, the masques! Dudley in his doublet, hose and gartered legs, dripping with jewels, eyes always on the Queen and hers always on him."

Sir Thomas sifted through the manuscripts before him. He handed one across.

"Read that, Mistress, you may keep it. A copy of an extract of a letter written by de Quadra, Bishop of Avila, Spanish envoy in England, to Margaret, Duchess of Parma, Ruler of the Netherlands who served as King Philip's lieutenant in matters appertaining to this kingdom. Now, before you read that letter," Sir Thomas held up a warning finger, "remember Cecil had joined the festivities at Windsor; but as you've remarked, since his return from Scotland he had been ignored by the Queen. In this," Sir Thomas passed across a small scroll, "are extracts from Cecil's own letters to Randolph the English ambassador in Scotland, Throckmorton our ambassador in Paris, and Chamberlain the English envoy to Spain. In all these dispatches Cecil claims he is so alarmed by the conduct of the Queen that he is thinking of retiring from public life."

"What?" I exclaimed. "The great William Cecil himself, the Queen's own shadow, about to leave public life?"

"Read de Quadra's letter," Master Reginald urged, "read it, Mistress, and keep it as yours."

I read the opening lines of the first document.

" 'De Quadra to the Duchess of Parma.' "

I lifted my head. "Why to her? I mean, I know she served as Philip's lieutenant but …"

"It was customary," Sir Thomas replied, "for the Spanish ambassador to write to Philip's lieutenant in Brussels before the letter was passed on to Madrid. The Spanish ambassador here could then receive fresh instructions and not have to wait for letters to travel to Spain and back."

Sir Thomas and Master Reginald moved back their chairs as if to leave.

"Sirs?" I queried.

Sir Thomas leaned over and pushed the entire leather wallet towards me.

"Mistress, you asked me a favour, you gave me a precious folio. This is one of my gifts in return. It contains most of the evidence about your Mistress, Lord Robert Dudley, later Earl of Leicester, and the curious death of Dudley's wife, Lady Amy Robsart at Cumnor Place on the 8th September 1560."

Something about Bodley's speech made me look sharply at him.

"It would be best, Mistress, if you studied it yourself and, perhaps, tomorrow … ?"

I nodded. Sir Thomas and Master Reginald bade their goodnights and quietly left the solar.

I gazed down the table ill at ease, unwilling to stretch forward and pull that leather wallet towards me. I was going back to that fateful day at Windsor. On Saturday, 7th September, 1560, I'd fallen ill and withdrawn to my own chamber. I remember being disappointed because I missed the festivities. By Sunday morning I was feeling better. Even so, the Queen sent a message that I was to stay in my quarters. I was still very young, kept well away from the hurly-burly of court and the Queen was always solicitous for my welfare. I had become rather bored, slept late and was woken by the sound of hasty goings-on, running feet along the gallery, doors being opened and shut. I remember standing at the small, diamond-shaped casement window staring down into the yard, glimpsing the pinpricks of torchlight. Royal messengers were taking horses from the stables. I returned to bed to the clatter of hooves. Little did I know then that something had occurred which would transform my Mistress's life forever …

I could not hesitate any further. I pulled the leather wallet towards me, pulled back the flaps and glanced down at the manuscripts. First I thumbed through them; some were originals, others were copies, the writing courtly and elegant, in other places ill-formed and hasty. The first folio contained de Quadra's letter of 11th September 1560 to the Duchess of Parma. De Quadra immediately moved to the heart of the matter.

After my conversation with the Queen, I met Secretary Cecil whom I knew to be in disgrace, as Lord Robert was trying to turn him out of his place. After exacting many pledges of strict secrecy, he said the Queen was conducting herself in such a way that he thought of retiring. He said it was a bad sailor who did not enter port if he could, when he saw a storm coming on, and he clearly foresaw the ruin of the realm through Robert's intimacy with the Queen, who surrendered all affairs to him and meant to marry him. He said he did not know how the country would put up with it. He would ask leave to go home, although he thought they would cast him into the Tower first. He ended by begging me, in God's name, to point out to the Queen the effect of her misconduct, and persuade her not to abandon business entirely but to look to her realm; then he repeated, twice over to me, that Lord Robert would be better in Paradise than here.

I expressed sorrow at what he said, and reminded him how earnestly I had always tried to advise the Queen to act aright and live peacefully and marry. He knew how little my advice had availed, although the Queen willingly listened to me. I would not tire of well-doing however, but would take the first opportunity of speaking again, although I understood that it was hopeless to expect a peaceful settlement of her quarrel with the French. Cecil answered me in a way that seemed as if he would like to excuse the French. He said the Queen did not like foreigners, and thought she could do without them, and that she had an enormous debt which she would not think of paying. She had, therefore, lost her credit with the London merchants.

He ended by saying that Robert was thinking of killing his wife, who was publicly announced to be ill, although she was quite well, and was taking very good care they did not poison her. He said surely God would never allow such a wicked thing to be done. I ended the conversation by again expressing my sorrow without saying anything to compromise myself, although I am sure he speaks the truth and is not acting crookedly.

This mishap of the Secretary must produce great effect, as he has many companions in discontent, especially the Duke of Norfolk, whom he mentioned.

The next day the Queen told me, after she returned from hunting, that Robert's wife was dead or nearly so, and asked me not to say anything about it. Certainly this business is most shameful and scandalous, and withal I am not sure whether she will marry the man at once or even if she will marry at all, as I do not think she has her mind sufficiently fixed. Cecil says she wishes to do as her father did.

These quarrels cannot injure our public business, as nobody worse than Cecil can be at the head of affairs, but the outcome of it all might be the imprisonment of the Queen and the proclamation of the Earl of Huntingdon as King. He is a great heretic, and the French forces might be used for him. Cecil says he is the real heir of England, and all the heretics want him. I do not like Cecil's great friendship with the Bishop of Valence. Perhaps I am too suspicious, but with these people it is always wisest to think the worst. The cry is that they do not want any more women rulers, and this woman may find herself and her favourite in prison any morning. They would all confide in me if I mixed myself up in their affairs, but I have no orders, and am temporising until I receive Your Highness's instructions. Your Highness should advise the King not to wait until the Queen mends matters.

Since writing the above I hear the Queen has published the death of Robert's (wife), and, said in Italian, "she broke her *neck." (che ha il rotto il colle). She must have fallen down a staircase – London, 11th September 1560.*

De Quadra's letter laid the scene. Lady Amy was in great danger, then she died most mysteriously. The next schedule of documents developed the story. Lady Amy's death at Cumnor Place caused consternation at Windsor. On Monday, 9th September 1560, Dudley sent a trusted henchman, Thomas Blount, 'his Kinsman', to ascertain the situation and the following five letters between Dudley and Blount describe matters.

Letter I
LORD ROBERT DUDLEY TO T. BLOUNT

Cousin Blount, Immediately upon your departing from me there came to me Bowes, by whom I do understand that my wife is dead, and, as he says, by a fall from a pair of stairs. Little other understanding can I have of him. The greatness and the suddenness of the misfortune does so perplex me, until I do hear from you how the matter stands, or how this evil should light upon me, considering what the malicious world will proclaim, I can take no rest. And, because I have no way to purge myself of the malicious talk that I know the wicked world will use, but one, which is the very plain truth to be known. I do pray you, as you have loved me and do tender me and my quietness and as my special trust is in you, that [you] will use all devices and means possible for learning of the truth; wherein you must have no respect to any living person. And, as by your own work and diligence, so likewise by order of law, I mean by calling of the Coroner, and charging him to the uttermost from me, to have good regard to make choice of no light or slight persons, but the discreetest and [most] substantial men for the jury, so their knowledge may be able to search thoroughly and duly, by all manner of examinations, to the bottom of this matter, they must earnestly and sincerely deal in this matter without respect. The body must be viewed and searched accordingly by them. In every respect they must proceed by order and law. In the meantime, Cousin Blount, let me be appraised from you, by this bearer with all speed, how the matter stands. For, as the cause and the manner of this, does marvellously trouble me, considering my case, in so many ways, so shall I not be at rest till I may be ascertained. Praying you, even as my trust is in you, and as I have ever loved you, do not dissemble with me, neither let anything be hid from me, but send me your true knowledge and opinion of the matter, whether it [Lady Amy's death] *happened by evil chance or by villainy. And fail not to let me hear continually from you. Thus, fare you well in much haste; from Windsor, this ninth of September in the evening* [1560]. *Your loving friend and kinsman, much perplexed, Robert Dudley.*

I have sent for my brother Appleyard, because he is her brother, and others of her friends also to be there, that they may be privy and see how all things do proceed.

Letter II
T. BLOUNT TO LORD ROBERT DUDLEY

May it please your Lordship to understand that I have received your letter by Bristow, the contents whereof, I do well understand. Your Lordship was informed by Bowes upon my departing that my Lady was dead. I also accept your strait charge given unto me that I should use all the devices and policies that I can for the true understanding of the matter, as well by mine own work as by the order of law, as in calling the Coroner, giving him charge that he choose a discreet and substantial jury for viewing the body and that no corruption should be used or person respected. Your Lordship's great reasons which makes you so earnestly search to learn the truth, the same, with your earnest commandment, does make me to do my best in this matter. The present knowledge I can give to your Lordship at this time is, too true it is that my Lady is dead, and, as it seems, due to a fall but, yet how or which way, I cannot learn. Your Lordship shall hear the manner of my proceeding since I came from you. The same night I came from

Windsor, I lay at Abingdon all that night. Because I was desirous to hear what news went abroad in the country, at my supper I called for mine host, and asked him what news was thereabout, taking upon me as if I was going into Gloucestershire. He said there'd occurred a great misfortune within three or four miles of the town; he said my Lord Robert Dudley's wife was dead; I asked how. He said, by a misfortune, as he heard, by a fall from a pair of stairs. I asked him by what cause: he replied, he knew not: I asked him what was his judgement, and the judgement of the people; he said, some were disposed to say well, and others evil. What is your judgement? said I. By my troth, said he, I judge it a misfortune because it occurred in that honest gentleman's house [i.e. Sir Anthony Forster]: *his great honesty, said he, doth much curb the evil thoughts of the people. Me thinks, said I, that some of her people that waited upon her should contribute to this. No sir said he, but little; for it was said that they were all here at the fair, and none left with her. How might that chance? said I. Then said he, it is said how that she* [Lady Amy] *rose that day very early, and commanded all her sort to go to the fair, and would suffer none to tarry at home.*

And truly, my Lord, I did first learn of Bowes, as I met with him coming towards your Lordship, of his own being that day and of all the rest of their being, who affirmed that she would not that day suffer one of her own sort to tarry at home, and was so earnest to have them gone to the fair so, that with any of her own sort who made reason of tarrying at home, she became very angry. Mrs Odingsells, the widow who lives with Anthony Forster, refused that day to go to the fair, [Lady Amy] *was very angry with her also. However, she* [Mrs Odingsells] *said it was no day for gentlewomen to go in, but said the morrow was much better, and then she would go. Whereupon my Lady answered that she might choose and go at her pleasure, but all hers should go; and she was very angry. They asked who should keep her company if they all went? She said Mrs Owen should keep her company at dinner. The same tale doth Pirto* [her maid], *who does dearly love her, confirm. Certainly, my Lord, as little while as I have been here, I have heard different tales of her* [Lady Amy] *that make me judge her to be a woman of strange mind. In asking Pirto what she might think of this matter, caused either by chance or villany, she said by her faith she doth judge by very chance, and neither done by man nor by herself. For herself, she said, she* [Lady Amy] *was a good virtuous gentlewoman, and daily would pray upon her knees. At different times she saith that she hath heard her* [Lady Amy] *pray to God to deliver her from desperation. Then, said I, she might have an evil toy in her mind. No, good Mr. Blount, replied Pirto, do not judge so of my words; if you should so take it that way, I am sorry I said so much.*

My Lord, it is most strange that this chance should fall upon you. It passeth the judgment of any man to say how it is; but truly the tales I do hear of her makes me to think she had a strange mind in her; as I will tell you at my coming. Now as for the inquest. You would have the jury so very circumspectly chosen by the Coroner for the understanding of the truth; your Lordship does not need to doubt their well choosing. Before my coming, most were chosen, and some of these were at the house. If I be able to judge of men and their ableness, I judge them, [and especially some of them], *to be as wise and as able men to be chosen upon such a matter as any men. They are but countrymen, as truly I saw, yet they are well able to answer to their charge before whosoever they shall be called. As for their true search, without respect of person, I have delivered your message to them. I have good hope they will conceal no fault, if any be; for, as they are wise, some of them, as I understand are very enemies to Anthony Forster. More knowledge at this time, I cannot give your Lordship; but, as I can learn so will I inform you. I wish your Lordship to put away sorrow, and rejoice, whatsoever happens, in your own innocence. Thus I humbly take my leave; from Cumnor, the xith of September. Your Lordship's life and loving,*
T.B.

Letter III
LORD ROBERT DUDLEY TO T. BLOUNT

Cousin Blount, Until I hear from you again how the matter falls out in very truth, I cannot be in quiet; yet you do well to satisfy me with the discreet jury you say are chosen already: unto whom I pray you say from me, that I require them, as ever as I shall think good of them, that they will, according to their duties, earnestly, carefully, and truly deal in this matter, and find it as they shall see it fall out; and, if it fall out to be a chance or misfortune, then so to say; and, if it appear a villany (as God forbid so mischievous or wicked a body should live), then to find it so. And, God willing, I have no fear of the due prosecution accordingly, whatsoever person it may appear any way to touch, for the just punishment of the act itself as for mine own true justification; for, as I would be sorry in my heart that any such evil should be committed, so shall it well appear to the world, my innocence in this matter, if it shall so fall out. So therefore, Cousin Blount, I seek chiefly truth in this case, which I pray you still to have regard unto, without any favour to be showed either one way or other. When you have delivered my message to them, I require you to stay, to search thoroughly yourself in all ways so that I may be satisfied, and do so with such convenient speed as you may. Thus fare you well, in haste, at Kew, this xith day of September. Yours assured,
R.D.

Letter IV
T. BLOUNT TO LORD ROBERT DUDLEY

I have done your Lordship's message unto the jury. You do not need to bid them to be careful: whether justice of the cause or malice to Forster do forbid it, I know not, they are taking great pains to learn the truth. Tomorrow I will wait upon your Lordship; and, as I travel, I will break my fast at Abingdon; there I shall meet with one or two of the jury and what I can, I will bring to you. They are very secret; yet I do hear whispering that they can find no presumption of evil. And if I may say to

your Lordship, according to my conscience, I think some of them may be sorry for this, God forgive me. And if I judge aright, mine own opinion is much quieted; the more I search of it, the more free it does appear unto me. I have almost nothing which can make me so much as to think that any man should be the perpetrator ... the circumstances, and as many things as I can learn, persuades me that only misfortune is the cause, and nothing else. I will wait upon your Lordship tomorrow, and say what I know. In the meantime I humbly take leave; from Cumnor, the xiiith of September. Your Lordship's life and loving,
T.B.

Letter V
LORD ROBERT DUDLEY TO T. BLOUNT
I have received a letter from one Smith, who seems to be the foreman of the jury. I perceive by his letters that he and the rest have, and do, work very diligently and circumspectly for the trial of the matter which they have charge of. As for anything that he, or they, by any search or examination can make in the world hitherto, it does plainly appear, he saith, a very misfortune; which, for mine own part, Cousin Blount, does much satisfy and quiet me. Nevertheless, because of my thorough quietness ... , my desire is that they may continue in their inquiry and examination to the uttermost, as long as they lawfully may; yea, and when these have given their verdict, though it be never so plainly found, assuredly I do wish that another substantial company of honest men might try again for more knowledge of the truth. I have also requested to Sir Richard Blount, who is a perfect honest gentleman, to help in the furtherance of this. I trust he be with you, and Mr Norris, likewise Appleyard, I hear, has been there, and, as I appointed, Arthur Robsart her brother. If any more of her friends had been at hand, I would also have caused them to have seen and been privy to all the dealings there. Well, Cousin, God's will be done. I wish he had made me the poorest creature that creepeth on the

*ground, so this misfortune had not happened to me. But, good
Cousin, according to my trust, have care about all things, that
there be plain, sincere, and direct dealing for the full trial of
this matter. Touching Smith and the rest, I mean no more to
deal with them, but let them proceed in the name of God
accordingly. I am right glad they be all strangers to me. Thus
fare you well, in much haste: from Windsor. Your loving friend
and kinsman.*
R.D.

I went through the rest of the diplomatic correspondence,
extracts from letters of ambassadors regarding the reactions of
foreign courts over the death of Lady Amy. Sir Henry Sidney, a
relation of Dudley, told the Spanish ambassador how he'd
examined the circumstances and found no trace of foul play.
However, he was forced to admit that Lord Robert would find it
difficult to persuade the world of his innocence as most believed
a crime had occurred. The Spanish ambassador also reported how
it was rumoured that the Queen and Dudley had planned the
assassination of his wife, since she'd been found in the country
house 'with a stroke from the point of a dagger in her head'.
Throckmorton, the English ambassador in Paris had also been
very busy. In a letter dated 19th October 1560, he told his brother
ambassador Chamberlain:

*My friends inform me from home that my Lord Robert's wife is
dead, and has by mischance broken her neck. Here, however, it
is openly rumoured by the French that her neck was broken for
her.*

So concerned was Throckmorton, not only by the death of
Lady Amy but at rumours of the Queen still persisting in her
resolution to marry Dudley, that he'd sent his own secretary, Jones,
to England for an interview with the Queen. On the 30th November
1560, Jones reported back. The letter itself, as I went through it,

was full of vague warnings until Jones, who must have been a very brave man, specifically raised the matter of Lady Amy's death. According to Jones, the Queen reacted as follows:

> She told me that the matter had been trialled at the country and found to be contrary to what had been reported. The Queen maintained that, at the time, Lord Dudley was then in Court and neither he or any of his people were at the attempt at his wife's house and that the conclusion had been that, the incident neither touched his honesty nor her honour.

I studied that passage, particularly the word "attempt". I drew across my own writing tray, plucked up a quill, uncapped the ink-pot and scored under "attempt". There were other memoranda and letters conveying Court chatter and gossip. One remark I recognised, because it became common knowledge around London, how Mary of France, later Queen of Scotland, had openly announced that the Queen of England was about to marry her horse-master who'd killed his wife to make place for her, a remark neither Elizabeth nor Dudley ever forgot. Much more interesting was the extract from the Spanish Papers which actually described Lady Amy's death. It declared:

> As the Lady Robsart was in the country playing with her Ladies at tables, [i.e. Gaming], she left the room, fell downstairs and broke her neck, being thrown down by order of her Lord, but he gave it out that it was by chance and no man dare say to the contrary.

What followed next from the sheaf of documents was truly surprising. Written out in Master Reginald's bold hand was the title 'Quieta non Movere' – 'Let sleeping dogs lie'. Apparently Dudley had believed the coroner's verdict of 'Death by Misadventure' would settle the matter, yet the storm rumbled on. Master Reginald had included an extract from the Spanish ambassador's report a year after Lady Amy's death, claiming Dudley's enemies at court, now he'd been created Earl of Leicester, were busy stirring up the Robsart affair and wanted it to be re-examined. At first this was ignored but, between 1566 and 1567, long after Lady Amy had been buried in St Mary's Church, Oxford, members of the council pushed for a fresh inquiry. Thomas Blount, Dudley's henchman during those stirring days of September 1560, was summoned and cross-examined. According to a letter Master Reginald had found, Blount immediately confessed how sorry he felt at not being able to speak with Dudley before he encountered this examination. According to Blount, Lady Amy's relations had been asking questions about her death. They were secretly supported by several noblemen, opposed to Dudley and, above all, by John Appleyard, Lady Amy's half-brother who'd been offered £1,000 by this faction if he came forward to provide evidence of wrongdoing. According to Blount, Dudley had granted Appleyard an interview and grown so furious with the man, Blount thought Dudley would have run him through the body with his own sword. The Councillors smelt blood and cast their net wider. Appleyard was summoned before the Council and examined. Appleyard, however, appeared to be a man of little steel: after some time in prison he eventually made his submission. Once again Master Reginald had recorded this. The extracts were as follows. First Appleyard's examination before the Council:

Item: In his speech furthermore he [Appleyard] *said that he had oftentimes moved the Earl to give him leave and to countenance him in the prosecuting of the trial of the murder of his sister, adding that he did take the Earl to be innocent thereof, and yet he thought it an easy matter to find out the offenders, affirming therewith, and showing certain circum-stances, which moved him to think surely that she was murdered. Nevertheless, he says that the Earl always assured him that he thought it not fit to deal any further in the matter, considering how, by order of the Coroner, it was already found otherwise, and that it was so presented by a Jury. Nevertheless the said Appleyard in his speech said upon this question that the Jury had not as yet given up their verdict.*

Item: *He said that he never made mention of any money to be given to the Earl of Pembroke or Secretary Cecil for the calling in of the Commission granted to Elliott and others.*

This was followed by Appleyard's most abject submission [extracted from him in the Fleet Prison] in which he fully accepted the verdict of the Coroner and the fifteen man jury that his half-sister's death was due to Misadventure.

APPLEYARD'S SUBMISSION

With remembrance of my most bounden duty my most singular good Lords, I received from your honours, by Mr Warden of the Fleet, the copy of the verdict which in my other letter I humbly sued for, by whom I yesterday returned the same to your Lordships again, in which verdict I do find not only such proofs testified under the oaths of 15 persons how my late sister, by misfortune, happened of death, but also such manifest and plain demonstration thereof as hath fully and clearly satisfied and persuaded me and my Lords (commending her Soul to God). I have nothing further say of that cause, for I have of your favours required nothing that might bring trial of her unhappy case to light, but I have, in all justice, received the same, yea, even with the offer of your noble assistance. [He then proceeds to beg for mercy.]

Master Reginald had also made his own enquiries and written out a question, "Were the Coroner and his Jury bribed to record their verdict on Lady Amy?" According to Master Reginald's memorandum, the Coroner was the Mayor of Abingdon, a Mr Elliott, whom Appleyard referred to in his confession. Master Reginald had been most careful in his researches and, in answer to his question, "Were the Coroner and Jury bribed?", he had extracted from Dudley's accounts the following entry for May 1566: "To one of his [Dudley's] servants: Mr Peacock, I pray you to deliver to the bearer four yards of black taffeta, and a short gown and three yards of black velvet to guard the same which my Lord will give to Mr Smith, the Queen's man." I glanced up. Smith! The same name as the Foreman of the jury at Cumnor? The entry continued: "and also 3¼ yards of crimson satin for a doublet which my Lord is giving to the Mayor of Abingdon and seven of black satin for two doublets which my Lord had given to two of the Mayor's relatives in the town of Abingdon, 16th May 1566." I put the parchment down, went across, plucked up a small log and thrust it onto the fire. Why was Dudley, about the same time Appleyard was raising the question of his half-sister's death, giving such expensive presents to the Mayor and Coroner of Abingdon as well as a man named Smith, termed the "Queen's Man", the same gentleman who had been Foreman of the jury at Cumnor? Was it to silence their tongues, to hide something? Deep in the house a bell tolled, the sign for my servants to retire for the night. I felt tired but still excited by what I had read. These were matters which had once been whispered along the galleries or in the chambers of palaces. Now I felt as if I was eavesdropping at doors where decisions had been made and a great secret hidden away.

I returned to the table and picked up the last piece of parchment. I quickly recognised what was written there. In 1585 Elizabeth and her Council had issued the most stringent proclamations against certain libels which had appeared in the country loosely entitled, *Leicester's Commonwealth*, a fictional dialogue between three individuals about the state of the country. In truth this proved to be the most vicious attack upon Robert Dudley, Earl of Leicester and all his doings. No one knew who wrote the *Commonwealth*. Some said it was the work of the Jesuits, others a gentleman called Charles Arundel, who fled abroad because he was a Papist. Whoever it was nourished a great hatred for Leicester and spent a great deal of time on the pamphlet. It raised, amongst other issues, the spectre of Lady Amy's death and the truth behind it. Master Reginald had transcribed the relevant passage:

As for example, when his Lordship was in full hope to marry her Majesty, and his own wife stood in his light, as he supposed; he did but send her aside to the house of his servant Forster of Cumnor in Oxford, where shortly after she had the chance to fall from a pair of stairs, and so to break her neck, but yet without hurting the hood that stood upon her head. But Sir Richard Varney, who by commandment remained with her that day along with one man only, and had sent away perforce all her servants from her, to a market two miles off, he (I say) with his man can tell how she died, which man being taken afterwards for a felony in the marches of Wales, and offering to publish the manner of the said murder, was made away privily in the prison; and Sir Richard himself dying about the same time in London, cried piteously and blasphemed God, and said to a gentleman of worship of my acquaintance, not long before his death, that all the devils in hell did tear him in pieces. The wife also of Bald Butler, kinsman to my Lord, gave out the whole fact a little before her death.

Secondly, it is not also unlike that he (Dudley) prescribed unto Sir Richard Varney at in his going thither, that he should first attempt to kill her by poison, if that took place, then by any other way to dispatch her howsoever. This I prove by the report of old Doctor Bayly, who then lived in Oxford … , and was Professor of Physic in the same University. This learned, grave man reported for most certain, that there was a practice in Cumnor among the conspirators to have poisoned the poor Lady a little before she was killed, which was attempted in this order:

They, seeing the good Lady sad and heavy (as one that well knew by her other handling that her death was not far off), began to persuade her that her disease was abundance of melancholy and other humours, and therefore would needs counsel her to take some potion, which she absolutely refused to do, as still suspecting the worst. They sent one day (unawares to her) for Doctor Bayly, and desired him to persuade her to take some little potion at his hands, and they would send to fetch the same at Oxford upon his prescription meaning to have added also somewhat of their own for her comfort. The Doctor, upon just causes suspected, seeing their great importunity, and the small need the good lady had for physic, flatly denied their request, misdoubting (as he after reported) lest if they had poisoned her under the name of his potion, he might have been hanged for the colour of their sin. Marry, the said Doctor remained well assured that if this was taking place, she should not long escape violence, as after ensued. And for that she being hastily and obscurely buried at Cumnor. … My good Lord, to make plain to the world the great love he bore to her in her life, and what a grief the loss of so virtuous a lady was to his tender heart, would needs have her taken up again and reburied in the University Church at Oxford, with great pomp and solemnity. Here, Doctor Babington, my Lord's chaplain, making the public funeral sermon at her second burial, did trip once or twice in his speech, recommending to their memories that virtuous lady so 'pitifully murdered', in stead of so pitifully slain.

I read the extract again: it reeked of sarcasm and spite. *Leicester's Commonwealth* had done great damage to Dudley. A year ago I had read the entire text. So authoritative did it sound, that any right-minded person would consider its author had been advised by someone very close to Dudley. It had certainly influenced me. If Dudley's henchmen had killed Lady Amy, had the Queen given that consent? Were her words, as well as the letters between Blount and Dudley, a sham, a tawdry veil to cover the truth? I placed the document back in the leather wallet with the rest and turned my chair, toasting myself in front of the fire. What sense could be made of all this? Had Dudley killed his wife? Had he bribed the jury? Was my Mistress involved? I narrowed my eyes, gazing at the hideous figure carved on the mantle of the hearth. What did these manuscripts I had just studied signify? If de Quadra was to be believed, if Cecil was telling the truth, Dudley, and perhaps my Mistress, had planned Lady Amy's death. On the other hand, those letters between Blount and Dudley of September 1560 demonstrated Dudley was sorely shocked at the news of his wife's death and realised he would be blamed. Even Appleyard never openly accused Dudley of murder; yet considerable evidence pointed to matters being smothered, persons bribed, manuscripts destroyed, mouths silenced. Why, if Dudley was innocent?

I picked up the leather wallet and a scrap of parchment fell out. It was in Sir Thomas' hand and commented on how strange it was that the verdict of the jury, mentioned in Appleyard's confession, had disappeared, as had the records of the Privy Council for those last months of 1560. Even more surprising, the letters of de Quadra, Bishop of Avila, such a busy body with a long nose for mischief, had disappeared for the same period. My unease deepened. I had few dealings with Robert Dudley, Earl of Leicester. However, what I'd seen of him from afar was that he was two men, the brilliant courtier and the sombre, sinister soul. I didn't really care for him, or for his doings. What concerned me was this. Had my own Mistress, Elizabeth of England been party to the death of Lady Amy? Did she bear any guilt for what had happened? I heard a knock on the door and turned in the chair as the maid entered.

"My Lady," she said, "surely it's time for bed?"

"Surely it is." I replied, gathering up the parchments in the leather wallet. I told the maid to tend to the fire and the lights and made my way slowly upstairs. In the long gallery I heard the sound of a rebec, low and mournful, and remembered how Master Reginald liked nothing better than to play some music before he retired at night. I was tempted to visit him to discuss what I'd read, yet the hour was late and I must wait until tomorrow. I entered my own chamber and undressed slowly. My maid came up all breathless, eager to help, but I wanted to be alone. I took my time, now and again moving to the window gazing out at the blackness, watching the snow drift from the eaves above. When I had finished, I pulled back the blankets, removed the warming pan and climbed between the sheets, dragging the thick woollen coverlet high over my face. I crouched as I did when I was a girl, recalling the events of the day. For some strange reason I went back to that Sunday evening at Windsor: no snow then, just clattering hooves, raised voices, and hasty footsteps. What had really happened at Cumnor? I imagined in my mind's eye, based on the little I had learnt about that fateful place. Cumnor was built around a quadrangle with different households in different wings. On that particular Sunday morning Lady Amy rose very early. There is no evidence that she was ill, not she, moving home from house to house, buying new clothes and fashionable items. Why these purchases? To look the best for her wayward husband? Lady Amy, if Blount and Pirto were to be believed, was in sound physical health though agitated in her mind. No wonder! Lord Robert was now a Great One in the Realm, the Queen's favourite. Lady Amy must have heard the rumours about a possible marriage to the Queen and divorce from her. If Master Cecil and others were to be believed, more sinister gossip was swirling. How Lord Robert wished to poison her or arrange some unfortunate accident? Yet, if Lady Amy was fearful, why did she want to be alone that day? A woman, wary of silent assassins, would demand protection, surely? According to the Spanish, she left a game of tables – so why was she wearing a cloak with a hood? What was the knife wound to her head? Would a fall down stairs be fatal? Which stairs? To her own chamber or, more probably, Mrs Owens? After all, this would accord with the evidence provided by Blount that Lady Amy wanted to dine with Mrs Owens, as well as the Spanish reports that her fall occurred after leaving a game of tables with her ladies. However, certain problems still festered:

> *Item: Why did Lady Amy want to be by herself on that particular Sunday?*
> *Item: If she were 'playing at tables' with Mrs Owens, why did she, on a warm autumn day, don a cloak with a hood?*
> *Item: If she fell down stairs, wouldn't Mrs Owens and the other 'ladies' realise something had happened? Why was it left to servants returning from Abingdon Fair to discover the body?*
> *Item: Why is Sir Anthony Forster mentioned in so many of the accounts – Blount's and Leicester's Commonwealth – as being depicted as assuming a leading role in this macabre tragedy?*
> *Item: What was happening at Windsor? Why was Cecil so certain something hideous would soon befall Lady Amy? Why, after the event, was Elizabeth the Queen so uncertain about what had truly happened to Lady Amy?*
> *Item: If my Royal Mistress and Dudley were totally innocent – why the subterfuge, the apparent bribes, the doubts of Appleyard and others? What was Dudley, with the implicit support of Elizabeth, trying to conceal?*

My mind turned and twisted even as my eyes grew heavy.

Commentary on Part IV

There is no doubt that Dudley and Queen Elizabeth were deeply infatuated with each other. The contemporary William Camden was so intrigued by their mutual fascination that he tried to explain it through astrology: William Camden's *History of Elizabeth*, Vol. I, p.44. An example of the scurrilous domestic rumours circulating about Elizabeth can be seen in *Historical Manuscripts Commission, Salisbury*, Vol. II, pp.252 to 253 and p.257, whilst the *Public Record Office (Kew) State Papers* 12 – 13 – 21; 21 (2) contain stories from the shires about how the Queen had borne children by Dudley. The Queen's passion for Dudley can be traced in the following documents: V. Klarwill, *Elizabeth I and Some Foreigners* (1928), pp. 114-115 and *Public Records Office State Papers* 31/3/26, folio 98.

On Amy Robsart there are a number of books and articles. The most important is G. Adlard, *Amy Robsart and the Earle of Leicester* (1870). Adlard published the correspondence between Dudley and Blount and his book carries articles on all aspects of this case. One very important article is J.E. Jackson's 'Amy Robsart' in the *Wiltshire Archaeological Magazine* (1878), Vol. XVII, pp.58-93. Jackson also prints correspondence from Lady Amy about her tailoring needs, which suggests she was enjoying good health. None of the books and articles published, however, develop the theory argued here.

Cumnor Place itself has now been totally destroyed, though a staircase from the old manor house is said to have been moved to Lower Whiteley Farm in Oxfordshire. There is a famous Victorian painting by W.F. Yemes depicting Amy's fall, which now hangs in the Tate Gallery. A portrait of Amy by an unknown artist, is in the possession of the Walpole family at Wolverton Park: the face which stares out at you is pretty in a childlike way.

The above-mentioned articles and books also describe Sir Anthony Forster and others at Cumnor. The ugly rumours that Dudley and the Queen were plotting to kill Lady Amy can be read in the *Calendar of State Papers, Spanish*, 1558 to 1567, pp.58 and 112. The important entries read as follows: "People talk ... they go so far as the saying that his (Dudley's) wife has a malady in one of her breasts and the Queen is only waiting for her to die to marry Lord Robert". The following remarks by de Quadra are even more sinister: "I have heard from a certain person who is accustomed to give me truthful news that Lord Robert has sent to poison his wife. Certainly the Queen is only keeping Lord Robert's enemies and other countries engaged with words until the wicked deed of killing his wife is consummated. The same person told me some extraordinary things about this intimacy which I would never have believed. Only that now I find Lord Robert's enemies in the Council making no secret of their evil opinion of it." There is a further entry in the *Calendar of State Papers, Spanish*, 1558-1567, p.27, which again, in 1559, mentions Lady Amy suffering from a "malady of the breast". The theory that Lady Amy Robsart was suffering from breast cancer which can lead to hardening of the bones, and so made her more vulnerable to the effects of a fall, are discussed by Professor I. Aird in his article 'The Death of Amy Robsart' (*English Historical Review*, Vol. LXXI, pp.69-79). Aird's article has been seized upon by many historians as the gospel truth. In fact, historians tend to be divided between those who think Lady Amy was suffering from breast cancer, making her more vulnerable to a fall, and those who maintain she committed suicide. They have sustained this theory despite the fact that the reports about Lady Amy having breast cancer surface as early as the spring of 1559 some sixteen to seventeen months before her death. Yet, the evidence published by Adlard and Canon Jackson, quoted above, indicate a young woman, quite vigorous and busy about her affairs. More importantly, Sir William Cecil, who kept himself well appraised of what was happening, had no doubt, when he spoke to de Quadra, that Lady Amy was in very good health and fully intended to remain so. This crucial report about conversations between de Quadra, Cecil and, later the Queen, can be found in the *Calendar of State Papers, Spanish,* 1558 to 1567, pp.174-175. It is also published in the text.

The correspondence between Dudley and Blount, described in the text, is mentioned in all articles and books on this mystery. In the main, historians believe these letters are genuine though they cannot decide whether they were later revised when Dudley (in 1566 and 1567) sustained fresh attacks regarding the mysterious death of his wife.

The political turmoil caused by the death of Lady Amy is apparent in the correspondence of the Spanish envoy, de Quadra, Bishop of Avila, *Calendar of State Papers, Spanish,* 1558 to 1567, pp.180 and 181-183, although it cannot be emphasized enough that so many important documents concerned with this case have now disappeared: these include some of de Quadra's correspondence, not to mention records of the Privy Council and, of course, more importantly, any documentation regarding the Coroner and jury which sat to decide on the true cause of Lady Amy's death.

The reference to Lady Amy "playing at cards" can be found in *Calendar of State Papers, Domestic,* Vol. 12, p.137. Reports regarding the "dagger wound to the head" are to be found in Gonzales Tomas, *Documents from the Simoncas relating to the Reign of Elizabeth (1558-1568),* (London, 1865), p.69.

The important letter quoted in the text about Throckmorton's man Jones in November 1560, can be read in its entirety in many record sources. The original is published in *Miscellaneous State Papers* (known as the *Hardwicke Papers*), edited by P. Yorke (1778), pp.162-169: these also contain Mary, Queen of Scot's jibe about Elizabeth marrying her horse-master who'd killed his wife. The protest of Parson Thomas Lever, written on 17th September 1560 as the scandal about Lady Amy Robsart's death swept the country, can be found in the *Historical Manuscripts Commission (Salisbury)*, Vol. I, no. 792, pp.251-252.

The machinations of Appleyard, Norfolk and other enemies of Dudley, can be clearly traced. The Earl of Arundel was searching as early as 1561; the Spanish knew all about this: *Calendar of State Papers, Spanish*, 1558 to 1567, p.213. The other Appleyard papers can be viewed in *Historical Manuscripts Commission (Hatfield)*, Vol. I, pp.1131, 1136, 1137, 1150 and 1155, as well as the *Pepys Manuscripts* at Magdalene College, Cambridge (Historical Manuscripts Commission), p.103 and following. For Appleyard's close involvement in Norfolk's rebellion of 1570 – see the *Acts of the Privy Council*, Vol. VIII, p.248. Cecil's two memoranda on Robert Dudley and the Queen are also extant. The one drawn up in the mid-1560s about Dudley's potential as a possible husband of the Queen, is published in S. Haynes, *Collection of State Papers left in the care of William Cecil*, p.444. Cecil's second memorandum, drawn up in 1579 on the Queen's childbearing potential, is cited by Conyers Read, *Queen Elizabeth and Lord Burghley* (London), p.210. Cecil often acted as the peacemaker between Dudley and the powerful Earl of Norfolk, who was eventually destroyed in 1570-1571. It is interesting to observe that the Dudley/Norfolk feud became public in 1565, a year before Appleyard became immersed in his mischief. It apparently happened over a tennis match at Whitehall in 1565 which the Queen was watching. Dudley and Norfolk were opponents. Dudley, to wipe the sweat off his face, took a napkin from the Queen's lap and began to mop himself; Norfolk protested and angry words were exchanged. The feud is described in a manuscript in the *Public Record Office State Papers*, 52/10, folio 68.

Leicester's Commonwealth is the source of many of the allegations about Dudley being a seducer and a murderer. (Another is Robert Naunton's *Fragmenta Reglia*, ed. J. Cervoski, 1824). The authorship of this brilliantly satirical text has been heatedly disputed: most agree that it appeared in the mid-1580s, probably printed and published abroad. Some consider it the work of the Jesuit priests, others now maintain it may have been the work of the English exile, Charles Arundel. The most recent and accessible edition of this work is that of D.A. Peck (Ohio) 1985. Dudley's bribes to Elliott and others in Abingdon can be traced in the *Dudley Papers* at Longleat (1.IV.18). The British Library also holds a *Contemporaneous Chronicle* which lays great emphasis on Dudley's management of the Coroner and jury at Cumnor, *British Library, Additional Manuscripts*, no. 48023, folio 353.

Part V

"You have read the papers, Mistress?"

"I have."

I had risen early that morning, gone straight to the frozen mullioned-glass window and looked out. No further snow had fallen but it was bitterly cold. I'd washed and dressed hastily, gone down to the buttery to break my fast and was waiting in the solar when Sir Thomas and Master Reginald hurried in after taking the air and examining the footprints of animals and birds in the snow. They had broken their own fast on soft bread and light ale and were ready for another day's work. Both men looked well slept and rested. They complimented me on my chambers as well as the food and drink they had taken in the buttery. I offered them cups of posset. Both men shook their heads, claiming they had drunk sufficiently the night before, whilst the business before them required a clear head. They were dressed soberly. Sir Thomas looked even more like a Puritan Divine in his black woollen doublet and white unadorned collar. Master Reginald was garbed in expensive brown fustian, his cambric shirt clipped at the neck with a silver pin. Both men wore cloaks as the cold was bitter. Even where we sat we could feel the draughts seeping through the windows despite the thick, well-clasped shutters and the fire leaping merrily in the hearth. They were eager to press on with the business in hand. Sir Thomas covered the bottom half of his face with his hand, one elbow resting on the table, as he watched me curiously. Master Reginald leaned forward like a lawyer in a court as if to catch every word of an important witness.

"Did you have knowledge of what you read?" Sir Thomas asked.

"Some," I half-laughed. "I was the Queen's lady-in-waiting but, as you know," I spread my hands, "what we learnt and what constituted the truth were two different things. Oh, I heard the chatter! I could keep you here for a week on that but what these records contain ..." I shook my head. "What they reveal for the first time ..."

"It's a wonder they still exist," Sir Thomas replied. "It is remarkable, Mistress, how many important documents touching this matter have now disappeared."

"Do you consider ..." Master Reginald cleared his throat. "Do you think, Mistress, your Queen was a murderess?"

I grasped the leather wallet I'd brought down from my chamber. "There is enough evidence here to make a jury to think so, otherwise it's all a mystery."

"Not necessarily so." Master Reginald rubbed his hands together. The more he talked the more he reminded me of a sharp-eyed lawyer, ready to reach his conclusion.

"I have read," I closed my eyes, "but I have not fully reflected. I am confused."

"Let me give you a summary." Master Reginald sat back in his chair. "I have been through these documents, Mistress, time and time again. I feel like a lurcher pursuing a hare through the brambles and tangle of undergrowth. The truth is just as evasive. What I will do ..." He glanced at Sir Thomas who nodded quickly. "I will summarise what you have read and then, as in the schools of Oxford, as I have seen Sir Thomas do, we will deposit a hypothesis, develop it, attack it, criticise it and if it doesn't stand move to the second. Are you in agreement?"

"I am."

"Good."

Master Reginald pushed back his chair, rose and began walking up and down. This was no longer a matter of buying this manuscript or that or mere curiosity about the past. Master Reginald has a sharp, lively mind. He was intrigued to be given the opportunity to stare into the doings of the great-ones, to peer into their minds and study their secret desires. Would others at Scottish James' Court want the same? I wondered about my own servant, Catesby. I trusted him but, there again, the government has a spy in every household.

I peered towards the window then glanced over my shoulder at the door, fearful that someone might be listening there. Yet, what did I fear? Me? An old lady from an ancient time, a forgotten reign, the Queen is dead, long live the King! A new Court now occupies our rooms at Whitehall and Richmond. What interest would the Council take in a person like me? Unless, of course, they suspected what I might know about them. True, I had certain papers, but I hid those well.

"Mistress?"

Sir Thomas was sitting in his chair, head back, peering at me from under heavy eyelids.

"Mistress, we are following you down a path, though where does it lead? Some of that path we know better than you, but – " he pointed his finger, "you seem to know what lies at the end of this journey."

"And so will you," I retorted, "when we reach that end, Master Reginald."

He paused before the fire and turned. "You have read the manuscripts, Mistress, so let me summarise matters very swiftly. Sometime in the winter of 1559 or 1560, Amy Robsart, wife of ten years to Lord Robert Dudley, Master of the Queen's Horse, Knight of the Garter and Member of the Council, transferred her residence from the Hyde family at Denchworth to Cumnor Place, the residence of her husband's treasurer, Sir Anthony Forster, who had leased it from its former owner, William Owen. Lady Amy set up residence there with her own staff of personal servants."

"Did Dudley visit Cumnor?"

"Not to our knowledge, Mistress." Master Reginald paused in his pacing. "The last time the Dudleys were together as man and wife was at Denchworth. We know that from a letter which still exists. We also learn from that same letter that Robert Dudley left his wife rather quickly on some weighty matter of state."

"Was she a prisoner there?" I asked.

"No, definitely not! I've heard such rumours," Sir Thomas spoke up. "Amy Robsart lived as any lady would in the countryside, free and unrestricted."

"Was she ill?"

"Certainly not."

"But there were rumours that she was so."

"Yes, there were." Master Reginald came back to the table and closed his eyes. "There is a letter from the Spanish ambassador in 1559. I have studied it very carefully." He picked up the leather pannier resting against his chair. He undid the straps, rummaged amongst its contents and brought out a small roll of parchment.

"Yes, in 1559 the Spanish ambassador informed his master how people were talking freely of Dudley's advancement and possible marriage to the Queen. He goes on ..."

Master Reginald came across and stretched the piece of parchment out on the table. "They say that his wife," he glanced up at me, "has a malady in one of her breasts and the Queen is only waiting for her to die to marry Lord Robert. Another report says something much more malignant." Master Reginald undid the roll even further. "Ah yes – this is the copy. The Spanish ambassador was writing about the different marriage proposals between Elizabeth and foreign princes. The ambassador concludes that the Queen is only keeping Lord Robert's enemies and country engaged with words until the wicked deed of killing his wife is consummated. He goes on. 'The same person told me some extraordinary things about this intimacy which I would never have believed. Only now I find that Lord Robert's enemies in the Council make no secret of their evil opinion of it.'"

"I, too, have read that," I declared. "So, on the one hand, they say Lord Robert's wife is ill with a malady of the breast but, on the other, if Lady Amy dies it's not because of any natural cause, or lack of physic, but her own husband's murderous contempt and the Queen was partial to that."

Master Reginald pulled a face.

"According to the evidence," I demanded, "was Lady Amy truly ill? Is there any proof?"

"No proof whatsoever," Master Reginald replied. "The only evidence we have about the final few months of her life concerns her clothes. She ordered embroidered velvet, a pair of velvet gloves, a gown of russet taffeta, the collar of which seemed to have pleased her greatly, so much that she sent her tailor one of her velvet gowns to be adorned with a similar collar. The letter was sent on 24th August, some two weeks before her death. Surely," Master Reginald shook his head, "a women who is seriously ill of a tumour, and had been for at least sixteen months, would not be so concerned about velvet gowns, shoes or a russet taffeta collar for her dresses. Nor does Blount in his letters to Dudley indicate any physical ailment. Of course, other references in Blount's letters to Dudley show that Lady Amy suffered some sort of," Master Reginald chose his words carefully, "spiritual distress?"

"And the household at Cumnor?" I asked.

Master Reginald gestured at the parchments on the table.

"They are listed there: Sir Anthony Forster and his wife, his wife's sister, Mrs Odingsells, whose husband had been a gentleman usher to Henry VIII, and Mrs George Owen, widow of the previous owner of Cumnor Place, whose husband had been a Royal Physician. Mrs Owen's son, William, owned Cumnor until he leased it to Anthony Forster."

"And the house itself?" I asked.

"Cumnor once belonged to the Benedictines of Abingdon. When fat Henry dissolved the Monasteries it was sold along with its grounds. Not the gloomy mansion," Master Reginald smiled, "of the legends and popular songs which have flourished about the death of Lady Amy. Cumnor was built of grey stone with a fine slated roof and served as a summer residence for the Abbots. The buildings themselves are two-storey and form a quadrangle set back a short distance from the road. The main entrance to this quadrangle is a vaulted gatehouse in the North side. The trackway leading up to this is lined with shadowy yews and elm trees. The entire building has a high curtain wall surrounding it. The principal buildings within the walls are as follows ..." Master Reginald came over to the table. He picked up a scrap of parchment from a tray, dipped a quill into the ink and drew crude drawings. "The Hall was on one side of the quadrangle with a buttery at the northern end and the butler's pantry on the southern. Lady Amy's apartment was above the butler's pantry. It's still called Lady Dudley's Chamber."

"You have visited the place?"

"Oh yes," Master Reginald agreed, "a very pleasing manor house with mullioned windows, gardens, terraced walks, stately trees and well-stocked fish ponds; a very pleasant place particularly in the summer. Near the manor house stands the village church, in fact there is an entrance from Cumnor Place which leads directly into God's acre."

"If Lady Amy's chamber was on the second storey, how was it reached?" I asked.

"From the quadrangle by a door which, in turn, opened onto a private wooden staircase which led to her quarters. On the south-side of the quadrangle were more apartments and a chapel overlooking the churchyard. The northern side consisted of a magnificent vaulted gatehouse. Chambers stood either side of it, connected by a long gallery. From what I understand the Forsters occupied the spacious apartments next to the chapel. Mrs Owen occupied apartments above the buttery – these were the most spacious and elaborate in the manor. They were reached from the buttery by a spiral stone staircase."

"You mention two flights of stairs?" I said. "A private staircase leading to Lady Amy's apartment and a stone spiral staircase leading to Mrs Owen. According to popular legend, at the foot of which staircase was Lady Amy's corpse found?"

"There is nothing in the records," Master Reginald conceded. "However, according to popular lore, rumour and local gossip, Lady Amy was found at the foot of the spiral staircase near the buttery."

"In other words the staircase leading to Mrs Owen's, not to her own?"

"Correct." Master Reginald smiled. "Why do you ask?"

I pointed to the leather wallet. "Something I read in Blount's letter. Mrs Owen was the only person Lady Amy really wanted near her that day."

"I agree!" Sir Thomas intervened.

"Secondly, amongst the reports from the Spanish ambassador, there is a reference to Lady Amy playing cards or 'tables', after which she left the game and fell down those stairs?"

"Again, correct," Sir Thomas echoed.

"In which case – " I lifted a hand, "that could account for Lady Amy's body not being found until the servants returned. In other words, she was found at the foot of a stone staircase which did not lead to her own apartments."

"But, if the ladies were playing at tables with her in a chamber," Master Reginald asked, "surely they'd miss her? They'd go out onto that staircase when they heard her scream."

I closed my eyes and sighed. "And the rest?" I asked.

"Well, I've studied the documents," Sir Thomas declared brusquely, "Elizabeth was at Windsor by Friday, 6th September to celebrate her 27th birthday. Robert Dudley, her favourite, was with her as was William Cecil, Secretary to the Council: de Quadra the Spanish ambassador arrived the same day. Lady Amy was residing at Cumnor Place. Now, from what I can gather, the Queen and Dudley spent Saturday, 7th September hunting. On Sunday, 8th, de Quadra had an interview with Elizabeth where problems with Scotland, as well as her marriage plans, were discussed. On the same day he met the Queen, de Quadra also talked to Sir William Cecil, probably in the latter's private chambers in the castle.

"Sir Thomas," I tapped the table, "I have read de Quadra's letter. What happened, surely, was treasonable? I mean for Cecil to utter such things to a Spanish ambassador?"

"I agree." Sir Thomas raised his eyebrows. "But, there again, Cecil was very depressed. He took the darkest view of the Kingdom's prospects with Dudley in the ascendant, possibly the man the Queen would marry, make her Consort, perhaps even King. Of course, what de Quadra said must be taken with more than a touch of cynicism, but I don't think he would lie. After all, Cecil's determination to resign and withdraw from public life had also been voiced to other ambassadors – Randolph in Scotland and Throckmorton in France. Indeed, Cecil apparently wanted Throckmorton to return home and assume his place as Secretary of the Council. So, by 8th September, Cecil must have been a very disappointed man, even a very jealous one; after all he had been in the north to bring a successful end to the troubles of Scotland. He may have lost his temper and said things to de Quadra he later regretted; that Robert Dudley was intending to marry the Queen; that both of them were thinking of putting Lady Amy to death."

"A strange remark," I interrupted. "He is virtually accusing his own Sovereign and her favourite of plotting murder."

"I have an answer to that," Master Reginald spoke up. "Though it must wait. What is interesting is what Cecil adds about Lady Amy being reported to be ill but that he, Cecil, knew otherwise, as well as that she was taking very careful precautions not to be poisoned."

"Which means," I replied, "that Cecil must have had someone at Cumnor Place who was reporting to him on everything which occurred there?"

"Precisely," Master Reginald declared, going across to the fire to warm his hands.

"But, of course, that would be natural. Cecil would have spies in any household worth watching."

"Then in which case," I sighed, "Cecil may have known the truth."

"Ah, the truth!" Sir Thomas shook his head.

"This Forster," I asked. "Sir Anthony Forster?"

"Son of a good family," Sir Thomas replied. "Educated, became a landowner in Worcestershire, Warwickshire and Shropshire. He later entered Dudley's service. He was trusted by him, being appointed treasurer."

"And Varney?" I asked. "The man mentioned in *Leicester's Commonwealth*?"

"There was a Richard Varney, a knight, but there were also other Varneys who acted as messengers or henchmen of Dudley. It is difficult to find which Varney the documents are referring to."

"And Thomas Blount?" I asked.

"Dudley's chief henchman," Sir Thomas replied, "his lieutenant, a distant kinsman, highly trusted by Lord Robert."

"What did happen?" I asked in exasperation. "Sir Thomas, do you know the truth of Cumnor Place?"

Master Reginald sat down opposite me.

"According to the evidence," Master Reginald began, "Lady Amy was found dead from a fall from a pair of stairs or, whatever it means, betwixt stairs on Sunday, 8th September 1560. On the 9th September, the Monday following, the Queen returned from hunting and informed de Quadra that Lady Amy had died, or was near to death, but to keep the matter quiet. Two days later de Quadra actually penned his letter, a copy of which you have. According to that, the Queen had issued a statement saying Lady Amy had died due to a fall from the stairs, adding '*Che il ha rotto il collo*', in Italian – 'she apparently broke her neck.'"

"So," I intervened, "on 9th September the Queen says Lady Amy was 'dead or near to it' but, by the 11th, the cause of her death was publicised."

"Agreed," Master Reginald nodded quickly.

"And what happened to her corpse?"

"Well, it would stay at Cumnor for the jury to examine it carefully. Once they had, it was probably sheeted and coffined and laid in the nearby parish church. According to *Leicester's Commonwealth* it was buried quickly there and later exhumed." Master Reginald shook his head. "*Leicester's Commonwealth* is very cunning; it doesn't lie, it just takes the truth and twists it. In fact, as you know, Lady Amy's corpse was conveyed to Gloucester College in Oxford from whence it was taken with much ceremony and buried in St Mary's Church in the same city."

"And Dudley?"

"Mistress," Sir Thomas declared, "he never visited Cumnor, as far as we know, to pay his last respects to his dead wife nor did he attend the funeral. From what we understand, Lord Robert stayed for a while at Windsor, probably on the orders of the Queen, before retiring to the Dairy House at Kew, a manor recently granted him by the Queen. He remained there until the Coroner and his jury had finished their task."

"According to the documents," Master Reginald pulled across the leather wallet, "Dudley's henchman, Blount, left Windsor for Cumnor early on Monday, 9th September. We do not know from his letters whether it was in connection with the death of Dudley's wife or other business he may have had with Forster, Dudley's treasurer. He had not travelled very far when he met another of Dudley's servants, Bowes, coming from Cumnor. Bowes was the bearer of sad news that Lord Robert's wife had been found dead. Bowes gave no particulars, only that it had happened the day before by a fall between a pair of stairs. The two men then parted, each going their respective way."

"But Blount didn't go direct to Cumnor?"

"No," Master Reginald agreed, "he went to Abingdon. Bowes would deliver the news to his master whilst Blount decided to fish at a nearby tavern as to the mood of the local citizens, Lord Robert's principal concern. True, Dudley shows no grief at his wife's death. He believes the tragedy will be put down to villainy and he'll be named as the culprit."

"I agree," Sir Thomas shook his head. "Blount's behaviour is extraordinary. His master's wife has been found dead yet he stays the night in Abingdon. At supper he invites the landlord to his table to hear what news there is in the neighbourhood, adding the lie that he was going on to Gloucester. The landlord gives the news about Lady Amy's death, declares he is highly suspicious, but praises Sir Anthony Forster as a man of great honesty, whose integrity would be sufficient to answer any accusation. We then get further revelations about events at Cumnor: Lady Amy rising early and trying to clear the house of her servants; but how some of them, led by Mrs Odingsells, objected."

"I can understand that." Master Reginald pulled his cloak closer about him. "Abingdon Fair was held on Lady's Day, 8th September. It attracted ruffians, moon people, tinkers, chapmen – not a place for ladies to resort on a Sunday afternoon. Anyway, to return to what was happening at Windsor. When Dudley does receive news of his wife's death, on that same day, Monday 9th, late in the evening, he writes to Blount. He expresses his deepest fears that his wife's death will be viewed as an act of murder and that he'll be held responsible. This second letter reveals how highly anxious and agitated Dudley has become. He advises Blount to do anything he can to ensure a fair hearing is held and a just decision is reached. Dudley protests his innocence and insists that if villainy occurred, the perpetrators should be found and named. Dudley asks Blount to do all he can to persuade the Coroner to call a jury. In fact," Master Reginald licked his lips, "when Blount arrived at Cumnor on Tuesday 10th September he found everything was already in place. The Coroner was present and a jury had been empanelled. All Blount could do was to deliver his master's charge that they should view and search the corpse then conduct their enquiry in an honest manner and be no respecter of persons. Blount was a little concerned about those serving on the jury, 15 in number. He recognised some as hostile to Sir Anthony Forster."

"Master Reginald?"

"Yes, Mistress?"

"Dudley shows little or no respect for his wife. He actually insists in a letter for her corpse to be stripped and carefully examined by the jury. He shows no feelings."

"Mistress, God knows what happened between Robert Dudley and Amy Robsart – whatever love did exist had long disappeared. Perhaps there was affection but, by 9th September 1560, you must imagine Dudley's feelings. He was no longer the Queen's favourite, no longer her soon-to-be husband. Instead, he faced disgrace, perhaps even a charge of capital murder for which he could hang. Blount tried to curb his Master's anxieties in his next letter, advising him to let his agitation be tempered by the fact that he knew himself to be innocent. Dudley, of course, would not be satisfied. He writes afresh on 12th September, begging Blount once again to convince the jury that they must find their verdict according to the evidence, whether Lady Amy's death was due to chance or villainy. If it were the latter, then prosecution for murder must certainly follow, whoever might be involved. Only in that way could the perpetrator of the vile act be punished and Dudley's own innocence be clearly vindicated. Blount answers these anxieties in his letter of Friday, 13th September – he assures Dudley that his master's repeated calls for prudence were unnecessary; the jury were taking great pains over the enquiry, even if it was for the reason that some of them bore Sir Anthony Forster considerable ill will."

"Master Reginald?"

"Yes, Mistress."

"Dudley asks for the jury to do their job properly, with integrity. However, Blount claims that on 14th September, he is to meet some of the jury in Abingdon. He was to dine with them and learn what he could, which intelligence he would bring to Dudley. Surely, this was tampering with the jury?"

"Not necessarily, according to the evidence!" Sir Thomas pushed back his chair stretching out his legs. "By then the jury must have reached their conclusion, or been close to it because, as Blount admits, he's heard rumours that they could find no grounds for presuming evil, that all the evidence pointed to the theory that Lady Amy's death was a result of pure mischance. True, Dudley's last letter from Kew," Sir Thomas continued, "demonstrates that Dudley himself had been in communication with the foreman of the jury: a gentlemen called Smith, who had assured him that their verdict was clearly one of misadventure. Dudley's relief was apparent. He even wanted to have a second jury empanelled composed of notables such as Sir Richard Blount, Lieutenant of the Tower of London and Master Henry Norris of Rycote Manor, Oxfordshire, a close friend of the Queen. Such a jury would, Dudley declared, vindicate his name." Sir Thomas narrowed his eyes. "You don't seem convinced, Mistress?"

"No, I am not," I replied. "Here is Smith, foreman of the jury, writing to Dudley, assuring him that Lady Amy's death was due to misadventure. We have Blount meeting members of that same jury for a meal in Abingdon. We have Dudley wanting a second jury empanelled composed of the likes of Norris of Rycote, men patronised by the Queen, clear friends of Dudley. Their verdict would have been an agreed conclusion. Finally, both you, Sir Thomas and Master Reginald, know about those entries from

Dudley's household book for 1566: cloths being sent to the 'Queen's man Smith' at Abingdon, gifts also to the Mayor and his brothers, the very time when Master Appleyard was whispering that Lady Amy's death was not properly examined or its true cause published for all to read. Appleyard's interrogation," I continued, "yields golden nuggets, precious jewels of information. He seems to have been well looked after by Dudley, given money, a post in Ireland well away from Cumnor. He also spent some time in France."

"And yet," Master Reginald spoke up relishing his lawyer's role, "Appleyard quite clearly states Dudley is innocent, although he adds it would be easy to find the true perpetrators behind what had happened to Lady Amy at Cumnor Place."

"But there is evidence," I persisted, "that the jury, which sat to determine Lady Amy's fate was tampered with and not only what I have cited. In his confession Appleyard alleges that Cecil might have interfered with the commission to Elliott, the Mayor and Coroner of Abingdon. My conclusion is that Mr Elliott's jury did find Lady Amy had died by accident, but that rumours persisted that her death might have been caused by something else. Her Majesty herself implies this when talking to Jones, Throckmorton's secretary. She states quite clearly 'that Dudley or none of his people were present at the attempt at his wife's house'. Now the word 'attempt', Master Reginald, can mean what we think, an attempt to do something. It can also mean an assault. Was her Majesty hinting that something vile and heinous did happen at Cumnor Place on that Sunday afternoon?" I paused. "But if it did, why didn't any of the other ladies hear any commotion? And Sir Anthony Forster? He is referred to time and again in the letters between Blount and Dudley, whilst *Leicester's Commonwealth*, Papist propaganda or not, seems to know a great deal about Lady Amy's death, placing it at the door of Forster and a man called Varney. It claims Lady Amy was murdered in a private chamber and her body taken to the foot of the stairs so it looked as if she'd fallen down without disturbing the hood on her head. It also refers to well-known stories about Dudley attempting to poison his wife. How he even tried to use a Doctor Bailey of Oxford, who was alive when *Leicester's Commonwealth* was published. But," I gestured at Master Reginald, "I can see that you're as eager as a greyhound to give your own theories. Yes?"

"Mistress, I've listened very carefully to what you have said. You've plucked at this and plucked at that. However, let's ignore the gossip and the chatter. Lady Amy's death was caused somehow but – "

Master Reginald sat upright in his chair like a prophet who'd come to judgement, hand raised as he emphasized his points. "We can fashion different hypotheses," he continued, "first let us say it was an accident. Yet – " he pointed his thumb in the air:

"Item: Isn't it strange that an accident occurred on the very day Lady Amy asked all her servants to leave her and go to Abingdon Fair?

"Item: Isn't it strange Lady Amy suffered her accident on the very day Cecil claimed the Queen and Dudley were plotting to kill her?

"Item: Isn't it strange that Lady Amy, married ten years to Lord Robert Dudley, suffered an accident at the very time when her husband's relationship with the Queen was approaching its zenith?

"Item: Isn't it strange that, when Lady Amy suffered this accident, no one heard her cries or noticed anything untoward so that she lay at the foot of some stairs with her hood pulled over her head?

"Item: Some found it hard to accept that an accident had occurred. The great Earls themselves, albeit Dudley's enemies, Norfolk, Arundel and Sussex, firmly believed there was something highly suspicious about Lady Amy's death.

"Item: If Lady Amy's death was an accident, why did Dudley try to interfere with the jury? I agree with you, Mistress. I know he did. We have Blount meeting jurors at a tavern in Abingdon. We have the foreman Smith writing privately to Dudley, whilst during the crisis of 1566 to 1567, Dudley gave presents to Master Elliott, Mayor and Coroner of Abingdon as well as further presents to the Queen's man Smith and relatives of Master Elliott.

"Item: Lady Amy's half-brother, Appleyard, clearly insinuates his half-sister's death was murder, not an accident. From what we can gather he was forced into silence.

"Item: The Queen herself does not describe it as an 'accident' but as an 'attempt' at the house of Lord Dudley's wife." He paused, sighed and stared into the fire. "Before we go any further," Master Reginald continued, "let's try and list what all the evidence agrees on: Lady Amy died of a fall. She suffered a broken neck. She was at Cumnor Place. Every piece of evidence we have looked at would agree with that. What we have to decide is, if it wasn't an accident, if she didn't break her neck," he paused and, chewing his lips, asked, "then who broke it for her?"

"Do continue," I murmured.

"And so we move to the second hypothesis; that Lady Amy's death was an accident but one caused by her illness; there being some connection between her fall and the malady in her breast."

Master Reginald returned to the attack:

"Item: Master Thomas James and Master John Norton are good friends of myself – " he gestured towards Sir Thomas, "and Sir Thomas. Master James is keeper of the new library at the University of Oxford, John Norton, a bookseller. They have in their possession every book on physic available, printed either in this country or abroad. I have made diligent search about the malady of the breast. I have consulted with the Guild of Physicians in London. There is an agreement: a malady of the breast can be light or it can be death-bearing. If the latter is the case, particularly in a young woman like Lady Amy, death is rapid, the tumour grows, the malignancy spreads and death occurs quickly. Yet Lady Amy is reported to be ill of a malady of the breast at least 16 months before her death.

"Item: The books on physic and the learned physicians all concede that a malady of the breast carries with it other infections as the humours of the body are disturbed: there is soreness, weakness, a fragility of the bone.

"Item: The books on physic, and those who write them, all agree that a fall for such a woman could be fatal. However, according to Master Cecil in September 1560, Lady Amy was in the best of health and taking very careful precautions that she remain so.

"Item: Mrs Pirto, Lady Amy's maid, never refers to any physical ailment, nor does Master Blount, nor does Appleyard or any of those involved during the crisis of 1566-1567.

"Item: In August 1560, only a few days before her death, Lady Amy, in her own letters, shows no indication of serious illness. On the contrary, she is more concerned with clothes, robes, dresses, shoes and a taffeta collar.

"Item: Let us say that *causa disputandi* – for the sake of argument – that Lady Amy did have some malignancy in her breast. Isn't it strange her malady caused such a crisis on that very day at that very time? I refer to matters I have already raised. The coincidence is too much, it cannot be accepted.

"Item: In conclusion, none of the records indicate in any way that Lady Amy was suffering from anything serious. A malady of the breast can be something mild; a soreness, a petty infection. I suggest it was this."

I could see Master Reginald was thirsty. I went across to the dressing table, filled goblets of apple juice and brought them back. Sir Thomas and Master Reginald lifted their cups in toast as I sat down.

"Do continue, Master Reginald," I asked. I found it difficult to stifle the thrill of excitement which turned my stomach and sent my heart fluttering. For over fifty years, Lady Amy's death had haunted me. I'd always toyed with suspicions. Had she been murdered? Had Elizabeth of England taken a hand in it?

"Let us move to the third hypothesis," Master Reginald sipped from his cup, "that Lady Amy committed suicide. According to Blount, who questioned the maid, Mistress Pirto, Lady Amy was in the habit of daily praying upon her knees. How she'd heard her, at different times, begging to God to deliver her from her desperation. Blount tried to hint at suicide, claiming Lady Amy may have had an evil toy or thought in her mind. Mrs Pirto disabuses him of this and explicitly states it was not what she said. Blount then goes on to relate that what he'd learnt about Lady Amy makes him think that she had a strange mind. So Blount still considers the possibility that Lady Amy committed suicide. But why should she?

"Item: In August, 1560 Lady Amy was in good humour enough to order new clothes, slippers and gowns. Master Cecil says Lady Amy was in good health and determined to remain so.

"Item: The jury didn't find any hint or indication of suicide.

"Item: The Queen's own statement to Jones, Throckmorton's secretary, gives no indication of suicide.

"Item: If Lady Amy did decide on suicide, surely she would have taken a less painful way than throwing herself down a staircase? There were other less sharp means to end her life.

"Item: I refer to matters already raised, why should Lady Amy decide to commit suicide on that very day? In view of what I have already said, isn't it the most remarkable of coincidences?

"Item: Master Blount is being disingenuous. He knew full well why Lady Amy should be distraught. She was separated from her husband, she was childless, rumours milled that her husband might divorce her, she had no home to call her own. It was natural for such a poor woman to be distressed and highly anxious. Indeed," Master Reginald concluded, "there is no evidence whatsoever that, on Sunday, 8th September 1560, Lady Amy took her own life."

I sat up in my chair and glanced at a painting, a likeness of King Edward IV which my father had bought from a merchant in

Huntworth. The King's face seemed to come alive, dark eyes glittering in a bland face and, although the King was smooth shaved, there was a cast about his eyes which reminded me of Cecil. I repressed a shiver and wondered if my wits and imagination were wandering. The silence in the solar had become oppressive. Master Reginald was sitting arms crossed, head slightly down, looking at his master out of the corner of his eye. Sir Thomas was clearing his throat, tapping his fingers against the table as if eager to proceed. I noticed how dark the room had become whilst outside I glimpsed the first fluttering flakes of impending snow. I stirred myself eager for any noise. A rook cawed in a tree outside, an animal shrieked in pain. I was almost relieved to hear the shouting of a servant hurrying along the passageway beyond. I had been young, very young when these happenings first occurred. I had followed the convention of the Court and kept both my mouth and my ears free of gossip. Yet, over the years, like a malignancy, the fear had grown. I'd seen a portrait of Lady Amy by some unknown artist, narrow faced, hair piled high, haunting eyes. I'd wondered if that poor lady had been killed on the orders of my Mistress. So much intrigue, so much subterfuge, so little truth, but now I was close to it. Despite the cold outside, the darkness, the snow, I felt a flicker of comfort; at least the truth would be known.

"We now come to our fourth hypothesis," Sir Thomas Bodley's voice echoed harshly in the solar, "that Lady Amy was murdered by Dudley and, if this is the case, certainly with the connivance of the Queen. There is," he sighed, "a great deal of evidence against Dudley. We have the rumours before Lady Amy ever met her death that Dudley was planning to kill her through poison. Certainly he wished to be rid of her either by death or divorce so as to marry the Queen. The Spanish ambassador reported as much. Master Cecil claimed as much. There are the rumours which followed Lady Amy's death, voiced by persons like Sir Thomas Lever. Now, Lord Robert Dudley certainly had a bloody reputation.

He was an intriguer, a conspirator, a soldier and in many ways, a violent man. Blount himself admits that when Dudley, then Earl of Leicester, interviewed Appleyard in the crisis of 1566 to 1567, he so lost his temper he could have run him through with his sword. Moreover, there are many murders ascribed to him. No wonder few people liked Dudley." He opened the writing case before him and picked up a parchment. "In 1566, Cecil drew up a memorandum on Robert Dudley, Earl of Leicester, categorising him under certain headings. Under that of 'friendship' Cecil puts 'none, but such as shall have of the Queen'; 'In reputation hated of many; ill-famed by his wife's death'. Other contemporaries are less than complimentary. Thomas Naunton, a virulent gossip at Elizabeth's court, claims Leicester 'to have died by that poison which he'd prepared for others of which they claimed he was a rare artist.' Naunton goes on to say: 'I fear Robert Dudley was too well versed in the aphorisms and principles of Nicholas the Florentine and the teaching of Cesare Borgia.' Another contemporary, Manningham, alleges how the Lord Chamberlain at the time declared: 'If he committed to prison everyone who spoke evil of Leicester, he should make as many prisons in London as there were dwelling houses.' Dudley was seen as an assassin. Nicholas Throckmorton, our ambassador in Paris, returned to England and Dudley feigned friendship with him. According to common report, in 1571 Sir Nicholas Throckmorton was at supper in Leicester's house where he was taken in the most violent manner by an impostumation of his lungs and died within a few days, but not without suspicion of poison."

Sir Thomas picked up another piece of parchment.

"According to *Leicester's Commonwealth*, Dudley was called away from table to attend court. He made Sir Nicholas Throckmorton take his place and be served – he was and, soon after, Throckmorton died of a strange and incurable vomit. The same pamphlet relates how, a few days before he died, Throckmorton had attacked the Earl's cruel and bloody disposition, affirming him to be the wickedest, most perjured and perfidious man under heaven. Now, of course, such evidence could be tainted being highly biased. However, Dudley himself wrote in a letter: 'We have lost on Monday our good friend Sir Nicholas Throckmorton who died in my house, being taken there suddenly in great extremity, his lungs were perished and a sudden cold he'd taken was the cause of his death.' Dudley was also accused of causing the death of Lord Sheffield whose wife he lusted after, as well as Walter Devereux, Earl of Essex and Thomas Ratcliffe, Earl of Sussex. The latter died suddenly on the 9th June 1583 at his home in Bermondsey. On his death bed, Ratcliffe reportedly said to his friends 'beware of the gipsy', that Dudley 'would be too hard to you all as you do not know the beast as well as I do'."

"But this is tittle-tattle, gossip, scandal," I intervened. "Robert Dudley, Earl of Leicester was feared, resented, envied. He may have assassinated others, removed rivals, but that does not mean he murdered his wife."

"I agree." Sir Thomas stretched in his chair and took a gulp of apple juice from the jewel goblet. "Oh, Mistress, I assure you, I do not believe Lord Robert Dudley – " the words rolled out of his mouth, " – Earl of Leicester, Knight of the Garter, Master of the Queen's Horse, killed his wife." He leaned forward.

"Item: Why should Dudley murder his wife? That was the very act which dashed all hopes he had of any marriage with the Queen.

"Item: It is obvious from the letters between Blount and Dudley that Dudley was beside himself with rage. He did not mourn his poor wife's death, he deeply feared he'd be held responsible. He moved heaven and earth to vindicate his own innocence.

"Item: Master Cecil, Secretary to the Council, no friend of Leicester, would have exploited any opportunity to strike at his rival; but, in 1560 and again in 1567, Cecil did nothing to encourage the rumours against Dudley. In fact, he did quite the opposite.

"Item: Even John Appleyard, that wayward, weak and vacuous

half-brother of Lady Amy, quite categorically stated before the Council how Dudley was innocent of Lady Amy's murder but that others could be held responsible and would be easily discovered.

"Item: Why should Dudley involve himself in such an act and make himself so vulnerable to his enemies?

"Item: Even the Queen herself makes it quite clear how, after her own secret searches, Lord Robert Dudley had been cleared of any charge. She quite explicitly states to Master Jones, Throckmorton's secretary, that neither Dudley nor any of his people were at that attempt at his wife's house. Of course it could be alleged," Master Reginald added smoothly, "that Dudley might be innocent but members of his own retinue took the law into their own hands, imitating those Knights of Henry II who thought that by killing Becket they would please their Master; but," he pulled a face, "the same arguments, which vindicate their master's innocence, can be applied to them. They would never have dared to carry out such a deed without his permission."

"Even so," I replied, "from the commencement, whether it be Blount's letters to Dudley or *Leicester's Commonwealth*, there is a constant thread that some of Dudley's servants were involved: Sir Anthony Forster is named time and again."

"We shall return to Forster," Master Reginald murmured, "but there were others who could have Lady Amy's blood on their hands. So we come to the next hypothesis involving William Cecil, Secretary of the Council, displaced by Dudley, fearful of Dudley, terrified that the Queen might marry Lord Robert Dudley. Cecil had written to his ambassador friends, Randolph and Throckmorton, that he was thinking of retiring from public life. He repeated the same to the Bishop of Avila, the Spanish ambassador, saying he didn't care any longer if the Queen sent him to the Tower. Wouldn't he have so much to gain by ordering the secret destruction of Lady Amy and so crown his rival with guilt and suspicion? He certainly was wary of Dudley. Look at the memorandum he drew up in 1566. Who gained most by Lady Amy's death?" Master Reginald spread his hands. "Why, Master Cecil. Within days his rival was consigned to a house in Kew where Cecil visited him, and Dudley later wrote begging for his favour and protection. What makes him even more suspect," Master Reginald persisted, "a mere coincidence, a subtle conceit, that the very day Lady Amy dies, Cecil is telling the Spanish ambassador how Dudley and the Queen could be plotting to kill her. He seems to know a great deal about Lady Amy, about her health, and her determination to stay healthy. It's not beyond the bounds of possibility," Master Reginald sipped from his cup, "that William Cecil, Secretary of the Council, decided to help matters along. Yet, in the end, the case against him is very weak. He may have gained from the death of Lady Amy. However:

"Item: If Cecil had a hand in Lady Amy's death, it was very dangerous and rendered him most vulnerable. William Cecil was no assassin of innocent ladies.

"Item: If he killed Lady Amy, Cecil would have to hire assassins. He would have no control over their mouths or any attempt by them to blackmail him.

"Item: Lady Amy lived in a house with at least three other ladies and her maid, not to mention Sir Anthony Forster and his family. The presence of strangers in such a house would be quickly noticed.

"Item: Finally, if Cecil was responsible, if the Queen and Dudley ever found out it would have brought both Cecil's office and his life to an abrupt end. No, although Master Cecil can be suspected, little can be proved of Master Cecil's guilt in these proceedings.

"There is one other person." Sir Thomas got up from his chair, walked to the fire and turned to face me. "Thomas Howard, third Duke of Norfolk, Dudley's inveterate enemy."

I held my breath. This was a path I walked along myself and often wondered about.

"Is it possible?" Sir Thomas came forward and made himself comfortable against the back of his chair. "There was some form of relationship between Howard of Norfolk and Lady Amy. After all, her father was a Norfolk Knight. Appleyard, her half-brother, became a member of his retinue and actually took part in Norfolk's conspiracy against the Queen. In 1570 Appleyard was arrested for treason and stayed under house arrest until his death. Is it possible," Sir Thomas continued, "that Lady Amy appealed to Thomas Howard, Duke of Norfolk for help; the one man strong enough to protect her against Dudley? Did Howard send his own men into Cumnor that Sunday afternoon to abduct Lady Amy, though armed with secret instructions that it would be best for her to be killed, as Lady Amy was more valuable dead than alive? We gather from Appleyard's confession that Howard had a hand in trying to rekindle the charges against Dudley in 1566 and 1567. Yet," Sir Thomas shrugged, "the case against Howard, like that against Cecil, is very weak.

"Item: Cumnor Place was a busy house. Howard's retainers, the Yellow Jackets, could hardly be expected to swagger in, wreak their damage and saunter off.

"Item: If Howard was involved, and this was discovered, it could have sent him and those involved to the scaffold.

"Item: Howard was keen to have the investigation resurrected. If he had been involved that would have been very unwise. People might have come forward, not only to vindicate Dudley but to convict Howard of a very serious crime.

"Item: The arguments against Cecil's involvement also apply to Howard: if the Duke had used assassins they might either betray or blackmail him."

"Yet could it not have been Howard, or one of the other Earls?" I demanded. "After all, isn't that what the Queen was hinting at when she claimed Lord Robert Dudley and none of his servants were at the attempt at his wife's house? Surely she's implying others were?"

Sir Thomas glanced at Master Reginald who shook his head.

"In which case," I cried in exasperation, "which hypothesis do we favour?"

"Let us look at the evidence again." Master Reginald laid his hands flat on the table. "Let us take each statement step-by-step, establish a chronology of what exactly happened.

"Item: On Sunday, 8th September Lady Amy Robsart suffered a mishap, a tragic one at her house in Cumnor Place, from a fall between stairs which broke her neck. On that very same day de Quadra, Bishop of Avila, the Spanish ambassador, had a meeting with the Queen and another with Cecil. At that meeting Cecil confides that Lady Amy is in the best of health but the Queen and Dudley may be plotting her death. I believe Master Cecil was as great as any actor who strode the boards. To put it bluntly, Mistress, I believe Lady Amy had already suffered a mishap. Cecil, who by his own report, had spies at Cumnor, had learnt of this."

"In other words," I declared, "the news of Lady Amy's accident, whatever you may call it, was brought by fast courier to Windsor only thirty miles away. Cecil had learnt of this as he would, being Secretary of the Council. He immediately seeks an interview with de Quadra to sow the idea that if Lady Amy had suffered some fatal accident, perhaps the Queen and her lover were involved. In the end his fears became fact, and any hopes Dudley had of marrying the Queen were cruelly dashed."

I stared open-mouthed at Master Reginald even as I recalled laying in my own chamber, hearing those hurrying footsteps, the shouts, the clatter of hooves on the cobbles outside.

"It's most feasible." Master Reginald shrugged. "Look at any chart or map. Cumnor is only thirty miles from Windsor. On a fine September evening, a swift horseman brings the news. The Queen, Dudley and Cecil are informed and each plays their part. Cecil seeks out de Quadra to plant the seeds of his own mischief. More importantly, when Lady Amy suffered her accident, she didn't die immediately, which is why, according to de Quadra, the next day, Monday, after she had returned from hunting, the Queen confided to him that Lady Amy was close to death. The same is true of Lord Robert. Master Blount was not sent on some minor errand to Cumnor. Dudley already knew that his wife was dead or nearly so. He sent Blount, not to discover the cause of her mishap (he knew that already) but what effect it would have in the countryside around. Look again at those letters which passed between Dudley and Blount. In his first letter to his 'Kinsman Blount', written on the evening of 9th September, Dudley categorically states 'immediately upon your departing from me there came to me Bowes, by whom I do understand that my wife is dead, by a fall from a pair of stairs.' If you read that sentence time and again," Master Reginald put the piece of parchment back on the table, "there is an implicit understanding that Dudley knew his wife was in serious danger, on the verge of death and that Bowes simply confirmed it, which explains Dudley's phrase: 'I do understand that my wife is dead'. In other words, Dudley knew long before Bowes arrived what had happened at Cumnor Place, though he was left in doubt whether his wife was mortally injured or had died. Bowes' arrival confirmed the latter. Bowes also confirms my hypothesis. Lady Amy had suffered a grave mishap on Sunday evening. I doubt whether someone like Sir Anthony Forster would wait till Monday to send a messenger. If you look at Blount's reply to Dudley, he declares that he'd read the letter brought by the messenger, Bristow, and that Dudley has been advised by Bowes that his Lady was dead. In other words, any doubt has now been cleared."

"Of course," I agreed, "it also explains why Blount didn't immediately go to Cumnor Place. He was Dudley's henchman, his principal lieutenant. You'd think he'd hasten there immediately, but he doesn't. What's the use of that? Dudley and Blount realised Lady Amy was dead." I paused. "And of course, Blount could not help matters at Cumnor. Dudley had his own representative there, his treasurer, Sir Anthony Forster. Blount is more concerned about discovering what effect Lady Amy's death will have on popular opinion about Dudley. So he stays in Abingdon to question that tavern keeper. He knows he can achieve nothing at Cumnor. The best he can do for his master is find out how the news is being received in the countryside."

"Precisely," Master Reginald agreed, "and when Blount does arrive at Cumnor, lo and behold, the Coroner and the jury are already empanelled. Lady Amy died some time late on Sunday, 8th September but, by Tuesday at the very latest, September 10th, the Coroner and jury have already taken over Cumnor. Appleyard, in his submission of 1567, talks of a commission given to Master Elliott by Sir William Cecil. Cecil could also make sure, at the Queen's bidding, that her own man, Smith, was foreman of that jury." Master Reginald folded back the sleeves of his gown, pulling back the cuffs underneath as if ready to write. "The only conclusion I can reach, Mistress, is that Blount's letters must not be taken at their face value, indeed they may have been redrafted some time later to depict his master in the best of lights. Nevertheless, the news of Lady Amy's mishap did reach Windsor on Sunday evening. Cecil moved immediately. He sent a fast courier to Elliot, the Mayor and Coroner of Abingdon, to empanel a jury and ensure that its members included people who could be trusted."

"But doesn't that bring Cecil under suspicion again?"

"No, no," Master Reginald pursed his lips. "Cecil acted on the orders of the Queen. Master Dudley ordered Blount not to go directly to Cumnor, where affairs would be taken care of by Sir Anthony Forster. Blount was to find out exactly what common rumour now reported, as this would determine how the jury would act. The jurors are drawn from the locality. In other words, Dudley has had time to reflect on what has happened and has proceeded to the next problem, the verdict. The Queen tried to go about her normal business but admits to the Spanish ambassador on that same Monday, 9th September, that something heinous had happened to Lady Amy, that she had either died or was near to death."

"So what did happen?" I exclaimed. "How did Lady Amy die? Was it a fall, was it an accident? Was it murder? Who killed her?"

"A mixture, I believe." Sir Thomas Bodley took his seat. "In a word, Mistress, I believe Lady Amy was killed, albeit unwittingly, by her own maids."

"Never!" I retorted. "They were never brought under suspicion."

"No, listen." Master Reginald beat excitedly upon the table. "Let us go back to the beginning again. The person at the centre of the storm is Lady Amy. We know that she was in good health but highly anxious, according to her own maid, often praying on her knees to be delivered and, of course, we know the reason why. Rumour bubbled throughout the kingdom, especially in the locality, that her husband Lord Robert was about to divorce his childless wife and marry the Queen; even worse, that Lord Robert was intending to kill her through some poison or evil potion. No wonder she was agitated. In a word, Mistress, Lady Amy had decided to flee Cumnor Place but was prevented – "

"I find that surprising," I exclaimed. "By widow women! Lady Amy's own companions?"

"You were at the Court at the time," Sir Thomas replied, "where everyone saw Lady Amy's death as a result of intrigue, rivalry, deceit, lust for power. In truth it was a mishap which should never really have occurred."

"I was at Court," I agreed, "but her Majesty was most insistent that the name of Lady Amy was never mentioned. Few dared to ask what was happening. Each person had their own thoughts but it was prudent to keep such considerations to oneself."

"As I have said before," Master Reginald returned to his hypothesis, "we know that Lady Amy was deeply agitated. We know the reasons why. Any woman in such circumstances would have fallen to her knees and begged God for deliverance. The word 'deliverance' is important. If she is to be delivered, who will deliver her, where and when? Who will protect her against Dudley? I strongly suspect she placed her trust in her half-brother John Appleyard and, perhaps, behind him lurked the shadowy figure of Thomas Howard, Duke of Norfolk. Lady Amy would turn to someone whom she could trust, a kinsman. She would not dare to put such things in writing, so a stratagem was plotted out, whispered in darkened chambers and shadowy corners, which is why Appleyard was to play such an important role in the circumstances following Lady Amy's death."

"Was Appleyard at Cumnor on that day?"

"Hardly." Master Reginald smiled. "He would not dare approach – just in case something went wrong – which it did. I suspect Lady Amy intended, either with Pirto or by herself, to flee to some other house for refuge."

"If that is the case," I answered, "to raise an earlier question put by you, Master Reginald, why did the incident occur on that particular Sunday, 8th September? Why didn't Lady Amy flee a week beforehand, two months beforehand? Why wait until then?"

"The answer to that is very simple, Mistress. First, Sunday is a day of rest: no work is done, servants have free time, the retainers in a house like Cumnor would not be so diligent. Secondly, on that particular day, there was Abingdon Fair bringing strangers into the area: the track-ways would be busy. More importantly, it was a place to send the servants, to empty Cumnor Place so that Lady Amy could plot her own secret way. Thirdly, Sunday, 8th September was the day after the Queen's birthday, Saturday 7th –"

"Of course," I intervened, "Lady Amy would know of the festivities, the banquets, the masques, the feasting which would be taking place at Windsor. These would have diverted her husband. He and his retinue would have drunk deep of the revelry. They would not be so sharp and vigilant."

"Lady Amy was not in prison, but she was closely watched," Sir Thomas declared. "Master William Cecil's remarks about her health prove that."

"And so, in your mind's eye, you can witness what happened," Master Reginald declared. "On that particular Sunday morning, Lady Amy rose early, eager to let the business proceed. She wants to send her servants from her. Why should a woman do that? To welcome someone who is going to kill her? Hardly! Mrs Odingsells, probably placed there to watch her, objected. Lady Amy is asked 'who is she going to dine with?' She replies 'Mrs Owens', the Lady whose chamber stood above the buttery, at the top of a spiral staircase, the one popular legend claims to be the place where Lady Amy fell to her death, not the more simple private wooden staircase to her own quarters above the butler's pantry. Remember what the reports say, Mistress, how Lady Amy died 'between stairs'?"

"Of course," I agreed. "A stone spiral staircase has little landing spaces between the flights."

"On that particular Sunday Lady Amy dined with Mrs Owens. According to the Spanish reports she was playing dice or cards, at tables. She left the table, an opportune moment; people expect her to return and finish the game but Lady Amy has her own private arrangements. She left that chamber, put on her cloak and hood and perhaps picked up baggage and attempted to go down that staircase. Inside the chamber, Mrs Owens, and probably other ladies including Mrs Odingsells, already suspicious, became alarmed. They try to stop her; the staircase is narrow, steep, sharply turning. They did not mean to harm her but Lady Amy falls. She would suffer head wounds, hence the reference in the Spanish manuscripts to a dagger blow to the head. Now," Master Reginald gestured, "the head is not the place to strike with any weapon but a deep gash on the head could be inflicted by the sharp rim of a stone step. The mishap occurs. The ladies, truly horrified, hurry down. Lady Amy is lying there, they panic, they do not know what to do. So they send for the most senior official in Dudley's household, Sir Anthony Forster, the treasurer. He arrives and realises the implications of what has happened. He makes the decision to give the only explanation of what truly occurred, an accident. The body would be left where it fell. Now, because he does not move it, he is not too sure whether she is alive or dead; the panic on those steps must have yielded to a deep fear. Dudley would demand an explanation. More importantly, if charges were laid they could stand accused of murder or of having carried out that murder on the orders of their master, who wished to rid himself of his wife so as to marry the Queen. Their story is concocted. A fast courier is dispatched to Windsor. Cecil is alerted. He acts his part with the Spanish ambassador. He whispers that something dreadful is going to happen to Lady Amy when Cecil knows it already has. At the same time he dispatches a courier to Abingdon, ordering Elliott, both Mayor and Coroner, to convene a jury. Dudley is distraught, Elizabeth so fearful she betrays her anxiety to the Spanish ambassador. Dudley realises the full implications of what has happened. Forster is at Cumnor taking prudent precautions and covering up whatever he can. Blount would leave the next morning to discover exactly what effect Lady Amy's death would have on the people around. The jury are empanelled, they view the corpse and certainly see enough to credit Lady Amy's injuries to a fall. Nevertheless, they are uneasy, not so much about the death itself, but the circumstances behind it. They deliver their verdict but this is not publicly proclaimed because it might contain matters injurious to Dudley. This is where Appleyard comes into his own. He can not fault the verdict but he is, probably, the most knowledgeable about the circumstances which led to Lady Amy's fall. Dudley rewards him, sends him off to Ireland and France. Appleyard is now a valuable man. Hence, he attempts in 1566 and 1567 to revive Lady Amy's ghost in an attempt to blackmail Dudley." Master Reginald paused and watched me intently.

"If you accept my hypothesis, Mistress, then I'll make a summation. Such an explanation accounts for many things:

"Item: It explains Lady Amy's early rising and her anxiety.

"Item: It explains her trying to send away her servants on that particular Sunday.

"Item: It explains why she chose that day to make her flight from Cumnor Place.

"Item: It explains why she wanted to dine with Mrs Owens alone, above those sharp, steep steps.

"Item: It explains the Spanish ambassador's report about her playing at tables just before the accident occurred.

"Item: It explains that strange remark in *Leicester's Commonwealth*, how Lady Amy wore a hood upon her head which was not disturbed by the fall. Why was she wearing a hood on a warm autumn's day, unless it was part of a cloak? She was preparing to flee, to hide her face and features until she was free of Cumnor Place."

I raised my hand; Master Reginald paused. "I accept what you say," I declared, "but *Leicester's Commonwealth* was a vicious attack on Dudley. How do we know it's the truth?"

"It may be a lie." Master Reginald nodded in agreement. "But, Mistress the best lies contains a great deal of truth. It is very easy to twist what did happen, or what might have happened. But, let me continue:

"Item: Lady Amy's flight is in agreement with her state of mind, her desperation to be delivered, the same state of mind Blount refers to constantly in his second letter to Dudley.

"Item: My hypothesis explains how Cecil knew that something dreadful was going to happen to Lady Amy on that particular day; it did, as his play-acting with de Quadra proved.

"Item: It explains the Queen's uncertainty of Lady Amy's fate, that she was dead or nearly so.

"Item: It explains those enigmatic remarks contained in the letters of Blount and Dudley. How does it go? 'My Lady is dead' and 'Your Lady has died'. Blount and Dudley had reached the hideous conclusion that Lady Amy was now dead under the most suspicious circumstances, which would have their own cruel consequences.

"Item: My hypothesis explains Blount's strange actions in not going direct to Cumnor, where the matters were now in the hands of Sir Anthony Forster, but in searching the area to discover anything else which may affect his master's reputation.

"Item: It explains Dudley's reaction. There is very little grief, true shock or mourning over his wife. Dudley has had time to reflect on that since Sunday evening. He has now moved to a greater problem, will he be blamed?

"Item: It explains how the Coroner and jury were already in session by Tuesday, 10th September. Only a 'Great One' of the land, such as Cecil, could have organised that with such speed. Appleyard's submission in 1567 makes reference to the jury and the Coroner being very much under the influence of Master Cecil.

"Item: It explains those strange letters between Blount and Dudley. Nothing is said about the particulars of her death except that it was from a fall. Blount questions no one except Mrs Pirto. He did that to create the illusion that if Lady Amy's death couldn't be judged as an accident, perhaps suicide should be considered. Blount and Dudley were very careful about what they wrote. Indeed those letters may have been redrafted later but, of course, Blount didn't need to tell Dudley about the circumstances behind his wife's death. Bowes would have already informed him whilst Dudley would have learnt the important facts when that mysterious messenger arrived at Windsor on Sunday evening. Mistress, the letters themselves indicate one fact. Dudley and Blount did not wish to proclaim the circumstances which caused the mishap. All Blount will say is that Lady Amy had what he called a strange mind upon her. She did; though it wasn't suicide Lady Amy had been contemplating, but escape. Finally, Mistress, we come to Dudley himself. The mishap placed him on the horns of a hideous dilemma. Oh, he was innocent. No one more than Dudley was fearful at the news of Lady Amy's death. Appleyard, himself, seven years later, bears witness to that. Yet, Dudley was caught in a quagmire. He would have to explain why his wife was trying to escape Cumnor. He would also have to defend why others like Mrs Odingsells tried to stop her."

"Do you think, Master Reginald, Odingsells was Dudley's spy?"

"She acted unofficially as Lady Amy's guardian, some would say jailor. She was a widow who lived with Anthony Forster – that was her title. If she resided with Forster then she really should have had nothing to do with Lady Amy. Nevertheless, Lady Amy became very angry when Mrs Odingsells refused to go to Abingdon Fair, because she knew Odingsells was watching her. In turn, Odingsells was adamant in her refusal to be told what to do and where to go. First, because she took her orders from Sir Anthony Forster. Secondly, because she wanted to stay and watch what Lady Amy intended."

"I have talked long and often with Master Reginald," Sir Thomas settled himself more comfortably. "Dudley was trapped, yet how could he blame his servants? After all it was an accident, yet, at the same time, they were carrying out his instructions. If he tried to pass the blame to them who would believe him? The gap between an accident and murder is very thin. What proof did they have? What evidence could they suggest that Lady Amy was not pushed to her death? Dudley was certainly beholden to them. He couldn't blame or castigate them. If he did, they might reveal the true circumstances of Lady Amy's life at Cumnor, about her desolation, her isolation, her desire to escape. All this would have done almost as much harm to Dudley's reputation and standing as if it had been proven that he was responsible for his wife's death. In turn Dudley had to buy their support. In 1561 Forster was allowed to purchase Cumnor without a licence, being pardoned for this a year later. In 1564 Forster's wife was granted the leasehold of lands in Derbyshire and 14 other counties which had once belonged to the Priory of Pitney in Norfolk. Appleyard's gifts are also listed, a commission to seize prizes overseas, the portership of Berwick, whilst Dudley also stood guarantee for Appleyard's debt of £400. Appleyard later became Sheriff of Norfolk and Suffolk. In 1564 he was appointed Keeper of the Marshalsea Prison, whilst Dudley also secured him a post abroad, first in Ireland then in France. No wonder Dudley's enemies were suspicious. From 1561 to 1567 they mined away to suborn Appleyard, to bribe him into offering new evidence which might reopen the case. Dudley was just as vigilant. He turned on Appleyard; yet, in the end, Dudley recognised he, himself, had done nothing wrong. By 1567 Dudley viewed Appleyard for what he was: a weather-vane, turning to whatever wind blew. Dudley also rewarded Elliott of Abingdon, Mayor and Coroner, as well as Elliott's brothers and the Queen's man, Smith, with gifts of costly cloth. Dudley wished to keep them hand-fast, to stand by the verdict they had published in 1560." Sir Thomas cleared his throat. "Appleyard makes a most illuminating remark in his submission. He clears Dudley of any guilt for Lady Amy's death but adds the surprising statement that it would be an easy matter to discover the true offenders. Why should Appleyard think it was so easy? Why does he mention offenders? If he were going to lay charges against Dudley, which of course he doesn't, Dudley would not be easy to prosecute. The same is true of any of the 'Great Ones' of the land, Cecil or Thomas Howard, Duke of Norfolk."

"I agree," I interrupted "But against two widow women, Mrs Owens and Mrs Odingsells, perhaps even Mrs Pirto herself."

"Precisely," Sir Thomas smiled. "Appleyard knew exactly what had happened and so did Dudley's enemies. The case would be reopened. Dudley would be cleared of any charge; but others, Odingsells and certainly Forster, would be implicated on a possible murder charge. More importantly, details would spill out about Dudley's treatment of Lady Amy and questions would be asked: 'Why was Lady Amy so determined to flee? Was Dudley threatening her? Was Dudley trying to poison her?' No, Dudley could not afford that. Moreover, by 1567, the situation had changed – the powerful William Cecil realised that any chance of Dudley marrying Elizabeth was shattered. Lady Amy's death had achieved what he'd hoped for, the complete and utter dashing of any hope by Dudley of becoming the Queen's consort, which is why Cecil, probably at the Queen's behest, supported Dudley in his confrontation with Appleyard."

"And Her Majesty," I asked, "the Queen?"

"Her Majesty." Sir Thomas scratched his bearded chin and peered across the chamber at a portrait of the Queen hanging on the far wall, not a true likeness but one made of a painting by Hilliard. "Of course, Her Majesty knew, hence her remark, 'Lord Dudley and none of his people were at the attempt at his wife's house'. The Queen was speaking the truth, the closest we shall ever come to it. The 'attempt' she mentioned was Lady Amy's attempt to flee. The people involved were those ladies and, as we have seen, none of them were of Dudley's retinue."

"One further piece of evidence –" Master Reginald plucked up a small square of parchment. "Appleyard was supported by the Howard/Arundel faction. In 1561 the Spanish ambassador reported," Master Reginald peered at the parchment, "yes, here it is: 'Great suspicions are entertained of the Earl of Arundel with whom Lord Robert had such words that the Earl went home and he and others are drawing up copies of the testimony given in the inquiry respecting the death of Lord Robert's wife. Robert is doing his best to repair matters as it appears that more is being discovered in that affair than he wishes.'" Master Reginald put the manuscript down. "Note, Mistress, it is the testimony given at the inquest which Dudley's enemies concentrated on – I suspect the witnesses – the household at Cumnor Place."

"Whilst the reference to more being discovered," Sir Thomas interjected, "is a reference to these matters we have already discussed. Dudley's enemies were shifting their assault, I believe, to the circumstances which caused Lady Amy's death."

"And remember," Master Reginald added, "Dudley never appeared before that Coroner. In his case, least said, soonest mended."

"So," I concluded, "Lady Amy did decide to flee Cumnor on Sunday, 8th September. Odingsells and others became suspicious. She tried to escape during a card game, whilst dining in Mrs Owens' quarters above the buttery. She fell down that stone spiral staircase, gashing her head and breaking her neck. Sir Anthony Forster then takes over, sending a dispatch to Windsor and so the play begins."

"It does," Master Reginald agreed. "Which is why, from the very outset, Forster's name is linked with Lady Amy's death. It is not just a matter of speculation but based on gossip and chatter. He was there at the time. He would certainly have taken matters over to protect his master's interests. He would have been questioned by the Coroner and jury. Forster was the one who made the decision that Lady Amy's death must look like an accident. This is all caught up by the anonymous author of *Leicester's Commonwealth*. The story that pamphlet publishes is actually true, only the writer has made a radical change so an accident is twisted to look like a murder. And, of course, what defence can Dudley make?"

Ah, I reflected, what defence could Dudley make? What defence could my Mistress make? They had all been caught in a cruel trap! Fickle Fortune's wheel had turned and dashed any hopes! I rose from my chair rubbing the side of my head, relieved yet sad, relieved that any suspicions against my Mistress had now disappeared like snow under the sun. Sad, because I know she truly loved Dudley. She lived for him, pined for him with all her heart. I glanced up – Sir Thomas and Master Reginald were now collecting their papers, shuffling them into order, pleased as lawyers who'd won their case and were about to adjourn to a nearby tavern for six bottles of wine.

"I am grateful," I murmured.

"Mistress, you seem distressed?"

"No," I forced a smile, "just hungry." I rang a small hand bell and we adjourned to a table which overlooked the garden. The servant brought in a collation of ham and eggs, freshly cooked quail meat in a broth, small loaves and pots of butter. The table was quickly laid. We ate hungrily. Sir Thomas complimented me on the ale I brewed. Master Reginald compared it to the best he had ever drunk in a London tavern. They were flattering me, trying to distract me. I wanted to go away and reflect upon what they had said, yet, what was the use of reflection? Master Reginald had already argued his case – one of the great mysteries of Elizabeth's reign shown to be a hideous tragedy which marred so many lives. Yet there was more. Despite their apparent bonhomie, Sir Thomas and Master Reginald were waiting for me to keep my side of the bargain: to tell them what I knew.

"You are writing a memoir, Mistress?" Sir Thomas wiped his lips on a napkin and picked up a knife as if to admire the silver filigree work along its handle.

"I am, for my own secret purposes, to impose some order on what I suspected, knew and discovered about Elizabeth of England, about her origins, her death, her relationship with Dudley."

I paused, listening to the fire crackle. The dancing shadows seemed to draw closer. "I have described how my Mistress died. How she lived is for others. I always wondered if her antecedents, the intrigue and scandal surrounding her own birth and mother, prevented her from truly loving. My Mistress," I whispered, "was a very great woman in love with her Kingdom but she did love Dudley, truly, deeply and …"

"And?" Master Reginald's voice was curt and clipped.

"And," I replied. "Does that conceal an even greater secret? Gentlemen." I made to rise, Master Reginald hastened round to draw back my chair. I placed the napkin on the table and bowed.

"For what you told me this morning, I am truly grateful. For the afternoon I wish to adjourn. I shall send you each a sheaf of documents, copied from the originals. I ask you to study them – then we'll meet again."

I returned to my own chamber. The servants had built the braziers high, fired the charcoal, lit the candles and lamps. I closed the door, turned the key, pulled the bolts across and hastened over to the wainscoting on the right of the great bay window overlooking the garden. I felt for the knot of wood and pressed it – the carved panel opened with a creak. I pushed it back, delved in and took out the greased leather satchel. I closed the panel door and carried the satchel over to the table. I undid the cord, breaking the seal on the neck and drew out the three hardback ledgers, each one sealed. Two of these I took to the door. I unlocked and unbarred it and went out to the gallery, summoning Master Catesby: "Give these to Sir Thomas and Master Reginald," I told him. "I do not wish to be disturbed. You know what they contain."

Catesby, a mute since birth, nodded, dark green eyes watchful in his pale, thin face. If I trust any man, I trust Catesby.

I returned to my own chamber, locked and barred it again. I made sure the secret panel was closed. I grasped my own ledger and went across to my writing desk close to the window. The light was poor so I brought more candles. I opened the ledger, and looked down at those documents: letters from Spain which maintained Elizabeth of England loved Dudley so much she even bore him a child.

The manuscripts constitute letters and memoranda drawn up by Sir Francis Englefield, an exiled Papist, regarding the mysterious Arthur Dudley. Englefield's purpose was to acquaint Philip of Spain with the news of this man's arrival in Spain. The documents are original, written in Englefield's personal way, his mastery of English interfering with his command of Spanish. He also refers to questions and memoranda which no longer exists; yet he, as well as an English spy named 'B.C.', clearly declare that, in 1587 to 1588, a young Englishman, calling himself Arthur Dudley, presented himself at the court of Philip II of Spain, claiming to be the son of the Great Elizabeth and Robert Dudley. The documents (bracketed with notes by me) read as follows:

Relation made to Sir Francis Englefield by an English- man named Arthur Dudley, claiming to be the son of Queen Elizabeth.

Imprimis, he named one Robert Southern, a servant of Catherine Ashley (who had been governess to the Queen in her youth, and was for ever afterwards one of her most beloved and intimate ladies). Southern was married, he lived 20 leagues from London and was summoned to Hampton Court. When he arrived, another lady of the Queen's court, named Harrington, asked him to obtain a nurse for a newborn child of a lady who had been so careless of her honour that, if it became known, it would bring great shame upon all the company, and would highly displease the Queen if she knew of it. The next morning, in a corridor leading to the Queen's private chamber, the child was given to the man, who was told that its name was Arthur. The man took the child, and gave it for some days to the wife of a miller at Molesey to suckle. He afterwards took it to a village near where he lived, 20 leagues from London, where the child remained until it was weaned. He then took it to his own house, and brought it up with his own children, in place of one of his which had died of similar age.

Some years afterward, the man Robert, who lived very humbly at home, left his own family, and took this Arthur on horseback to London, where he had him brought up with great care and delicacy, whilst his own wife and children were left in his village.

When the child was about eight years old, John Ashley, the husband of Catherine Ashley, who was one of the Queen's gentlemen of the chamber, gave to Robert the post of lieutenant of his office as keeper of one of the Queen's houses called Enfield, three leagues from London; and during the summer, or when there was any plague or sickness in London, Arthur was taught and kept in this house, the winters being passed in London. He was taught Latin, Italian, and French, music, arms and dancing. When he was about 14 or 15, being desirous of seeing strange lands, and having had some disagreement, he stole from a purse of this Robert as many silver pieces as he could grasp in his hand, about 70 reals, and fled to a port in Wales called Milford Haven, with the intention of embarking for Spain, which country he had always wished to see. Whilst he was there, awaiting his passage in the house of a gentleman named George Devereux, a brother of the late Earl of Essex, a horse messenger came in search of him with a letter, signed by seven members of the Council, ordering him to be brought to London. The tenor of this letter showed him to be a person of more importance than the son of Robert Southern. This letter still remains in the castle of Llanfear, in the hands of George Devereux, and was seen and read by Richard Jones and John Ap Morgan, then magistrates of the town of Pembroke, who agreed that the respect thus shown to the lad by the Council proved him to be a different sort of person from what he had commonly been regarded.

When he was conveyed to London, to a palace called Pickering Place, he found there Wootton of Kent, Thomas Heneage, and John Ashley, who reproved him for running away in that manner, and gave him to understand that it was John Ashley who had paid for his education, and not Robert Southern. He thinks that the letter of the Council also said this.

Sometime afterwards, being in London, and still expressing a desire to see foreign lands, John Ashley, finding that all persuasions to the contrary were unavailing, obtained letters of recommendation to M. de La Noue, a French colonel then in the service of the States. He was entrusted for his passage to a servant of the Earl of Leicester, who pretended to be going to Flanders on his own affairs, and they landed at Ostend in the Summer of 1580, proceeding afterwards to Bruges, where he remained until La Noue was taken prisoner. This deranged his plans, and, taking leave of the Earl of Leicester's gentleman, he went to France, where he remained until his money was spent: after which he returned to England for a fresh supply. He again returned to France, whence he was recalled at the end of 1583 by letters from Robert Southern, saying that his return to England would be greatly to his advantage.

When he arrived in England, he found Robert very ill of paralysis at Evesham, where he was keeping an inn, his master having sold the office of keeper of Enfield. Robert, with many tears, told him he was not his father, nor had he paid for his bringing up, as might easily be seen in the different way in which his own children had been reared. Arthur begged him to tell him who his parents were, but Robert excused himself, saying that both their lives depended upon it, besides the danger of ruining other friends who did not deserve such a return.

Arthur took leave of Robert in anger, as he could not obtain the information he desired, and Robert sent a lad after him to call him back. Arthur refused to return unless he promised to tell him whose son he was. Robert also sent the schoolmaster, Smyth, a Catholic, after him, who gravely reproved him for what he was doing, and at last brought him back to Robert. The latter then told him secretly that he was the son of the Earl of Leicester and the Queen, with many other things unnecessary to be set down here. He added that he had no authority to tell him this; but did so for the discharge of his own conscience, as he was ill and near death. Arthur begged him to give him the confession in writing, but he could not write, as his hand was paralysed, and Arthur sent to London to seek medicines for him. He got some from Dr Hector (Nunes), but they did no good; so, without bidding farewell to Robert, he took his horse and returned to London, where, finding John Ashley, and a gentleman named Drury, he related to them what Robert had told him. They exhibited great alarm at learning the thing had been discovered, and prayed him not to repeat it, recommending him to keep near the court; and promising him if he followed their advice, he might count upon their best *services whilst they lived. They told him that they had no means of communicating with the Earl, except through his brother, the Earl of Warwick.*

The great fear displayed by John Ashley and the others, when they knew that the affair was discovered, alarmed Arthur to such an extent that he fled to France. On his arrival at Eu in Normandy he went to the Jesuit College there in search of advice. After he had somewhat obscurely stated his case, the Rector, seeing that the matter was a great one and foreign to his profession, dismissed him at once, and told him he had better go to the Duke of Guise, which he promised to do, although he had no intention of doing it, thinking that it would be impolitic for him to divulge his condition to Frenchmen. When he was in Paris, he went to the Jesuit College there, with the intention of divulging his secret to an English priest named Father Thomas but, when he arrived in his presence, he was so overcome with terror that he could not say a word. The Commissioners of the States of Flanders being in Paris at the time, to offer their allegiance to the King of France, and there being also a talk about a league being arranged by the Duke of Guise, Arthur feared that some plans might be hatching against England, and repented of coming to France at all. He thereupon wrote several letters to John Ashley, but could get no reply. He also wrote to Edward Stafford, the English ambassador in France, without saying his name, and when the ambassador desired to know who he was, he replied that he had been reared by Robert Southern, whom the Queen knew, and whose memory she had reason to have graven on her heart.

He remained in France until he had cause to believe that the Queen of England would take the State of Flanders under her protection, and that a war might ensue. He then returned to England in the ship belonging to one Nicholson of Ratcliff. The said master threatened him when they arrived at Gravesend that he would hand him over to the justices for his own safety. Arthur begged him rather to take him to the Earl of Leicester first, and wrote a letter to the Earl, which Nicholson delivered.

The Earl received the letter, and thanked the bearer for his service, of which Nicholson frequently boasted. The next morning, as the ship was passing Greenwich on its way to London, two of the Earl's gentlemen came on board to visit him, one of them named Blount, the Earl's equerry ... When they arrived at Ratcliff, Flud, the Earl's secretary, came to take Arthur to Greenwich. The Earl was in the garden with the Earls of Derby and Shrewsbury and, on Arthur's arrival, the Earl of Leicester left the others, and went to his apartment, where by his tears, words, and other demonstrations he showed so much affection for Arthur that the latter believed he understood the Earl's deep intentions towards him. The secretary remained in Arthur's company all night, and the next morning, on the Earl learning that the masters and crews of the other ships that had sailed in their company had seen and knew Arthur, and had gone to Secretary Walsingham to give an account of their passengers, he said to Arthur, 'You are like a ship under a full sail at sea, delightful to look upon, but dangerous to deal with.' The Earl then sent his secretary with Arthur to Secretary Walsingham, to tell him that he [Arthur] was a friend of the Earl's and Flud was also to say that he knew him. Walsingham replied that if that were the case he could go on his way. Flud asked for a certificate and licence to enable Arthur to avoid future molestation. Walsingham therefore told Arthur to come to him again, and he would speak to him. On that day Arthur went with the Earl to his house at Wanstead, and returned with Flud in the evening to Greenwich. The Earl again sent to Walsingham for the licence; but Walsingham examined him very curiously and deferred giving him the paper, so Arthur was afraid to return to his presence. He, therefore, went to London and asked M. de la Mauvissiere to give him a passport for France, which, after much difficulty, he obtained in the guise of a servant to the ambassador. He supped that night with the ambassador, and was with him until midnight, but, on arriving at Gravesend the next morning, he found that the passport would carry him no further without being presented to Lord

Cobham. As he found there an English hulk, loaded with English soldiers for Flanders, he entered into their company and landed at Begten-op-zoom. He was selected to accompany one Gawen, a lieutenant of Captain Willson, and a sergeant of Colonel Norris, to beg the States for some aid in money for the English troops, who were in great need.

The paper then relates at length Arthur's plot with one Seymour to deliver the town of Tele to the Spaniards, which plot was discovered; his adventures at Cologne and elsewhere are also recounted. He opened up communications with the Elector of Cologne and the Pope. Indirectly the Duke of Parma learnt of his story and sent Count Paul Strozzi to interview him. After many wanderings about Germany, Arthur received a message from the Earl of Leicester at Sighen, but to what effect he does not say. He then undertook a pilgrimage to Our Lady of Montserrat, and, on learning in Spain of the condemnnation of Mary Stuart, he started for France, but was shipwrecked on the Biscay coast, and captured by the Spaniards as a suspicious person, and was brought to Madrid, where he made his statement to Englefield. (The latter portion of the statement is not here given at length, as it has no bearing upon Arthur Dudley's alleged parentage.)

The above statement was accompanied by a private letter from Arthur Dudley to Sir Francis Englefield as follows:

As time allowed I have written all this, although as you see my paper has run short. If God grants that his Majesty [Philip II] should take me under his protection, I think it will be necessary to spread a rumour that I have escaped, as everybody knows now that I am here, and my residence in future can be kept secret. I could then write simply and sincerely to the Earl of Leicester all that has happened to me, in order to keep in his good graces; I could also publish a book to any effect that might be considered desirable, in which I should show myself to be everybody's friend and nobody's foe. With regard to the King of Scotland, in whose favour you quote the law, I also have read our English books, but you must not forget that, when the din of arms is heard, the laws are not audible; and if it is licit to break the law for any reason, it is licit to do so to obtain dominion. Besides which, if this reason was a sufficiently strong one to bring about the death of the mother, [Mary Stuart] *the life of the son,* [James of Scotland] *might run a similar risk. Those who have power, have the right on their side. As for the Earl of Huntingdon, and Beauchamp, son of the Earl of Hertford* [possible claimants], *both of them are descendants of Adam, and perhaps there is some one else who is their elder brother.* [Arthur Dudley: a possible stronger claimant].

Attached to this document is another memorandum to Philip II from Englefield. It reads as follows:

I recollect that this Arthur Dudley, amongst other things, repeated several times that for many years past the Earl of Leicester had been the mortal enemy of the Queen of Scots, and that the condemnation and execution of Throckmorton and Parry [Mary's supporters] *and many others had been principally brought about in order to give an excuse for what was afterwards done with the Queen of Scots.*

I think it very probable that the revelations that this lad is making everywhere may originate in the Queen of England and her Council, and possibly with an object that Arthur himself does not yet understand. Perhaps, if they are determined to do away with the Scottish throne, they may encourage this lad to profess Catholicism, and claim to be the Queen's son, in order to discover the minds of other Princes as to his pretensions. The Queen may thereupon acknowledge him, or give him such other position as to neighbouring Princes may appear favourable. Or perhaps in some other way they may be making use of him for their iniquitous ends. I think also that the enclosed questions should be put to him to answer in writing (these are not extant) – whether all at once or at various times I leave to you. I also leave for your consideration whether it would not be well to bring Arthur to San Geronimo at Atocha, or some other monastery, or other house, where he might be more commodiously communicated with – 17 June 1587.

SIR FRANCIS ENGLEFIELD TO THE KING
Very late last night Andres de Alba sent me what Arthur Dudley has written, which being in English, and filling three sheets of paper, will take some days to translate and summarise in Spanish.

As, however, I have read it, I think well in the meantime to advise your Majesty that the effect of it is a discourse about his education, with the reasons and arguments which have led him to believe to be, as he calls himself, the son of the Queen. He then gives an account of his voyages away from England, in France and Flanders, showing that they had no other intention or motive than a desire, on his first voyage, to see strange countries. He returned in consequence of poverty, and subsequently set out on his second voyage for his own safety's sake. He mentions several things that happened in France and Flanders, and speaks of the letters which passed between him and the Elector of Cologne, and says that his reason for coming to this country was a vow he had made to visit Our Lady of Montserrat, where he was shriven on the 13th of October of last year. He enumerates certain places in Spain where he has stayed, and the persons he has been living with. He adds that his intention was to go to France when he was detained in Guipuzcoa, and ends by begging his Majesty to accept and esteem him as the person he claims to be, and to protect him [although with the utmost secrecy]. *He indicates a desire also to write something in English, to publish to the world, and especially to England, who he is, as well as the matter that those who have put the Queen of Scotland out of the way, will endeavour to send her son after her.*

As he replies in this discourse to some of the questions I sent to your Majesty on Monday, they may be modified accordingly before they are sent to him – Madrid, 18th June 1587.

SIR FRANCIS ENGLEFIELD TO THE KING

I send your Majesty herewith a summary of all that Arthur Dudley had sent to me, and as it appears that some of the questions your Majesty has are answered therein, I have eliminated the 4th, 5th and 6th questions and have added those I now enclose [these are no longer extant].

I also send enclosed what I think of writing with the questions, as I think I had better defer my going thither until after he has sent his answers to them, as I find many things which he told me verbally have been omitted in his statement.

When your Majesty has altered what you think fit, I will put my letter, which I will take or send as your Majesty orders, in conformity. As he says he is in want of paper, your Majesty had better order him to be supplied with as much as may be needed; as the more fully he writes the better shall we be able to discover what we wish to know – Madrid, 20th June 1587.

SIR FRANCIS ENGLEFIELD TO THE KING

Although the statement sent to me by Arthur Dudley omits many things that he told me verbally, which things must be inquired into more particularly, yet it appears evident from what he writes that he makes as light of the claims of Huntingdon, and of the sons of the Earl of Hertford, as he does of the life of the King of Scotland [all these were claimants to the English throne]. *It is also manifest that he has much conference with the Earl of Leicester, upon whom he mainly depends for the fulfilment of his hopes. This and other things convince me that the Queen of England is not ignorant of his pretensions; although, perhaps she would be unwilling that they should be thus published to the world, for which reason she may wish to keep him* [Arthur Dudley] *in his low and obscure condition, as a matter of policy, and also in order that her personal immorality might not be known, the bastards of princes not usually being acknowledged in the lifetime of their parents, and she has always considered that it would be dangerous to her for her heir to be nominated in her lifetime, although he alleges that she has provided for the Earl of Leicester and his faction to be able to elevate him* [Arthur Dudley] *to the throne when she dies, and perhaps marry him to Arabella* [Stuart: another possible claimant]. *For this and other reasons I am of opinion that he should not be allowed to get away, but should be kept very secure to prevent his escape.*

The final document I studied corroborated Englefield's documents, being a hasty letter from an English spy, Mr. 'B.C.', to London in May 1588. It reads as follows:

About xvi months ago was taken a Youth entering Spain out of France, about Fontarabie. He has given out his person to be begotten one between our Queen and the Earl of Leicester; born at Hampton Court, and forthwith by the elder Ashley delivered into the hands of one Southern, the servant to Mrs Ashley, with a charge upon pain of death that the said Southern should not reveal the matter, but raise the infant. Southern brought the child to a miller's wife at Moseley to give it suckle, and afterwards the said Southern going into his county which was Worcester or Shropshire, carried with him the child, and there brought him up in learning and qualities. In the end, revealing unto this youth the whole secret, he took flight over seas, where many years he has remained until his coming here. His name is Arthur, and of 27 years of age, or thereabout. This indeed is his claim, and he takes upon him the likeness to the man he pretends to be. Whereupon he wants no keepers, and is very solemnly warded and served with expenses to this King of vi crowns a day. If I had my alphabet, I would say more touching his lewd speeches. If I may, I will do him pleasure, specially being called to account about him, as it is told me I shall shortly be. The King [Philip II] *being informed that about that time I served*

in [the English] *Court, whereby I may say somewhat to this matter.*
Madrid the xxviiith of May 1588.
Yours to use,
B.C.

I picked up the final manuscript, a memorandum I had drawn up since receiving the Englefield papers, listing the conclusions I had reached.

> **Item:** *Englefield's letter of 17th June 1587, describing Arthur Dudley's birth and upbringing is easy to follow; the places he mention exist as did the people. But, there again, that would be easy for anyone to concoct. It is a matter of public knowledge that George Devereux was a great land owner in Pembroke: that John Ashley was known to the Queen, that Edward Stafford was the English ambassador to Paris. The same is true of Francis Walsingham, Secretary to the Council and Master of Intelligence. The passage really hinges on Robert Southern and the school master, Smyth of Evesham. I have made careful scrutiny of the Parish and Probate Records at Worcester. These excited my interest, Arthur Dudley did not lie. I discovered Southern's will. He'd owned a tavern there and had fallen so sick his will had to be transcribed by a man called Smyth.*
>
> **Item:** *Arthur Dudley's private letter to Sir Francis Englefield. The young man was educated and erudite; he did not wish to be supported but rather protected. His letter hints of secret matters about possible successors to the Great Elizabeth, be it James of Scotland, or English claimants such as the Earls of Huntington and Hertford.*
>
> **Item:** *Englefield's memorandum was genuine, particularly in his analysis of Dudley's opposition to Mary, Queen of Scots.*
>
> **Item:** *Englefield's second letter to Philip dated 18th June 1587, is again genuine and reveals English opposition to James of Scotland.*
>
> **Item:** *Sir Francis Englefield's third letter to the King of Spain*

dated 20th June 1587. My only regret is that it did not include the questions Englefield put to Arthur Dudley or the replies he obtained.

Item: *Sir Francis Englefield's final letter to Philip II. In this Englefield seems more convinced about Arthur Dudley. He now regards the young man as most useful to Dudley's faction.*

Item: *The letter of the Spy known as 'B.C.' dated 28th May 1588. The letter had been written almost a year after Englefield's. It demonstrates that Arthur Dudley had not changed his story whilst his importance in the eyes of the Spanish Court appears to have grown. He had been given a generous pension and was held in great respect. 'B.C.' is very intrigued and, so alarmed, scribbled the letter off without using his alphabet or cipher. The phrases, "and if I may I will do him pleasure", and, "yours to use", sound sinister.*

I let the memorandum slip from my fingers. I thought of James of Scotland desperate to acquire the English Crown, ruthless in removing any rivals. I dared not think any further but, pushing the manuscript away, went to kneel on my prie-dieu before a triptych of the crucifixion.

I met my friends later that day. We dined in the Painted Chamber. The cupboards shimmered with the silver and gold vessels placed around, their rubies and diamonds catching the light. A fire roared in the hearth against the cold whilst beeswax candles and braziers, fragranced with incense, drove back the encroaching darkness. The table was lavish and costly with its white damask cloths, glittering pewter, gold and silver knives, porringers, bowls and platters. The air was rich with the sweet odours from the ovens and stoves. My cook and servants served pottage and soups, quail and pheasants, ham and beef, all spiced and basted with herbs. I truly enjoyed that meal. Sir Thomas Bodley and Master Reginald Carr sat like boys who'd been given a treat and expected more. They ate hastily while I conversed about the price of wool or the laxity of local magistrates. I recognised what they truly wanted to talk about but, of course, with servants milling about, doors open, eyes watchful, ears sharp – that is not the time to discuss the Great Elizabeth's love-child. Such a matter must wait until we retired to the solar, to drink white wine cooled in small vats of iced water. This time there were no documents. I knew my script, I'd learnt my lines. Catesby had moved my great chair before the fire. Sir Thomas sat on my right, Master Reginald on my left. For a while I just sat and watched the logs break and shatter, whilst Catesby pulled the drapes, secured the shutters and closed the door firmly behind him. I lifted my head and smiled at Master Reginald.

"You are intrigued?"

"Of course," he replied hoarsely. "That the Great Elizabeth had a child! Haven't you heard in London, Mistress, what they are saying – that one chip of her greatness would be worth anything from Scotland."

"If King James heard that," I retorted, "we'd all be arrested for treason, accused of supporting a possible pretender."

"But that's not true," Sir Thomas observed sharply. "We are not traitors. Yet what you showed us, Mistress, it may all be a masque, a mummers' play – all froth and no ale?"

"There are three possibilities," I replied. "First, that Arthur Dudley is a liar, a pretender, a villain. Secondly, that he is a by-blow of Dudley, a base-born, a bastard by some wench. After all, the allegations against Dudley come thick and fast like the snowflakes outside, his lechery, his licentiousness, his love of soft flesh. We know that he seduced Lady Douglas, the wife of Sheffield, and later married the widow of the Earl of Essex by whom he had a son."

I stretched out my toes towards the fire to catch the warmth.

"Dudley may have seduced some serving wench, a lady-in-waiting. According to *Leicester's Commonwealth* whilst at Elizabeth's court he was offering women of the Queen's entourage £300 to spend the night with him."

"And the third possibility?" Sir Thomas asked.

"Well that is logical," I replied. "That Arthur Dudley is what he claims to be, the son of Elizabeth and Dudley – the harvest of their passion, the fruit of their love."

"It is the most searing accusation," Master Reginald declared. "Elizabeth played the naughty, was promiscuous, lusted after another man, had a bastard child by him."

"Not so," I replied, "not so! My Mistress was of pure heart and good soul. She'd not played the doxy; her court was not some lewd place, a brothel-house like that of Francis I. You talked about a hypothesis, Master Reginald. Let me give you mine. Here we have Elizabeth of England, a woman passionate about everything; passionate in her studies, knowledgeable in Latin and Greek, French and Italian. She was more conversant with Holy Writ than her own bishops. She patronised the poetry and music of her Court – she could converse with the best and debate with the sharpest, a skilled politician, a woman of outstanding charm who could break any man's heart, rule this country for 45 years whilst fighting Scotland, Mary its Queen, the Papacy, France, Spain, not to mention her enemies within. My hypothesis is this: is it so foolish to imagine that she who was always alone, always by herself, never able to enjoy the small things of life, a woman of great intellect, great heart, vigorous in all she did – can she be blamed for being passionate in her love for one man?" Tears, hot and bitter, stung in my eyes. "Is it beyond the bounds of possibility, the realm of reason, that she loved one man, and why not Dudley? True, in many ways he was a villain, a rogue, a charlatan, a liar – perhaps even a murderer. He kept passion in his pocket, he could hide his feelings, be devious and sly, but he was also a superb horseman, a dancer beyond comparison, learned in languages, a delighter in all things beautiful, a peacock of a man, yet a lion, a soldier, a braggart. Above all, Master Reginald, I know he did something which few men could do – he made Elizabeth laugh, he made my Queen relax."

"I can see this," Sir Thomas replied quietly. "Mistress, we do not wish to trouble you but …"

"But what, Sir Thomas?"

"Well, Lady Amy's death?"

"Lady Amy's death did not put an end to the passion," I affirmed. "The Queen loved Dudley more than any woman loved any man. Have you, Sir Thomas, loved? Have you, Master Reginald? I have. When you really love, reason is forgotten. What we apply to ourselves, can't we apply to the Queen? Lady Amy died in the September of 1560. No, Elizabeth did not give up on Dudley. For five years she struggled against that passion. On one occasion, only a year after the affair at Cumnor Place, she, Dudley and de Quadra were on the Thames, relaxing on the Royal Barge, enjoying the sights and scenes of the river. Dudley always made Elizabeth laugh. On that lovely day he drew the Bishop into 'mock' conversation – he pointed out that de Quadra was a Bishop of the Catholic Church and, if he wished, could marry them there and then. De Quadra, of course, stiff as a board, protested and quibbled. Dudley and the Queen laughed at him. Yet beneath Dudley's offer was serious intent. Sir Henry Sidney, as the Spanish ambassador reported, came secretly to him and said that if Spain would support Dudley's marriage with the Queen, Elizabeth might turn the Realm Catholic. Jests and japes apart, Master Reginald, if the Great Elizabeth was prepared to abandon the religion of her Kingdom for her love of Dudley, how great was her passion? I could point to many instances following the death of Lady Amy when the Queen's love of Dudley became so apparent, that even great Lords like Norfolk confronted Dudley and asked him to desist."

"My Lady." Sir Thomas sipped his wine and placed it carefully on the small table beside me. "Elizabeth's passion for Dudley, I accept. But the matter of Arthur – that is another matter. Look at the facts. Sir Francis Englefield was a member of Mary Tudor's Council. He was a Papist, a high ranking English official; he went into exile rather than accept the Protestant faith. He was, in many people's eyes, a traitor. He travelled to Spain and became advisor to Philip II. If you look at his commentary on Arthur Dudley's statement, well – " Sir Thomas pulled a face, "Englefield does not believe the young man. He mocks him, he even hints that Arthur could be a spy, deliberately planted at the Spanish Court to cause confusion."

"I could turn that on its head, Sir Thomas. True, Sir Francis Englefield was a Papist. He'd served high in the Council of Elizabeth's sister, Mary Tudor. He was a well-known Catholic who'd held great office. True, he was allowed to go to the Spanish Court. But did you also know, Sir Thomas, that Sir Francis Englefield, even though exiled, in many ways a traitor, was allowed to draw his revenues from England?"

"What!"

"Oh yes, Sir Thomas," I retorted. "I've done my searches as well. Sir Francis Englefield may have been in exile, but to quote his verse back to him, he may have been the traitor. Let us create the hypothesis that Sir Francis Englefield was actually what you might call an agent for both sides. A man who wanted to drink from both cups, a Papist, an enemy of England, yet also secretly an agent of Queen Elizabeth, prepared to confuse Philip of Spain and mislead him. There is some proof of that, so it is only logical that he should reject young Arthur, perhaps dismissing him as an imposter. Now, let's turn to Arthur himself. If you look at what he says, and remember, we are reading a hostile witness' account of this young man: Sir Francis Englefield does not support his claims. Nevertheless, what shoots through the last few phrases is that this young man did not wish to be recognised publicly. He did not want to be used as some cat's-paw, but be hidden away, to be cared for. Arthur Dudley did not nourish ambitions. He did not want to be declared, 'A Prince in Exile'. He did not seek to raise Spanish forces; all he wants is refuge, a sanctuary, a place of rest."

"I did agree with Sir Thomas," Master Reginald spoke sharply.

"True, Englefield is dismissive but, in his second letter to Philip, Englefield has changed his stance – he is more supportive." Master Reginald smiled at me. "That does not contradict you, Mistress – Sir Francis could well have been playing out his Janus-like role of quietly supporting both camps."

"I have more on Englefield," I replied, "but it can wait."

"I will concede." Sir Thomas, who'd sat slumped in his chair, chin on his chest, drew himself up. "I will concede," he repeated, "that Elizabeth of England loved Dudley with great passion. I, too, have studied the records, Mistress. When Dudley died the Queen closeted herself in her own chamber for so long the Council ordered the doors of her private apartment to be forced." He leaned his elbow on the arm of the chair and scratched his brow. "I will also concede that in a casket found after Elizabeth's death, Dudley's last letter to her was found – the Queen had marked it so. I accept your hypothesis that Elizabeth of England loved Dudley with great passion, she called him on one occasion her "Lord", she adored him. Oh, they argued and, now and again, Elizabeth made her authority felt. There is the famous incident of Bowyer, Gentleman of the Black Rod, whose task was to ensure that no one entered the Royal Presence Chamber whom he did not recognise. One day Black Rod Bowyer checked a swaggering Captain and told him to go no further. This officer, a protégé of Dudley's, went off and complained to his patron. Dudley appeared in fury; he attacked Bowyer, calling him a knave, said he would no longer act as Black Rod and made to go directly to the Queen. Bowyer was too quick for him; he went in, fell on his knees before the Queen and put his case, begging to be told whether Dudley was King or Her Majesty, Queen? Elizabeth's response was eloquent, 'God's death my Lord, I have wished you well,' she shouted at Dudley, 'but I will have here one Mistress and no Master.' She then added. 'And I hold you responsible for this man –' she pointed at Bowyer, 'that no evil falls to him.'"

Sir Thomas paused. He passed his cup from hand to hand and

glanced quickly at Master Reginald. "Mistress, you brought us here to examine the evidence. In the end I concede Elizabeth could bear a child – the question here is, did she bear Dudley's?"

"If Arthur Dudley is a liar," Master Reginald declared softly, "he will lie about the small things as well as the great. How much truth is there in his statements? These names he mentioned?"

I glanced towards the casement window. The snow was falling again. It was almost dark.

"Mistress," Sir Thomas murmured, as if anxious not to disturb me, "what Master Reginald says is the truth; if this Arthur can be found to be a liar in the small things then why not in the large?"

I wondered whether I should tell them in a rush all I knew. I went back so many years clasping the rope of time, going down the dark gallery with the candle of truth glowing at the far end. I had been so relieved after the storms caused by Lady Amy's death had passed, I scarcely thought about other things. It wasn't until those letters had been given to me, did I remember the Queen swelling up, dropsy or so they said, secluding herself from the Court. Oh, I know what goes on in the mind of many a man. How could the Queen conceal her pregnancy? My answer is very easy; some of her ladies-in-waiting did, right until the very birth. There were times when the Queen was withdrawn. In the early years I was only a mere chit of a girl, allowed to bring the Queen this present or that, or stand in the withdrawing chambers reading a book or jabbing at a piece of tapestry with a needle. I had yet to grow accustomed to the gossip and scandals. Naturally, any whisper that the Queen was 'enceinte' would be regarded as the utmost blasphemy.

I glanced up at Sir Thomas and Master Reginald. They were seemingly intrigued by the mystery but not yet convinced.

"Let me help you, Mistress," Master Reginald spread his hand. "Here we have the accounts of Sir Francis Englefield, letters written by him to Philip of Spain in 1587 as well as the memorandum of the spy, Mr. 'B.C.'"

"One of Cecil's minions," I replied. "I don't know who. During my searches, after the Englefield manuscripts were sent to me, that letter came into my hands."

"The spy in Spain," Sir Thomas declared, "agrees very much with what Sir Francis Englefield has related, except he provides a few more details. How Arthur Dudley was about 27 years of age, certainly a man who provoked the spy's anger. 'B.C.' was looking forward to questioning him, or so he says. Arthur may have been revealing things about the private life of the Queen and perhaps his reputed father, Lord Robert. 'B.C.' was certainly agitated by Arthur Dudley. He writes 'I wish I had my alphabet with me'. He is talking about his cipher, isn't he, the code spies use when they dispatch letters? He's in such a passion to write, he can't wait to get his message sent." Sir Thomas' face creased into a smile. "He should have sent that letter using his alphabet. Master Cecil would be ill pleased; such information could be opened and read by anyone."

"Let us summarise, Mistress." Master Reginald raised his hand diplomatically. "Here we have a young man, 27 years of age in 1588 therefore born around 1561. He claims that Catherine Ashley, governess, friend, confidant of the Queen, a person known to us all, summoned Robert Southern to Hampton Court where another lady-in-waiting gave him a new born child, claiming the infant was the by-blow of some well-known lady who wanted to keep the matter hidden. The next morning, even though they are trying to hide this child from Her Majesty, in a corridor leading to the Queen's private chamber, the infant is delivered to Southern who is told that his name is Arthur." Master Carr moved his head from left to right. "A choice name! It was also given to Henry VIII's elder brother who first married Catherine of Aragon. The Tudor family regarded the Great Arthur of the Britons as their ancestor. Anyway, noble ancestors or not, this child is taken to a miller's wife at Moseley, very near Hampton Court, to be suckled. Arthur remains there until he is weaned. For a while he lives with the

Southerns but is later taken from the family home to be raised in London with every care and delicacy. Southern is paid for his work, being appointed keeper or bailiff of a Royal House in Enfield. Arthur spends his summers there but, in winter, when the prospect of plague recedes, he is brought back to London. He was given a gentleman's education in Latin, Italian and French, music and fencing. Between the age of 14 and 15 he slips away to Pembrokeshire. He visits George Devereux and other Welsh notables, before being brought back to London; here, he meets Thomas Heneage 'et al'. They make it very clear that John Ashley, and not Robert Southern, was responsible for financing his education. Arthur then travels on to the Netherlands where he stayed sometime before returning to England. He goes to his foster father, Robert Southern, who's now moved from Enfield to keep a tavern in Evesham, Worcestershire. Arthur tries to discover the truth about his birth; eventually Southern confesses the truth. Southern is now very ill. Arthur leaves for London then on to France where he visits a Papist seminary. He later returns to England and meets certain notables of the Earls at Greenwich, Fludd the Earl's Secretary, Thomas Blount, as well as the Earls of Derby and Shrewsbury. He is later taken before Secretary Walsingham. Arthur is described as 'like a ship under a full sail at sea, delightful to look upon but dangerous to deal with'". Master Reginald paused to clear his throat.

"Arthur Dudley was certainly learned in his letters. He writes to Englefield and Englefield makes a judgement – he wonders if Arthur Dudley is a cat's-paw of the English, sent to Spain to distract them. However, before Arthur Dudley left England and began his wanderings over France and elsewhere, he had a long conversation with Robert Dudley, the Earl of Leicester. In his second letter to the King of Spain of 22nd June," Master Reginald sniffed, "as I remarked earlier, Englefield has changed his position. Arthur Dudley has revealed a great deal about what he'd learnt in England. Englefield has revised his opinion and advises the King of Spain to keep Arthur Dudley under close scrutiny. Cecil's spy, 'B.C.' whoever he is, seems to confirm that Arthur Dudley went up in the estimation of both Englefield and his Spanish masters because he was being shown at Court, not detained, and living on a generous pension of six crowns a day." Master Reginald waved his hand. "It's the change in Englefield's tone as well as the contents of his letter which fascinate me. Arthur Dudley apparently had a detailed conversation with the Earl of Leicester. He knows about other claimants to the English Crown, once Elizabeth has died, as well as the pretensions of James of Scotland. In other words, Arthur Dudley must have convinced Englefield there was a case to answer. If he hadn't, Arthur Dudley would have been turned out in his shirt and certainly not given a place of honour and security at the Spanish Court. Arthur Dudley is free to walk around, act the part of a nobleman and live on a pension of six crowns a day." Master Reginald picked up his wine cup and sipped it carefully. "I don't truly know, Mistress. What I will concede is that Arthur Dudley is more than some simple pretender. Such creatures are common. In the same year Englefield wrote to Philip of Spain, the Queen's Council in London was examining one Ann Bernel who claimed to be the daughter of King Philip of Spain and Queen Mary Tudor, because she bore upon her back the Arms of England – " Master Reginald pulled a face, "some form of birthmark. When Ann was examined most carefully, the Council concluded that she was a woman who'd been through great misery and penury, much abused by her husband, her wits gravely disturbed." He tapped the parchment. "But this does not seem to have happened here."

"So," Sir Thomas picked up the copies of the letters I had provided, shuffling them into place, "there is no doubt that in 1587 a 27-year-old man called Arthur Dudley presented himself to the Spanish Court claiming to be the son of Robert Dudley and Elizabeth of England. He seems to be of good wit, sharp intelligence and much travelled; a Papist, though Englefield wonders if he is as devout a one as he claims to be. The real source of all this is Sir Francis Englefield – how do we know that he wasn't the puppet master and Arthur Dudley his creature?"

"There is no proof of that," Master Reginald retorted. "Yet it would be a very dangerous game for Englefield to play. What fascinates me is how Englefield himself can't make his mind up; on the one hand he doubts Arthur Dudley's devotion to Catholicism but, on the other, does not really deny his claims. In his first letter he hints that Arthur Dudley could have actually been sent to Spain by Elizabeth herself, being used as a cat's-paw; yet what Arthur Dudley said to Englefield seems to have resolved some of his doubts. Englefield certainly decided that Arthur Dudley was a man to be watched. Philip of Spain, no fool at intrigue, must have also been impressed to give him a place and pension at Court."

"Englefield," I replied, "could have been walking down the centre of the lane because that is the only path he could take."

"What do you mean?" Sir Thomas asked. "Englefield was an English exile, a Catholic openly hostile to Elizabeth and Dudley but, as you've remarked, you have doubts about that?"

"Sir Francis Englefield," I replied, "was the son of Sir Thomas Englefield of Berkshire. He became Chief Officer of Mary Tudor's Council. A devout Catholic during the reign of Edward, he spent some time in the Tower for his faith. Once Edward was dead and Mary Tudor had assumed the Crown, Englefield was given every honour Queen Mary could think of. He was made a member of the Privy Council, the Master of the Wards, a Knight of Shire. He sat in every parliament during Mary's reign. A powerful man with a retinue of over a hundred people. There is no doubt of his devotion to the Old Faith. When Elizabeth succeeded to the throne, Englefield fled to Spain and his goods were seized. In 1563, according to my searches, Englefield wrote to the Privy Council explaining that he had followed his conscience which was not fashioned out of wax. Now, in October 1585, Elizabeth of

England's Council decreed that Englefield, because of his exile and refusal to return home, was guilty of high treason. Ten years earlier, Sir Francis, through attorneys, had tried to settle his estates and goods on his nephew. According to one source, Elizabeth of England refused to accept that. My Mistress seized all of Englefield's lands and revenues. However, according to another source, Englefield was allowed to draw revenues from all his estates in England except for a small part which was kept back for the sustenance of his wife."

"The double-backed traitor?" Master Reginald interposed, "a man who played with cogged dice."

"Possibly," I agreed. "I believe Sir Francis Englefield was a devout Catholic rather than a devoted Spaniard. He may have come to some sort of understanding with the Queen and Cecil that he stay in Spain, sit at Philip's Council, follow his conscience but, where possible, do no harm to Elizabeth of England. A subtle man, Englefield," I conceded. "A man who could play both ends and still succeed."

"I concede," Sir Thomas replied, "that Englefield may have acted as the honest broker, the man in the middle; but, of course, the truth is centred on Arthur Dudley."

"What convinces me," I retorted, "or half convinces me, is that change in Englefield, after he had listened to Arthur's description of his conversations with Lord Robert Dudley. Amongst other issues, Arthur Dudley describes how Elizabeth and her Council were implacably hostile to Mary, Queen of Scots, which we know to be the truth. Dudley and his coven were also desirous of getting their hands on her son, James, who, if they could seize him, might suffer the same fate as his mother. All that could be dismissed as mere speculation, tittle-tattle. Nevertheless, I know through my place-men in the Spanish Embassy how, in the winter of 1574-5, Elizabeth of England planned to send one of her most trusted Captains, Killigrew, with three ships into Edinburgh, to seize young James and bring him to England. The

Spanish ambassador also says that the Queen and Leicester plotted to marry a daughter the Queen allegedly had by Leicester to an English claimant to the throne, the son of the Earl of Hertford."

"Fiddle-fuddle nonsense," Sir Thomas broke in. "Are you now saying Elizabeth had a daughter as well as a son?"

"No, no," I lifted a hand, "I shall deal with that later. What I am saying now is that the Spanish ambassador's report of the winter of 1574-5 talks about a plot to seize young James of Scotland, which Arthur Dudley repeats to Englefield. This was not the first such plot. In 1567 the Spanish ambassador referred to a similar scheme of which Lord Robert Dudley was the fount and origin." I opened the leather parchment holder and picked up a manuscript. "This is an extract from the Spanish envoy to his masters about the matter of James of Scotland, – it is dated May 1567 and reads as follows:

> There is a talk of delivering the prince of Scotland to this Queen to be brought up by his grandmother [the Countess of Lennox, mother of Henry Darnley], who sent to me a few days since to say, that as she heard the Earl of Leicester was coming to consult me as to the advisability of this Queen's receiving the child here, the subject having been discussed in the Council, she begged me to advise that it should be done. Lord Robert came, but did not ask for my advice direct, although he introduced the subject in a way that compelled me to give it. I therefore told him they should make every effort to get the child here, because if it was desirable that he should inherit the crown, they could have him in their own hands, and thus keep in check other claimants in this country, whilst if he were not to succeed, they could put him into a safe place, so that in no case would any harm come to them from it. I said it was meet that the Queen should act promptly about it, as it was notorious that the French were endeavouring to get the child."

I placed the manuscript down. "If there was such a plot, and there seems to be a great deal of truth in the matter, the only person in England from whom Arthur Dudley could have learnt about such a confidential but important stratagem was Robert Dudley himself. Secondly, what the Spanish ambassador's report of 1574-5 does prove, whether they had the sex of the child right or wrong, is that amongst foreign ambassadors and envoys a story flourished about Elizabeth and Leicester having a child. More importantly," I continued, "how does Arthur Dudley appear to Englefield? The English spy, 'B.C.', quite categorically states Arthur had assumed the likeness or role of the man he pretended to be. That same impression, Gentlemen, I deduce from these letters. Arthur Dudley has literary pretensions. He boasts of good schooling in Latin, Italian, French, music, arms and dancing. Why should he make such a boast which could be quickly tested? He can write, he can read, he has knowledge of the English Court and is conversant with the secret politics of the time. He even makes a classical allusion when he is talking about the situation regarding Scotland and James' claim to the English throne. He says – " I pulled the parchment towards me and positioned the candle more closely searching for the place. "Ah, yes, here it is: 'with regard to the King of Scotland, in whose favour you quote the law.' That is," I glanced up, "the law of succession. Arthur Dudley continues, 'I have also read English books, you must not forget that, when the din of arms is heard, the laws are not audible': Sirs, that, as you know, is a direct quotation from Cicero's 'Pro Milone': *Inter arma, leges tacent*' – 'laws are silent in war'. So the first claim of Arthur Dudley that he is a gentleman, and well educated, is certainly proved by his own writing. Englefield, who was also a scholar and a man of letters, could have easily tested him and did. So, where did Arthur Dudley obtain such learning?"

"Mistress," Sir Thomas glanced up under his brows. "Why doesn't Englefield support Arthur Dudley without reservation? I appreciate Master Reginald's point that he changed his position; but why should Sir Francis Englefield be worried about how

Elizabeth of England would take the news?"

"Oh, Sir Thomas", I laughed, "Englefield wasn't worried about how Elizabeth would take the news, but how he might be depicted in this business. If he was seen to support Arthur Dudley without reservation, perhaps those revenues from England would quickly dry up?"

"Oh, come Mistress." Sir Thomas hitched his cloak about him. "How would Elizabeth of England get to know?"

"Oh, come Sir Thomas," I mimicked back. "First, Elizabeth's own spy had learnt about Arthur Dudley's existence. I have also been searching amongst the papers – you have met my servant Catesby, a deaf mute but still a very skilled clerk. Years ago, when I first thought of writing my memoir, I obtained a post for him in the Office of the Green Wax and Secret Seal. He worked for Cecil's son, Robert, whom Elizabeth designated her 'little man' or 'Pygmy'. Now I have learnt from him, indeed as gospel truth, that one of Cecil's creatures, a spy in Spain called Thomas Honeyman, openly boasted to his master, and I quote directly." I closed my eyes. " 'Postmasters in Spain give out the letters of their servants for 28 ducats a month. The one at Madrid, Pedro Martinez,' Honeyman continued, 'lets me read all of Englefield's letters. I return those I dare not keep.' Englefield," I opened my eyes, "must have known this, perhaps he even tolerated it. Englefield was a skilled gambler, hedging his bets. He'd be only too pleased to make known these startling revelations to his master but prudent enough not to let Elizabeth of England learn that he fully supported this extraordinary young man."

"But if a child was born," Sir Thomas pushed back his chair, "surely, other people would have known?"

"Would they?" I replied. "Look at Arthur Dudley's statement. Catherine Ashley, the Queen's close counsellor, and the lady-in-waiting, Harrington; perhaps even they didn't know the full truth about the child being sent away so urgently. Now," I agreed, "there was gossip. In 1560 Ann Dowe of Brentford was brought before the magistrates for scurrilous chatter about the Queen. Francis White, in 1561, was summoned because he claimed Dudley had swived the Queen; Burney in 1572 on a like charge; Henry Hawkins in 1581; Edward Francis of Dorset in 1592 – all claimed the Queen had an illegitimate child by Dudley. Of course, this was scurrilous gossip round the village well or in the local tavern, but I do wonder if it was a wisp of smoke from the fire of the truth. The gossip of royal servants may not have been silenced, hence these local legends, whilst the same stories were gleaned by diplomats, envoys and ambassadors. In November 1575 the Venetian ambassador claimed that Elizabeth was going to marry her illegitimate daughter to James of Scotland. In the same year the Papal envoy in Spain talked of a child of 13 years, whilst we have the Spanish ambassador's report during the same period talking of an illegitimate daughter. The Papal envoy talks of a child of 13 years, which takes us back to the year 1562 or thereabouts. Cecil's spy in Spain claimed Dudley was 27 years in 1588, which again points to the period 1561 to 1562, during the months following Lady Amy's death. On 18th April 1559 the Spanish ambassador reports that Elizabeth was visiting Dudley in his chambers day and night. In another report Dudley had chambers very close to the Queen. There is nothing lewd or naughty about this," I continued. "My main thesis, Sirs, is that Elizabeth of England loved Robert Dudley passionately – is it possible that such passion led to the conception and birth of a child and, if so, is that child Arthur Dudley? Listen now." I pushed back my chair and walked to the fire. I picked up two logs and placed them carefully on the flames; sparks flew out. I offered to fill my visitors' wine cups but both refused.

"Listen now," I repeated as I sat down. "By 1562 I was maturing. The Queen, as you may know, fell ill of smallpox. She was attended to by Lady Sidney who contracted that same disease herself. At one point Her Majesty's life was despaired of: she summoned members of the Privy Council to her. She told them that, if she died, Dudley was to be made Protector of the Realm, he was to be given a title, a pension of £20,000 and, harken to this, John Tamworth, the valet of his chamber, was to be given £500 a year for life." I enjoyed the surprise on both men's faces.

"Now it could be alleged," I continued, "that at the time Elizabeth of England was delirious with fever; but that doesn't mean she wasn't speaking the truth, expressing her great love for Dudley." I paused. "What is remarkable about this outburst during her illness, is not so much giving Dudley the Protectorship but that very generous pension to the valet of Dudley's chamber. Why is that? Why reward John Tamworth with a pension of £500 a year? What great work had he done for Crown and Kingdom? I only learnt this much later, but I believe that Tamworth knew something and that pension was mentioned to seal his lips. I do wonder, as I did when I read these letters," I lifted the parchments, "whether the secret Tamworth held is the same secret Sir Francis Englefield revealed?"

A clatter against the casement window made me jump. I glanced across. A twig picked up by the breeze had become entangled in the ivy outside. It was beating vainly at the glass like a lost soul from the frozen plains of hell, desperate to break in and bask in the warmth. I glanced round the chamber and repressed a shiver; the fire was burning merrily, the candles flaming strong, but the light they cast around made our shadows seem like other people. Were these ghosts from the past, eager to return and listen to the chatter of the living? I glanced down at the documents strewn around me.

"Master Reginald," I spoke brusquely trying to dismiss my feeling of unease. "Sir Thomas, you talked of Arthur Dudley lying about small things. However, go through Englefield's papers, where is the lie in the places he mentions? Greenwich, Pickering Place, Wanstead House: these were all well-known habitations of Robert Dudley. The same is true of some of the people mentioned, such as Blount and Heneage."

"And Secretary Flud?" Sir Thomas queried.

"He was certainly employed by Dudley in 1585, carrying messages from Secretary Walsingham when Dudley was serving in the Low Countries. Catherine Ashley's relationship with Her Majesty was well known. George Devereux was a power in Pembrokeshire, having a house and property there. Richard Jones and John Ap Morgan were magistrates in the town of Pembroke."

"And Southern?" Master Reginald asked.

"My searches were thorough," I replied. "Robert Southern did exist. He was keeper of a Royal House in Enfield. He later moved to Evesham where he kept a tavern until he fell ill – so ill that in 1585 the local school master, a Papist, Smyth, drafted his will for him." I heard their gasp of surprise. "That same Smyth whom Arthur Dudley mentions in his confession. This is the truth," I affirmed. "I have seen a copy of Southern's will from the archives at Worcester."

"Does it tell us much?"

"Nothing," I shook my head, "except that Robert Southern did not die a rich man. He makes no reference to any member of his family. The items listed are those which could be found in any alehouse. Arthur Dudley certainly wasn't lying. If Southern was his foster-father, where did Arthur Dudley receive such an education, acquire such knowledge that he convinced the likes of Sir Francis Englefield, as well as high-ranking officials of the Spanish Courts?"

"But the practical implications," Sir Thomas declared. "If the Queen became pregnant others would notice."

"Perhaps they did," I retorted. "We have the scandalous gossip. We all know the phrase 'no smoke without a flame', whilst the diplomats and ambassadors also seemed to have acquired some sort of rumour that Elizabeth had a child. But," I held up my hand, "I saw nothing scandalous, though," I added, narrowing my eyes, "I glimpsed the Queen from afar like a blaze of light through a mist. I lived my own life, more concerned about giving coy glances to this young nobleman or that. It was like attending some service in a Church: I worshipped the Queen from a distance. Now I am much older and, perhaps, a little wiser, I have seen the passing of the days. It's possible." I glanced sideways at both men. "It's possible that Elizabeth, Queen of England may have conceived a love-child."

"When?" Master Reginald asked. "If the Queen became pregnant it must have been sometime during those two years 1560 to 1562."

"How the Queen disguised it is a mystery," I mused. "In September 1561 rumours around the Court talked of the Queen swelling up due to dropsy before becoming extremely thin, the colour of a corpse. Indeed in 1563, during the January of that year, the Council investigated a certain Robert Garrard, his wife and their manservant regarding specific allegations which dated back to August 1561 when Lady Willoughby and other ladies in Suffolk claimed that, during the Queen's recent visit to Ipswich, she looked very pale as a woman might after childbirth. Now, of course, this is scurrilous gossip, but taken with all the other evidence it has made me think. Oddly enough, after Elizabeth fell ill in 1562 and demanded that Tamworth, a mere valet, be given £500 per annum pension for life, well," I paused, "Elizabeth recovered and travelled to Windsor to watch Dudley shooting at the butts in the Great Park. The Queen approached and whispered to him how beholden he was to her, for had she not passed the pikes on his behalf?"

"Passed the pikes?" Sir Thomas exclaimed. "To run the gauntlet!"

"Elizabeth," I agreed, "appears to be inferring that, not only had she done something extraordinary for Dudley, but exposed herself to great danger by doing so." I shrugged. "As to the practical possibilities, why, Sirs, look at any Court. I shall give you one example from Elizabeth's. In 1581, one of the Queen's principal maids-in-waiting, Anne Vavasour, gave birth to a child in the maids' lodging in the Coffer Chamber at Richmond. The Queen was so surprised and angry that she immediately dispatched the woman to the Tower. Now my argument is this, if a lady-in-waiting could hide her pregnancy beneath thick robes and dresses whilst at Elizabeth's Court, why not the Queen herself?"

Sir Thomas and Master Reginald nodded in agreement.

"And yet, if it is true," Sir Thomas remarked, "the Queen gave up her only child."

"Which could explain," I retorted, "why the Queen became so angry with those ladies of her court who became pregnant outside marriage or conceived a child so as to marry their beloved. Those stories about her being fearful of the love-act, not liking children, her fury at those ladies who did conceive, could all have had their origin in the birth of that love-child, Elizabeth's great secret. Remember the looking-glass image, Spenser's two bodies? Elizabeth was devoted to her role of the Virgin Queen, of being married to her Kingdom as passionately and devotedly as any Papist to a saint in a stained-glass window. However, as a woman, she seethed with passions, loss, grief and resentment."

"Do you think she ever married Dudley?" Sir Thomas asked. "I mean secretly?"

"No," I replied. "Later in her reign Dudley may have clandestinely married Lady Douglas, the wife of Lord Sheffield – he certainly married Lettice Devereux, widow of the Earl of Essex. If Dudley was hand-fast to the Queen he would have never have dared to have done that. Of course, on both occasions Elizabeth was furious, but what could she do? Both she and Dudley were growing older, he desperately wanted an heir, yet the passion still continued. Sir Thomas here spoke the truth. After her death I found Dudley's last letter to Elizabeth in an old casket beside her bed. When Dudley died, the Queen was so grieved that for days she shut herself in her chamber, alone. She refused to speak to anyone until the Council had the doors broken down."

I paused. "Elizabeth the mother," I mused. "Do you know what,

Sirs?" I scraped back my chair dabbing at the sweat gathering around my neck. "If Elizabeth had acknowledged this child she would have been as good a mother as any woman in her realm. However, Elizabeth the Queen could not pay the price for one moment of passion. If that conception had become common knowledge, she would have become the object of ridicule to everyone both at home and abroad. They would have raised the ghost of her mother, the lewdness of her father, they would have destroyed her. She did not sacrifice her child on the altar of ambition but on that of sheer necessity. Perhaps that is why, towards the end of her reign, she talked darkly of things she'd done, secrets best kept hidden." I sighed. "And once the child was gone, what use was there in pursuing the matter? Who would have recognised him as her true heir? What proof could she put forward? Elizabeth had to close the door firmly, lock and bolt it. There would be no return."

"And the Spanish?" Master Reginald asked. "Why didn't they use Arthur Dudley against the Queen?"

"Political necessity," I replied. "Arthur Dudley was at the Spanish Court in 1588, the very same year the Armada sailed and was defeated. Dudley died the following September. Strange ..." I mused, "close to the anniversary of Lady Amy's mysterious death. What could the Spanish do with Arthur Dudley? If they acclaimed him, he would be dismissed as a poltroon, a pretender and the Spaniards as simply desperate, politicking, beating the drum. Both England and Spain wanted peace, Elizabeth was growing old. James of Scotland was her successor. Why should the Spanish wish to alienate him? Of course, Arthur could have died but, there again," I straightened in my chair and gestured towards them, "that is one of the reasons I have asked you here. Sir Thomas, Master Reginald, you sweep the courts of Europe, their libraries and archives and search for books for your collection in Oxford. Sir Thomas Bodley," I lifted my cup towards him, "you may be a bibliophile, a great scholar, but I know you have done secret work for the Crown in foreign countries. You have friends and acquaintances everywhere. I beg you to use those people in Spain you both know and trust, to seek out what truly happened to Arthur Dudley."

"Why?" Sir Thomas asked.

"Why?" I repeated. "For over 30 years, Sir Thomas, I served the Great Elizabeth of England, a woman to whom I was passionately devoted. I have always wondered, for a Ruler who spent so much of her time and energy, her life, her personal desires on behalf of her country, did she have one moment of happiness?"

"And there's another reason, isn't there?" Master Reginald asked.

"Yes, Sir, there is. Elizabeth has gone to death, her reign a matter of dusty books and parchments. She left no trace of herself, like a comet, glorious and burning, searing the sky. If Arthur Dudley was her son, if it was possible, if only I could meet him once, converse with him," I gestured round the chamber, "I'd give up all my wealth, the legacy of three marriages, the manors and the fields, the treasures I have collected, even my library, just to sit here, in this secret chamber, with the wind howling, the snow falling, the log fire crackling and stare into the eyes of a man who may well have been my great Mistress' son."

"But do you believe in Arthur Dudley?" Master Reginald insisted. "Surely Elizabeth of England must have betrayed herself, let slip, confessed to some confidant."

"I thought the same," I replied, "until I recalled Elizabeth's motto, 'Video et taceo' – 'I see but keep silent'. Elizabeth did not make windows into men's souls; she was equally determined no-one would make windows into hers. Oh, I have searched the records and the manuscripts." I lowered my voice. "I thought my errand was fruitless." I stared down the table. "I thought I was pursuing a will-of-the-wisp," I murmured. "Yet," I glanced up, "I have found some proof, evidence from Elizabeth's own lips, her words!"

"Impossible!" Sir Thomas breathed.

"I would not think that," Master Reginald whispered.

"I thought the same." I opened the leather wallet in front of me and took out a slip of paper. "Elizabeth was a great scholar, a deeply religious woman. She often reflected on the psalms from Scripture, sometimes she wrote her own prayers. You'll find examples of her prayers to God, that she might be a good ruler or for the safety of her Kingdom. I am sure," I added dryly, "that Philip of Spain, Henry of France, even the old Pope in Rome did the same. Such prayers can be found at the back of any psalter. Elizabeth's prayers," I continued slowly, "belong to a certain pattern, until I discovered two prayers, written strangely enough, in 1563, in Latin. They read as follows ..." I pulled the candle closer, picked up the piece of parchment and tried to keep the tears from both eyes and voice. I glanced up quickly. Sir Thomas and Master Reginald were now leaning against the table fascinated: "Listen, this is what the Queen wrote during that stirring time of 1563! Two years after Lady Amy's death, around the same time as the whispers and the gossip that she'd had a child, close to the day when she asked that, if she died, Dudley should be made Protector, and his servant Tamworth be given a £500 pension a year, when Lady Willoughby and the other Suffolk ladies were making their remarks; above all, at the very time when Elizabeth finally decided that she and Dudley would never be man and wife." The tears came hot and scalding.

"Do you want us to read it?" Sir Thomas offered kindly.

"No." I picked up the napkin from the arm of my chair and dabbed at my eyes.

"You must excuse me," I smiled through my tears, "but my sight is not as good as it once was, but let me read my translation of what Elizabeth wrote. You can find the prayers yourself. It's really a collection of versicles, followed by a collect. The versicle reads as follows." I paused. "First," I picked up another piece of parchment, "let me give you a flavour of one of Elizabeth's other prayers. It goes as follows:

> *May your Grace attend upon those appointed as your Ministers,*
> *so that they be pious, upright and prudent. Send your Holy*
> *Spirit to them; that they may administer justice in your fear*
> *without exception of person. Grant me faithful councillors who,*
> *by their wisdom, would advise me about my Kingdom. Grant*
> *good shepherds who may care diligently about your word and*
> *may discharge their good offices."*

I stared at the two men. "The prayer goes on and on; it is replicated many times in Elizabeth's Prayer Book. But the prayers of 1563 are unique. Written in Latin, they stand in sharp contrast to the rest. This is what they say:

> *Do not enter into judgement with your handmaid,*
> *For in your sight no living man can be justified.*
> *If you will mark our iniquities, O Lord,*
> *Lord, who will be able to stand before you?*
> *From my secret sins cleanse me;*
> *From the sins of others spare your handmaid.*
> *Many sins have been forgiven her because*
> *She has loved much.*

The second," I glanced up "reads as follows:

> *Merciful God and most compassionate Father, patient and of*
> *great mercy, and true to your Word. You do not want the death*
> *of the sinner, but rather that she be converted and live: Create*
> *in me a pure heart O God, which may truly declare your mercy*
> *and my wickedness. For You are my God and my King; I am*
> *your handmaid, the work of Your hands. To You, therefore, I*
> *bend the knees of my heart; against myself I confess my fault. I*
> *have sinned, I have sinned, Father, against heaven and in Your*
> *sight; I do not deserve your compassion, I have not yet kept*
> *your covenant, nor have I walked in Your law. I have abandoned*

You, O God, my Maker, I have withdrawn from You, my Saviour. I have strayed from Your counsels. Do not deal with me according to my sins but make me favourable in your sight according to the greatness of Your mercy. May goodness conquer my evil. May your patience overcome my sins."

I paused to sip from my goblet.

"Strange," Sir Thomas mused, "in the second prayer, Elizabeth uses the words of the Prodigal Son from the Gospel when he returns to his father: 'I have sinned against heaven and in your sight'. It appears Elizabeth likens herself to him – as if she has done something which has gravely estranged her from God and now wishes to return to him."

"But what?" I asked.

Sir Thomas and Master Reginald studied the parchment I handed across.

"What was Elizabeth of England confessing?" I asked. "The Great Queen, the mighty ruler. Look at the versicles when she talks of secret sins, to be delivered from her secret sins and those of others. Study the last two lines of the versicle: Many sins have been forgiven her because, she has loved much."

"I follow your meaning, Mistress." Sir Thomas pulled a face. "Those are the words of Christ in Scripture about the woman of ill repute who anointed his feet whilst he was at dinner with the Pharisees. The Pharisees objected, claiming that if Jesus was a Prophet he would know what sort of woman was touching him. Jesus' reply was that 'many sins have been forgiven her because she had loved so much'."

"Did Elizabeth of England," Master Reginald interposed, "see herself as a woman who had committed adultery, perhaps conceived and given birth to an illegitimate child?"

"The collect prayer is just the same," I persisted deliberately, ignoring Master Carr. "What is Elizabeth talking about? She asks for God to create in her a clean heart. She confesses: 'I have sinned,

I have sinned … I have not kept your covenant … I have abandoned You'. Surely this is a reference to something Elizabeth knows she has done. And the verses themselves," I continued, "are a clear reinterpretation of Psalm 51: the very prayer King David in the Old Testament is said to have composed when he lusted after Bathsheba, the Wife of Uriah the Hittite. David sent Uriah into the forefront of the battle line and had him killed. He took Bathsheba into his own house. She conceived a child, the fruit of their illicit union. David was taken to task by the prophet Nathan. According to tradition, Psalm 51 was David's response to God: 'Have mercy on me, Oh God, have mercy on me and in thine infinite compassion blot out my offence.'"

"Could it be reference to murder?" Master Reginald asked. "These prayers were composed in 1563 a short while after the death of Lady Amy?"

"I have proved, or rather you have," I smiled, "how Lady Amy died. Certainly Elizabeth of England may have felt, as David did, hideous guilt about being the lover of someone whose spouse had died so mysteriously and violently; but she was not responsible."

"I concede," Sir Thomas leaned back in his chair, "in these prayers of 1563, Elizabeth is confessing to some secret, grievous sin. Something on her conscience which separated her from God. Adultery? Sharing her bed with Dudley? Yet what proof is there that she also conceived and gave birth to a child?"

"None," I retorted. "But the prayer itself was written at a time when Elizabeth was coming to her senses, when she realised that Dudley was not to be her husband. She is now repenting of her passion, of any act of love she shared with him. However, if they loved each other so passionately, if they intended to be man and wife, surely it's not too far-fetched to believe that during those days of passion a child was conceived? Forget the nonsense," I continued, "about Elizabeth not being able to conceive a child. It's part of the farrago of half-truths Elizabeth herself fostered to protect her reputation. In 1579, and Cecil reports this, when Elizabeth was thinking of marrying the French Prince Alençon, she was examined by French doctors. Even at that late age, when Elizabeth was 46 years of age, the physicians pronounced she was more than capable of conceiving a child."

Sir Thomas heaved a great sigh, rose to his feet, stretched and went to stand with his back to the fire, his face deep in the shadows.

"The evidence you have produced, Mistress, is overwhelming," he declared. "A jury would say there is a case to answer. You want me and Master Reginald to pursue this matter further?"

There was something in Sir Thomas' voice which created a prickle of cold across my shoulders, something sombre, almost despairing.

"Mistress," Sir Thomas walked to the window and stared out. "It's dark," he murmured. He pressed his face against the glass looking upwards. "I can see no stars: the snow will come again. Mistress," he turned sharply, "I need to have words with Master Reginald. We have to reflect on what you have said and shown us. Perhaps in the morning?"

I agreed. Sir Thomas and Master Reginald collected their papers, refusing any further offer of drink or food. They said they would retire to their chamber, adding they would rise early, break their fast and meet me afterwards in the solar. I let them go. I moved to the fire and sat on a small stool. I crouched like a servant wench, hands out to the flames. I stared into the fiery depths. What was Sir Thomas so concerned about? Vague thoughts came and went. I dozed for a while, dreaming I was back in the Presence Chamber at Hampton Court. Elizabeth, garbed in her gorgeous blue and gold gown, her red hair splendid, spangled with diamonds, a white ruff pushing under her chin. She slouched in a chair, slippered feet resting on a footstool, her long white fingers to her face, eyes sparkling as she watched some play with Dudley standing beside her whispering in her ear. Now and again the Queen would glance at him. I will always remember that look of pure devotion. She'd then turn her head back so that Dudley could continue his whispering. The Queen would laugh behind her fingers, eyes bright with merriment …

"Mistress?" I shook myself from my reverie. The maid was standing in the door. "Mistress, you are sleeping – it is dangerous to crouch like that before the coals."

I rose stiffly to my feet, thanked the girl, left the chamber and went up the darkened staircase to my own room. The maids had prepared it well. Catesby was there, sprinkling herbs on the charcoal. He lifted a candle, came forward and stared at me.

"They believe me," I mouthed the words slowly so he could read my lips. "I think they believe me." He smiled, his sombre scraggy face rather pale, eyes watchful.

"There's no danger," I whispered, "no danger whatsoever."

I retired immediately and was up even before the first grey light of dawn. Sir Thomas was correct, the snow had fallen again during the night, the sky was leaden grey. I washed, dressed slowly, went down to the kitchen and joined the servants for a bowl of oatmeal laced with nutmeg, honey, and sprinkled with sugar. I sipped some cold ale and went out through the postern door to stand in the small yard. It was bitterly cold but I walked to the gateway leading to the sunken garden. For a while I amused myself by studying the different animal tracks in the snow, trying to decide which was fox or badger whilst above me the rooks in the nearby trees cawed noisily. A servant called: "Sir Thomas and Master Reginald are already in the solar."

They stood before the roaring fire warming their fingers, sipping mugs of ale brought from the buttery. Sir Thomas talked about staying a little longer, how the roads would be impassable. I agreed and said they'd be most welcome guests. We talked about books and their binding, the preservation of parchment. Although Sir Thomas and Master Reginald were trying to be merry, they were clearly uneasy. I pushed the footstool away and leaned towards the fire.

"You wished to have words with me, Sir Thomas?"

He cleared his throat noisily, glanced at Master Reginald and nodded. "Mistress, what you have told us is a revelation and perhaps it would not be too difficult to search out if Arthur Dudley still survives." He emphasized the word "if", and that dark glimmer of a nightmare dream came to mind, a matter I'd considered myself but dismissed, as you would a sharp pain, something passing not to be reflected upon.

"Continue, Master Reginald." I glanced up at the ceiling.

"Mistress, you must remember Sir Francis Walsingham?"

My unease deepened – as if someone had opened the casement window and allowed in a bitter draught of icy air. "Of course," I murmured. "Who could forget Sir Francis Walsingham, Secretary of State, the subtle searcher of hidden secrets?" I glanced at Master Reginald. "I often met him at Court, keen-eyed, long-faced, dour looking with his dark features and sharp beard. He liked to dress in black apart from a white ruff. A man of dark obsession, Elizabeth used to tease him, calling him her 'Moor' or 'Black Tom'. She once confided to her ladies that he was the only man in England who frightened her."

"Sir Francis," Master Reginald conceded, "was a fierce man. Cecil's agent when they shattered the Ridolfi Plot, the first serious conspiracy to free Mary, Queen of Scots. Sir Francis' skill was much valued by Cecil. In the early 1570s he spent some time in Paris as the English ambassador before being recalled to be the Council's Intelligencer. A man who had a finger in every pie, who would cherish a plot for years before unmasking it. A king of spies, who always had his ear pressed to the keyhole; who would find a crack in the thickest door and peer through. If Elizabeth did not wish to make windows into men's souls, Sir Francis Walsingham certainly did."

"And what was he to do with this?" I asked.

"Murder," Master Reginald replied. "We talked about the death of Lady Amy in 1560. Has it ever occurred to you, Mistress, or to anyone else, that the lessons Cecil learnt there, he later played out in another place? I refer to Mary, Queen of Scots and the blowing up of her husband Henry Darnley at Kirk O'Fields on 10th February 1567. You must know the story. Henry Darnley had been sent into Scotland to marry Mary. The marriage began happily enough but Darnley soon revealed his true colours. He was vain, empty-headed, raddled with disease, licentious, of loose living. He plotted against his own wife; but, to cut to the quick, Mistress, Darnley was residing at Kirk O'Fields, a house on the edges of Edinburgh, when it was mysteriously blown up on the night of 10th February 1567. What happened later cost Mary, Queen of Scotland her throne. Her wits wandered. She put her trust in James Bothwell, Earl of Hepburn and later married him. Darnley's death was laid at Bothwell's door; but, I have heard it whispered, Mistress, that Kirk O'Fields was the work of Cecil's agents. They blew up the house, then strangled Darnley and his servant, Taylor, whose corpses were found in a nearby garden."

"I see what path you are following," I intervened. "The responsibility for the explosion was levelled at Bothwell."

"Precisely," Master Reginald agreed.

"And Mary married him?"

"Again the truth," Master Reginald smiled. "What I am saying, Mistress, is that in 1567, Mary of Scotland faced the same choices as Elizabeth did after the death of Lady Amy in September 1560. Mary's husband had been murdered in mysterious circumstances, the responsibility for that murder was laid directly with Bothwell. Mary, infatuated with Bothwell, married him and, that cost her dearly. If Mary had not allied herself with Bothwell, either in war or in his bed, her story might have been much different."

"Are you saying," I exclaimed, "that the plot at Kirk O'Fields may have been conceived after what happened at Cumnor Place?"

"So it is whispered," Master Reginald assured me. "It is possible. In 1560 Elizabeth hovered over the abyss. If she had married Dudley, a man who many people considered to have murdered his wife, civil war might have ensued. In 1567 Mary, Queen of Scots was given the same choice and made the wrong decision. Walsingham was a master plotter, a serpent in the grass. He was also a killer. If the Spanish plotted to kill Elizabeth and free Mary, rest assured Elizabeth of England's ministers also plotted against Philip of Spain. In the 1570s the Spanish ambassador was Mendoza, also a cunning schemer, a master of plots. Time and again Mendoza warned his own master to be wary of people dispatched to Spain to carry out his assassination or those of his advisers or military commanders. On 16th May 1578 Mendoza specifically warned Philip of Spain that an English spy, Egremont Ratcliffe, brother of the Earl of Sussex, who'd been involved in the Northern rising, was being freed from the Tower and allowed to go into exile. Mendoza believed that Ratcliffe was an agent dispatched to Spain to kill Don John of Austria, Philip's half-brother and one of the most able naval commanders of his time. Don John had won a great victory against the Turks at Lepanto. In England, many people believed that, if the Spanish launched their Armada against England, Don John of Austria might lead it and could achieve great success. Now as you know, Mistress," he leaned over and touched the back of my hand, "Don John of Austria died suddenly and mysteriously in 1578. We talked of Sir Francis Englefield. An English agent, Gabriel Davey, wrote a long letter to Englefield claiming Don John suddenly became ill when Egremont Ratcliffe joined his retinue. The English exiles in Spain believed Ratcliffe was dispatched from England to poison Philip's able commander."

"Are you saying," I exclaimed, "that Arthur Dudley could have been sent from England as a spy to assassinate Philip of Spain or someone Cecil or Walsingham had marked down for destruction?"

"No, Mistress, I'm not. I shall come to that. What I'm saying is that if the Court of Philip of Spain was a nest of vipers, Elizabeth I's was no different. You've heard the story, haven't you? Dudley became ill in September 1588 and died complaining of severe stomach pains; his widow Lettice later married Christopher Blount, Leicester's Gentleman and Master of Horse, not the Blount who dealt with Lady Amy. According to William Haynes, one of the Earl's pages, Dudley was murdered by his own wife and Christopher Blount, so they could dispose of him and marry, which they later did."

"But that was only an ugly rumour," I declared. "The Earl's corpse was carefully inspected: there was no trace of poison, whilst his wife built the most splendid tomb to Dudley in Warwick Castle."

Master Reginald laughed. "People who build tombs, Mistress, can often see it as an act of reparation, but I concede your point. The stories about Dudley being murdered are probably fable; but the argument I'm trying to fashion is that Dudley himself was hated. Spenser the poet, after Dudley's death, commented that the dead favourite's life had been 'like a glass upon the water' for, when he'd gone, no one came forward to praise the dead Earl. Now, Mistress, bear with me. My hypothesis is that those in the secret councils of Elizabeth of England would not stop at murder to achieve their aims. In 1588 Leicester died. A few years later Walsingham and Cecil ..."

I could follow Master Reginald's argument. I could glimpse his conclusion as you would a gate which emerges through a mist. I'd thought of it too, after the Great Elizabeth died in such mysterious circumstances. I'd posed the question myself but became too terrified to consider the answer. If they, the masters of shadowy politic, the likes of Cecil and the Howards, had struck at her Majesty, against whom else would they raise the sword?

"If Dudley was hated," Sir Thomas took up the story, "can you imagine how those around Elizabeth would resent the possibility that Dudley had a son by Elizabeth? That this young man was being sheltered, protected and patronised by the Spanish Court? Think, Mistress, the Armada was defeated, Elizabeth was growing older, Robert Cecil has taken over from his father. He now looks to Scotland and the smooth succession of young James. Do you think they would allow a possible impostor, a pretender, to threaten their subtle plans? Even more so, if they believed Arthur Dudley was what he claimed to be?"

Sir Thomas picked up his leather wallet resting against the leg of the chair, opened it and took out a piece of parchment.

"I refer, Mistress, to the report of that English spy, dispatched to England in May 1588." He passed his copy over to me. "Study it carefully, Mistress. This spy, whoever 'B.C.' is, is extremely angry at what he'd seen and heard. He is so impetuous, he does not use his alphabet, his secret cipher, but describes exactly what has happened. His letter also proves," Sir Thomas paused, "that if Arthur Dudley was someone dispatched to Spain by the English Council, this spy would have been briefed and kept silent on the matter but, clearly, he is very angry. He resents Arthur Dudley's airs and graces, he even insinuates he will challenge him. But, what is more important, is the phrase 'whereupon he wants no keepers and he is very solemnly warded and served'. In other words, Arthur Dudley is being treated as a person of some importance but not under close guard. Alphabet or not, cipher or not, Master 'B.C.' is informing his master that Arthur Dudley is vulnerable."

"'For you to use,'" Master Reginald whispered. "That's how the spy finishes his letter. It's an invitation, Mistress, to murder. You know it is!"

I repressed a shiver. "Never!" I whispered. "Elizabeth of England would never agree to the murder of her own son – that is what you are saying, Sir Thomas, and you, Master Reginald?"

"We are." Sir Thomas pushed his chair back from the heat and glare of the fire. "Think, Mistress," he whispered, "a son of Dudley and Elizabeth could have caused so much trouble, so much confusion. Yet you, by your own admission, say you have searched and found no other reference to him. There is no demand by the English Council that Arthur Dudley be returned, or dismissed from the Spanish Court as an impostor. It is my view, Mistress, and that of Master Reginald, the reason Arthur Dudley disappears from the records of Spain and anywhere else very shortly afterwards, probably during the lifetime of Master Walsingham, is that Arthur Dudley was secretly assassinated by English agents in Spain. Whether the Queen was consenting or not." He shrugged. "I doubt if she was ever consulted. Again, Mistress, think upon Mary of Scotland, shut up at Fotheringay, convicted of treason, of plotting Elizabeth's death. Elizabeth did not wish her executed but Walsingham and others on the Council took matters into their own hands. The first that Elizabeth knew of it was when she heard the Bells of London pealing for joy, that Mary of Scotland was at last dead, head separated from her body on the scaffold at Fotheringay Castle. Mistress, we will search for Arthur Dudley but I do not think we will find him amongst the living."

I put my hand to my face, my fingertips were cold. Of course, I'd considered such a possibility but dismissed it; like some phantasm of the night; the relic of a dream or hideous nightmare. But, listening to Sir Thomas' and Master Reginald's precise phrases, I realised there was every possibility they were speaking the truth.

"I beg you, Sirs," I muttered, "perhaps if you would give me some time to myself?"

Sir Thomas and Master Reginald scraped back their chairs. Sir Thomas lifted my hand and kissed my fingertips gently. Master Reginald stroked me on the shoulder – an affectionate touch. I heard them leave, closing the door quietly behind them. I gazed at the vine leaves carved on the mantlepiece and fought back the tears. What Sir Thomas and Master Reginald had said could well be true. Elizabeth of England had been sacrificed and would have sacrificed herself for her Kingdom. The likes of Walsingham would view the death of Arthur Dudley as part of that same sacrifice, for the good of the Realm. The Queen herself would never be consulted, perhaps never informed, which is why the young man disappeared so quickly and so mysteriously.

"All gone," I whispered. I pulled a handkerchief from the cuff of my gown and dabbed my eyes. I rose stiffly and went across to the dressing table. The hour was early but the cause was right. I lifted the jug and poured some red wine into a little silver-chased cup and took it over to a portrait of my Mistress. I lifted it in toast and studied that face. I wondered about Arthur Dudley, whose likeness did he have?

"Whatever happened," I whispered, toasting the portrait, "may his life be long, and his death a gate to eternal life!"

I suddenly started at the laughter of one of my maids in the gallery outside. For some strange reason it reminded me of the laughter of Elizabeth of England lounging in a chair with Dudley whispering in her ear and then, many years later, finding her Majesty sitting beside a pool at Hampton Court staring at a miniature portrait of the man she called 'My Lord', the love of her life. I'd come up swiftly, quietly behind her. I heard her words as Elizabeth of England studied the portrait of the man she truly loved, now gone, lost for ever. What were those lines? Time has mixed my memories yet I remember their music, their terrible heart-wrenching beauty. Ah that's it!

"For he being dead, with him is beauty slain and beauty being dead, black chaos comes again!"

Commentary on Part V

Sir Francis Englefield and Arthur Dudley – Sir Francis Englefield's reports can be found in the *Calendar of State Papers, Spanish*, Vol. IV, pp.101-105 and 111-112. The report of the spy calling himself 'B.C.' may be found in the British Library, *Harleian Manuscripts*, 295, folio 190. Sir Francis Englefield's career can be easily traced in the *Dictionary of National Biography*. On Englefield's ability to draw on his estates in England: J. Strype, *Annals of the Reformation* I: 410 and II: 275 (Oxford, 1824). It is interesting to note that in 1560, Englefield was in correspondence with no less a person than Throckmorton, the English ambassador in Paris: *Calendar of State Papers, Foreign*, Vol. 3. No. 963, p.531. Walsingham, that sinister creature, was certainly tracking Arthur Dudley. Master 'B.C.' wrote to Cecil in the June of 1588. By September of that year, Edward Palmer, one of Walsingham's most skilled spies, was on the case informing his master about how Arthur Dudley was under tighter security, being under house arrest in Madrid. *Calendar of State Papers, Domestic*, Vol. 12. No. 110, p.256. The last reference to Arthur Dudley which I can trace, speaks of him in the past tense, whilst any reference to Elizabeth has disappeared: *Calendar of State Papers, Foreign*, July 1590 to May 1591, p.392, para. 697. Here, Arthur is described as "of good quality and comely personage avowed himself Leicester's son by no small personage". Regarding Honeyman's dexterity in opening letters – see the *Calendar of State Papers,*

Domestic (Elizabeth), 1598 to 1601, pp.47-48. Regarding the contents of Arthur Dudley/Englefield's statements – most of the places mentioned are associated with Dudley. The same can be said of the people listed there. Thomas Blount, of course, was Dudley's henchman and played a prominent role in the Amy Robsart affair. Sir Thomas Heneage (*Dictionary of National Biography*) was a close associate of Dudley who, in his will, called Heneage "my good friend". Flud, or Fludde, was a secretary/ messenger of Dudley, active in his service when Dudley was in the Netherlands: G. Bruce, *The Correspondence of Robert Dudley, Earl of Leicester during his Government of the Low Countries, 1585-1586*, Camden Society (1844), Vol. XXVII, p.37. *The Dictionary of National Biography* also demonstrates that the Devereux were powerful landowners in Pembrokeshire. The key person, of course, is Southern. He was definitely a keeper of the Queen's house in Enfield, *Historical Manuscripts Commission (Salisbury)*, Vol. II, p.239. His will can be found in the Worcester Records, Worcester Probate Registry, File AD 1585.11. It was drawn up and approved in May 1585, which accords with the context of Arthur Dudley's statement. This will also proves Southern had fallen ill. He may have been semi-illiterate: the inventory of Southern's will was written out by a Papist school master, John Smyth. The will proved Southern did own a tavern at Evesham and was friendly with a Smyth as mentioned by Arthur Dudley. The document demonstrates relative poverty but nothing remarkable or significant. It should be noted that the only modern historian to mention the Arthur Dudley case is Jasper Ridley in his excellent biography *Elizabeth I: the Shrewdness of Virtue* (Viking Press, 1988). Ridley simply relates the story and moves on. The case of the imposter Anne Bernel is mentioned in the British Library Landsdowne Mss: No. 53 p.79.

The plot to seize James of Scotland is mentioned in the *Calendar of State Papers, Venetian*, Vol. VII, p.538 (13th November 1575). The Tamworth incident is mentioned in the

Calendar of State Papers, Spanish, 1558-1567, pp.262-264. For the crisis over Mary, Queen of Scots' death warrant: J. Ridley, *Elizabeth I*, pp.260-262.

On Elizabeth having 'dropsy' or 'swelling up' shortly after the Amy Robsart incident – see the *Calendar of State Papers, Spanish* 1558-1567, under 13th September 1561, de Quadra's letter to Madrid. On Lady Willoughby's remarks – see the *Calendar of State Papers, Domestic*, Vol. 6. p.534.

Rumours about a possible child of Elizabeth by Dudley amongst the diplomatic corps can be seen in the *Calendar of State Papers, Venetian*, Vol. VII, p.538: the *Calendar of State Papers, Elizabeth, Rome*, Vol. II, 1572-1578, p.238; the *Calendar of State Papers, Spanish*, 1558-1567, p.408. For Elizabeth's remark about "passing the pikes" – see the *Historical Manuscripts Commission (Conway Manuscripts)*. E. Jenkins also refers to this in her *Elizabeth and Leicester*, pp.89-90.

On ladies of the Court hiding their pregnancy: for the case of Anne Vavasour – see B.M. Ward, *The Seventeenth Earl of Oxford* (John Murray, 1926), pp.102-126. This interesting extract from J. Nichols, *The Progresses of Queen Elizabeth I* (3 Vols.) 1823, also proves such 'surprise births' were not uncommon. The entry reads as follows: (Vol. 3, pp.612-613): "two days after the Lady Effingham was brought to bed of a daughter altogether and unlooked for. As she and nobody else supposed she was with child."

Elizabeth's harshness with her maids was well known and led one of Elizabeth courtiers, Edward Stafford, to claim, "the Queen was angry with love". *Calendar of State Papers* (ed. A. Stevenson) 21.1. p.86.

The Prayers of Elizabeth I were published in the *Precationes Privatae Regiae* (T. Purfoot), London, 1563. They are available in a modern edition: *Elizabeth I's Autograph Compositions and Foreign language originals*, (ed. J. Mueller and L. Marcus, University of Chicago, 2003), pp.113-114. Some commentators would argue that the Queen was talking about her recent illness. I would claim, bearing in mind their content and Scripture references, they betray something much deeper. They were published for all who could, to read and study, albeit in Latin. I would argue that Elizabeth may have seen this as part of her penance, as David, according to the Old Testament, published his prayer of sorrow, whilst the woman of ill repute in the Gospels publicly made reparation.

Sir Francis Walsingham was the most consummate of 'Master Spies'. One of the best studies on the man and his methods is Charles Nicholl, *The Reckoning*, (Jonathan Cape), 1992.

The best studies of the Kirk O'Fields murders are two outstanding works: Antonia Fraser, *Mary, Queen of Scots* (Panther Books, 1970), p.339 and Alison Weir's scholarly and most readable work *Mary, Queen of Scots and the Murder of Lord Darnley* (Ballantyne Books, 2003). I doubt very much that Arthur Dudley would have been allowed to live. The Spanish watched James VI of Scotland smoothly succeed to the English throne as James I. Little wonder, English spies, as early as 1601, were intercepting James' letters to Spain in order to achieve just that – *Calendar of State Papers, Venetian*, 1592-1603, Vol. 9, No. 1001, p.467.

On Mendoza's warning about English assassins in Spain – *Calendar of State Papers, Spanish*, Vol. II, 1568-1579, p.584.

On Dudley's last letter to Elizabeth – see the *Public Record Office (Kew) State Papers*, 12-215-65. The Council did have to break down the door to Elizabeth's private chamber to persuade her from her solitary mourning over Dudley – *Calendar of State Papers, Spanish*, Vol. IV, p.431. The phrase describing Dudley's life as "a glass upon the water" comes from Spenser's poem 'The Ruines of Time'.

P. Doherty
Website: www.paulcdoherty.com

GREENWICH EXCHANGE BOOKS

Next book in the series by Paul Doherty
THE DEATH OF THE RED KING
to be published in the coming year

LITERATURE & BIOGRAPHY

Matthew Arnold and 'Thyrsis' *by Patrick Carill Connolly*
Matthew Arnold (1822-1888) was a leading poet, intellect and aesthete of the Victorian epoch. He is now best known for his strictures as a literary and cultural critic, and educationist. After a long period of neglect, his views have come in for a re-evaluation. Arnold's poetry remains less well known, yet his poems and his understanding of poetry, which defied the conventions of his time, were central to his achievement.
The author traces Arnold's intellectual and poetic development, showing how his poetry gathers its meanings from a lifetime's study of European literature and philosophy. Connolly's unique exegesis of 'Thyrsis' draws upon a wide-ranging analysis of the pastoral and its associated myths in both classical and native cultures. This study shows lucidly and in detail how Arnold encouraged the intense reflection of the mind on the subject placed before it, believing in " … the all importance of the choice of the subject, the necessity of accurate observation; and subordinate character of expression."
Patrick Carill Connolly gained his English degree at Reading University and taught English literature abroad for a number of years before returning to Britain. He is now a civil servant living in London.
2004 • 180 pages • ISBN 1-871551-61-7

The Author, the Book and the Reader *by Robert Giddings*
This collection of essays analyses the effects of changing technology and the attendant commercial pressures on literary styles and subject matter. Authors covered include Charles Dickens, Tobias Smollett, Mark Twain, Dr Johnson and John le Carré.
1991 • 220 pages • illustrated • ISBN 1-871551-01-3

Aleister Crowley and the Cult of Pan *by Paul Newman*
Few more nightmarish figures stalk English literature than Aleister Crowley
(1875-1947), poet, magician, mountaineer and agent provocateur. In this
groundbreaking study, Paul Newman dives into the occult mire of Crowley's
works and fishes out gems and grotesqueries that are by turns ethereal, sublime,
pornographic and horrifying. Like Oscar Wilde before him, Crowley stood in
"symbolic relationship to his age" and to contemporaries like Rupert Brooke,
G.K. Chesterton and the Portuguese modernist, Fernando Pessoa. An influential
exponent of the cult of the Great God Pan, his essentially 'pagan' outlook was
shared by major European writers as well as English novelists like E.M. Forster,
D.H. Lawrence and Arthur Machen.
Paul Newman lives in Cornwall. Editor of the literary magazine *Abraxas*, he
has written over ten books.
2004 • 222 pages • ISBN 1-871551-66-8

John Dryden *by Anthony Fowles*
Of all the poets of the Augustan age, John Dryden was the most worldly.
Anthony Fowles traces Dryden's evolution from 'wordsmith' to major poet.
This critical study shows a poet of vigour and technical panache whose art
was forged in the heat and battle of a turbulent polemical and pamphleteering
age. Although Dryden's status as a literary critic has long been established,
Fowles draws attention to his neglected achievements as a translator of poetry.
He deals also with the less well-known aspects of Dryden's work – his plays
and occasional pieces.
Born in London and educated at the Universities of Oxford and Southern
California, Anthony Fowles began his career in film-making before becoming
an author of film and television scripts and more than twenty books. Readers
will welcome the many contemporary references to novels and film with which
Fowles illuminates the life and work of this decisively influential English poetic
voice.
2003 • 292 pages • ISBN 1-871551-58-7

The Good That We Do *by John Lucas*
John Lucas' book blends fiction, biography and social history in order to tell
the story of his grandfather, Horace Kelly. Headteacher of a succession of
elementary schools in impoverished areas of London, 'Hod' Kelly was also a
keen cricketer, a devotee of the music hall, and included among his friends the
great trade union leader Ernest Bevin. In telling the story of his life, Lucas has
provided a fascinating range of insights into the lives of ordinary Londoners
from the First World War until the outbreak of the Second World War. Threaded
throughout is an account of such people's hunger for education, and of the
different ways government, church and educational officialdom ministered to

that hunger. *The Good That We Do* is both a study of one man and of a period when England changed, drastically and forever.

John Lucas is Professor Emeritus of the Universities of Loughborough and Nottingham Trent. He is the author of numerous works of a critical and scholarly nature and has published seven collections of poetry.

2001 • 214 pages • ISBN 1-871551-54-4

In Pursuit of Lewis Carroll *by Raphael Shaberman*
Sherlock Holmes and the author uncover new evidence in their investigations into the mysterious life and writing of Lewis Carroll. They examine published works by Carroll that have been overlooked by previous commentators. A newly-discovered poem, almost certainly by Carroll, is published here.

Amongst many aspects of Carroll's highly complex personality, this book explores his relationship with his parents, numerous child friends, and the formidable Mrs Liddell, mother of the immortal Alice. Raphael Shaberman was a founder member of the Lewis Carroll Society and a teacher of autistic children.

1994 • 118 pages • illustrated • ISBN 1-871551-13-7

Liar! Liar!: Jack Kerouac – Novelist *by R.J. Ellis*
The fullest study of Jack Kerouac's fiction to date. It is the first book to devote an individual chapter to every one of his novels. *On the Road*, *Visions of Cody* and *The Subterraneans* are reread in-depth, in a new and exciting way. *Visions of Gerard* and *Doctor Sax* are also strikingly reinterpreted, as are other daringly innovative writings, like 'The Railroad Earth' and his "try at a spontaneous *Finnegans Wake*" – *Old Angel Midnight*. Neglected writings, such as *Tristessa* and *Big Sur*, are also analysed, alongside better-known novels such as *Dharma Bums* and *Desolation Angels*.

R.J. Ellis is Senior Lecturer in English at Nottingham Trent University.

1999 • 294 pages • ISBN 1-871551-53-6

Musical Offering *by Yolanthe Leigh*
In a series of vivid sketches, anecdotes and reflections, Yolanthe Leigh tells the story of her growing up in the Poland of the 1930s and the Second World War. These are poignant episodes of a child's first encounters with both the enchantments and the cruelties of the world; and from a later time, stark memories of the brutality of the Nazi invasion, and the hardships of student life in Warsaw under the Occupation. But most of all this is a record of inward development; passages of remarkable intensity and simplicity describe the girl's response to religion, to music, and to her discovery of philosophy.

Yolanthe Leigh was formerly a Lecturer in Philosophy at Reading University.

2000 • 56 pages • ISBN: 1-871551-46-3

Norman Cameron *by Warren Hope*

Norman Cameron's poetry was admired by W.H. Auden, celebrated by Dylan Thomas and valued by Robert Graves. He was described by Martin Seymour-Smith as, "one of ... the most rewarding and pure poets of his generation ..." and is at last given a full-length biography. This eminently sociable man, who had periods of darkness and despair, wrote little poetry by comparison with others of his time, but it is always of a consistently high quality – imaginative and profound.

2000 • 220 pages • illustrated • ISBN 1-871551-05-6

POETRY

Adam's Thoughts in Winter *by Warren Hope*

Warren Hope's poems have appeared from time to time in a number of literary periodicals, pamphlets and anthologies on both sides of the Atlantic. They appeal to lovers of poetry everywhere. His poems are brief, clear, frequently lyrical, characterised by wit, but often distinguished by tenderness. The poems gathered in this first book-length collection counter the brutalising ethos of contemporary life, speaking of, and for, the virtues of modesty, honesty and gentleness in an individual, memorable way.

2000 • 46 pages • ISBN 1-871551-40-4

Baudelaire: Les Fleurs du Mal *Translated by F.W. Leakey*

Selected poems from *Les Fleurs du Mal* are translated with parallel French texts and are designed to be read with pleasure by readers who have no French as well as those who are practised in the French language.

F.W. Leakey was Professor of French in the University of London. As a scholar, critic and teacher he specialised in the work of Baudelaire for 50 years and published a number of books on the poet.

2001 • 152 pages • ISBN 1-871551-10-2

'The Last Blackbird' and other poems by Ralph Hodgson *edited and introduced by John Harding*

Ralph Hodgson (1871-1962) was a poet and illustrator whose most influential and enduring work appeared to great acclaim just prior to, and during, the First World War. His work is imbued with a spiritual passion for the beauty of creation and the mystery of existence. This new selection brings together, for the first time in 40 years, some of the most beautiful and powerful 'hymns to life' in the English language.

John Harding lives in London. He is a freelance writer and teacher and is Ralph Hodgson's biographer.

2004 • 70 pages • ISBN 1-871551-81-1

Lines from the Stone Age *by Sean Haldane*

Reviewing Sean Haldane's 1992 volume *Desire in Belfast*, Robert Nye wrote in *The Times* that "Haldane can be sure of his place among the English poets." This place is not yet a conspicuous one, mainly because his early volumes appeared in Canada, and because he has earned his living by other means than literature. Despite this, his poems have always had their circle of readers. The 60 previously unpublished poems of *Lines from the Stone Age* – "lines of longing, terror, pride, lust and pain" – may widen this circle.

2000 • 52 pages • ISBN 1-871551-39-0

Martin Seymour-Smith – Collected Poems *edited by Peter Davies* (180pp)

To the general public Martin Seymour-Smith (1928-1998) is known as a distinguished literary biographer, notably of Robert Graves, Rudyard Kipling and Thomas Hardy. To such figures as John Dover Wilson, William Empson, Stephen Spender and Anthony Burgess, he was regarded as one of the most independently-minded scholars of his generation, through his pioneering critical edition of Shakespeare's *Sonnets*, and his magisterial *Guide to Modern World Literature*.

To his fellow poets, Graves, James Reeves, C.H. Sisson and Robert Nye – he was first and foremost a poet. As this collection demonstrates, at the centre of the poems is a passionate engagement with Man, his sexuality and his personal relationships.

2006 • 182 pages • ISBN 1-871551-47-1

Shakespeare's Sonnets *by Martin Seymour-Smith*

Martin Seymour-Smith's outstanding achievement lies in the field of literary biography and criticism. In 1963 he produced his comprehensive edition, in the old spelling, of *Shakespeare's Sonnets* (here revised and corrected by himself and Peter Davies in 1998). With its landmark introduction and its brilliant critical commentary on each sonnet, it was praised by William Empson and John Dover Wilson. Stephen Spender said of him "I greatly admire Martin Seymour-Smith for the independence of his views and the great interest of his mind"; and both Robert Graves and Anthony Burgess described him as the leading critic of his time. His exegesis of the *Sonnets* remains unsurpassed.

2001 • 194 pages • ISBN 1-871551-38-2

The Rain and the Glass *by Robert Nye*

When Robert Nye's first poems were published, G.S. Fraser declared in the *Times Literary Supplement*: "Here is a proper poet, though it is hard to see how the larger literary public (greedy for flattery of their own concerns) could be brought to recognize that. But other proper poets – how many of them are left? – will recognize one of themselves."

Since then Nye has become known to a large public for his novels, especially *Falstaff* (1976), winner of the Hawthornden Prize and The Guardian Fiction Prize, and *The Late Mr Shakespeare* (1998). But his true vocation has always been poetry, and it is as a poet that he is best known to his fellow poets. "Nye is the inheritor of a poetic tradition that runs from Donne and Ralegh to Edward Thomas and Robert Graves," wrote James Aitchison in 1990, while the critic Gabriel Josipovici has described him as "one of the most interesting poets writing today, with a voice unlike that of any of his contemporaries".

This book contains all the poems Nye has written since his *Collected Poems* of 1995, together with his own selection from that volume. An introduction, telling the story of his poetic beginnings, affirms Nye's unfashionable belief in inspiration, as well as defining that quality of unforced truth which distinguishes the best of his work: "I have spent my life trying to write poems, but the poems gathered here came mostly when I was not."

2005 • 132 pages • ISBN 1-871551-41-2

Wilderness *by Martin Seymour-Smith*
This is Martin Seymour-Smith's first publication of his poetry for more than twenty years. This collection of 36 poems is a fearless account of an inner life of love, frustration, guilt, laughter and the celebration of others. He is best known to the general public as the author of the controversial and bestselling *Hardy* (1994).

1994 • 52 pages • ISBN 1-871551-08-0

STUDENT GUIDE LITERARY SERIES

The Greenwich Exchange Student Guide Literary Series is a collection of critical essays of major or contemporary serious writers in English and selected European languages. The series is for the student, the teacher and 'common readers' and is an ideal resource for libraries. The *Times Educational Supplement* praised these books, saying, "The style of [this series] has a pressure of meaning behind it. Readers should learn from that ... If art is about selection, perception and taste, then this is it."

(ISBN prefix 1-871551- applies)
All books are paperbacks unless otherwise stated

The series includes:
W.H. Auden by Stephen Wade (36-6)
Honoré de Balzac by Wendy Mercer (48-X)
William Blake by Peter Davies (27-7)

The Brontës by Peter Davies (24-2)
Robert Browning by John Lucas (59-5)
Lord Byron by Andrew Keanie (83-9)
Samuel Taylor Coleridge by Andrew Keanie (64-1)
Joseph Conrad by Martin Seymour-Smith (18-8)
William Cowper by Michael Thorn (25-0)
Charles Dickens by Robert Giddings (26-9)
Emily Dickinson by Marnie Pomeroy (68-4)
John Donne by Sean Haldane (23-4)
Ford Madox Ford by Anthony Fowles (63-3)
The Stagecraft of Brian Friel by David Grant (74-9)
Robert Frost by Warren Hope (70-6)
Thomas Hardy by Sean Haldane (33-1)
Seamus Heaney by Warren Hope (37-4)
Joseph Heller by Anthony Fowles (84-6)
Gerard Manley Hopkins by Sean Sheehan (77-3)
James Joyce by Michael Murphy (73-0)
Laughter in the Dark – The Plays of Joe Orton by Arthur Burke (56-0)
Philip Larkin by Warren Hope (35-8)
Poets of the First World War by John Greening (79-X)
Philip Roth by Paul McDonald (72-2)
Shakespeare's A Midsummer Night's Dream by Matt Simpson (90-0)
Shakespeare's *Macbeth* by Matt Simpson (69-2)
Shakespeare's *Othello* by Matt Simpson (71-4)
Shakespeare's *The Tempest* by Matt Simpson (75-7)
Shakespeare's *Twelfth Night* by Matt Simpson (86-2)
Shakespeare's Non-Dramatic Poetry by Martin Seymour-Smith (22-6)
Shakespeare's Sonnets by Martin Seymour-Smith (38-2)
Shakespeare's *The Winter's Tale* by John Lucas (80-3)
Tobias Smollett by Robert Giddings (21-8)
Dylan Thomas by Peter Davies (78-1)
Alfred, Lord Tennyson by Michael Thorn (20-X)
William Wordsworth by Andrew Keanie (57-9)
W.B. Yeats by John Greening (34-X)

BUSINESS

English Language Skills *by Vera Hughes*
If you want to be sure, (as a student, or in your business or personal life), that
your written English is correct, this book is for you. Vera Hughes' aim is to
help you to remember the basic rules of spelling, grammar and punctuation.

'Noun', 'verb', 'subject', 'object' and 'adjective' are the only technical terms used. The book teaches the clear, accurate English required by the business and office world. It coaches acceptable current usage and makes the rules easier to remember.

Vera Hughes was a civil servant and is a trainer and author of training manuals.

2002 • 142 pages • ISBN 1-871551-60-9

The Essential Accounting Dictionary of Key Financial Terms

by Linda Hodgson

This is a key aide for students seeking examination success in Accounting A-Level and GNVQ Advanced Business. It results from work with teachers and students and addresses common difficulties. Straightforward, easy to read definitions of key financial terms – which form the basis of understanding and better performance at tests and examination. There is a multiple choice quiz to crosscheck how much the student knows.

Linda Jane Hodgson, graduate in History and Politics, is a former Tax Inspector and qualified teacher. Professionally, she also advised accounting firms on taxation. She now teaches business and finance at a London college.

1999 • 150 pages • ISBN 1-871551-50-1